Edward Everett Hale

Mr. Tangier's Vacations, a Novel

Edward Everett Hale

Mr. Tangier's Vacations, a Novel

ISBN/EAN: 9783337025922

Printed in Europe, USA, Canada, Australia, Japan

Cover: Foto ©Andreas Hilbeck / pixelio.de

More available books at **www.hansebooks.com**

MR. TANGIER'S VACATIONS

A Novel

By EDWARD E. HALE

AUTHOR OF "THE MAN WITHOUT A COUNTRY," "IN HIS NAME,"
"TEN TIMES ONE IS TEN," "HIS LEVEL BEST,"
"UPS AND DOWNS," "FRANKLIN IN
FRANCE," ETC., ETC.

BOSTON
ROBERTS BROTHERS
1888

University Press:
JOHN WILSON AND SON, CAMBRIDGE.

MR. TANGIER'S VACATIONS.

CHAPTER I.

MR. TANGIER stood at the door of his office, with his hand on the handle, about to go out.

"Say to Mr. Willoughby that the deed will be ready at nine to-morrow morning; that I will have witnesses here, so that his sons need not come."

"Yes, sir," said the intelligent office-boy, who stood respectfully, and fixed "Willoughby" in his memory, by processes known to himself.

"If Mr. Sennett comes in, ask him to wait, if it is possible; say I have only gone to lunch, and will be back at two."

"Yes, sir," said the intelligent office-boy, and, by mental hooks known to him, fastened "Sennett" next to "Willoughby" in the mental box.

"Take a press-copy of the two letters on my desk, then address them, give them both to George for the mail, and make a neat copy, as if in my handwriting, of the long one, for the mail, also. Make that from the press-copy; there is not time for you to copy it direct."

"Yes, sir," said the boy again, and Mr. Tangier left the room. The office-boy had but just time to call

George, who was his boy, to bid him wet some paper, when Mr. Tangier returned. He had met Mr. Sennett and had brought him back with him. The office-boy gathered up the long letter and the short letter, and was retiring to his lair, so that the gentlemen might be alone, when Mr. Tangier called him back.

"If Mr. Willoughby comes, show him into the sitting-room, give him the paper and the 'Forum,' and ask him if he will have the kindness to wait a few minutes. Do not call me if you can help it."

And, as the boy retired, Mr. Tangier turned to Mr. Sennett and said, "I liked the looks of the captain more than you did. His story is horribly improbable, and probably true. I told him —" and here the boy was obliged to shut the door, and neither he nor this reader will ever know what the captain's story was.

The office-boy made the copies of the long letter and the short. He sent George to the post-office with both, and then addressed himself to his other task of copying ten pages of the long letter, in Mr. Tangier's handwriting.

While he did this, Mr. Willoughby came, and was put into the comfortable "sitting-room." A fellow of the copying-clerk's came from Curtis & Choate and made an appointment for a consultation at three the next day; the chairman of a reception committee came up to know if Mr. Tangier would be a vice-president at a public meeting for the reception of Baron Kittening; the junior partner of Severance & Hildreth came to retain Mr. Tangier, and to ask for an appointment. Punctually at two, Mr. Heeren came in, who was Mr. Tangier's junior partner. He had finished his lunch, and the attentive, observant, and intelligent office-boy subsided, on the moment, into all his native obscurity. He gave to Mr. Heeren a memorandum of the visits he had received, and the requests which had been made. He covered his copy, only begun, in his portfolio. He told Mr. Heeren who was in the inner office, and where Mr. Willoughby was, and he went for his lunch.

As he went, the cheerful office-boy reflected that, though he should only have fish-balls, followed by two doughnuts, for his lunch, while the chief could have, if he chose, roast turkey, followed by peach pie, followed by frozen pudding, — and these, at that moment, happened to be the ideal bill of fare in the office-boy's mind, — he reflected, I say, that he, the office-boy, had a chance to eat the fish-balls, while Mr. Tangier had no chance to eat those other dainties.

Had the copying-clerk's thoughts expressed themselves in words, he would have said, " A Fish-Ball in the Mouth is worth a Turkey on the Wing," and so a new proverb would have been born.

Mr. Heeren went to soothe Mr. Willoughby's indignation in the reception-room. Mr. Willoughby was an important person, or thought he was, and even in that office must not be snubbed. For a moment, therefore, George, the slave of the slave of the copying-clerk of the clerk of the junior partner of the firm, reigned at the head of the hierarchy in the outer room. The hierarchy, however, had been reduced to one person, when there were no visitors. George was that lowest person in this world, who can give orders to no one.

In a moment Mr. Sennett came out with Mr. Tangier, talking as earnestly as they went in. It was clear enough, even to George, that the case was more perplexing than the average. He explained to his master, whom he did not often address personally, how the other parts of the machine were at work, and where; and then, as Mr. Tangier took his hat again, but turned back to his inner office for his gloves, George received at the door two foreign-looking gentlemen, who presented their cards, which he took to Mr. Tangier. That gentleman came out, with perfect cordiality, welcomed them both, led them into the inner office, and again the door was shut.

George reigned alone once more till the copying-clerk returned from his fish-balls. In a few minutes more Mr. Heeren came in, and finding that the chief had shut the door, took his seat at a desk he had in the outer room. The copying-clerk completed the letter in Mr. Tangier's handwriting, and then began, with a type-writer, on the regular correspondence of the morning, writing from his short-hand notes. One and another visitor, in steady succession, called, and made their appointments, as before. At half-past three the foreign gentlemen left.

"George," said Mr. Tangier, "I am too late for my lunch. Go across to Hyde's and bid them send up a bowl of soup, whatever there is, and a cup of coffee. Mr. Grace will be here before I can go." And, as George left on this errand, Mr. Grace came, was welcomed, and took his turn in the inner office. When the waiter from Hyde's came in with his tray, Mr. Heeren sent him back, and bade him duplicate the order, that there might be the pretence of asking Mr. Grace to join in this hurried repast.

The two cups of coffee and the two bowls of soup were sent in, and from that time forth no one even knocked on the outside of the door of the inner office. Visitors came and went. Mr. Heeren soothed them, or encouraged them, or postponed them until to-morrow, or to a day certain, or indefinitely. The student came in who had been at work all the morning in the Registry of Deeds. He sat at his desk, plotting, so to speak, the results of his investigations. The copying-clerk copied, in one fashion or another, as the exigencies of the case required. Even George copied, also, in such methods as he had acquired, — not the best known, but gradually improving; — and he took such lessons as were suggested by the copying-clerk. He was even permitted to try the type-writer, when the copying-clerk was at work with a more primitive instrument, called a steel pen.

But no one ever suggested an appeal, not for one moment, to Mr. Tangier. All men and boys knew that Mr. Grace was there by appointment of great significance, and all boys and men knew that Mr. Grace was making his will.

At half-past five, George found it difficult to withdraw his attention from the window and the street outside. In the dignified discipline of this office, he made no report whatever of his observations. But even the copying-clerk was so impressed by George's continued study of outward Nature, that he was obliged to cross the room to raise the curtain. And it was noticed that, even to his jaded eye, the spectacle on which he looked attracted him for a minute from the type-writer. Even the student then found it necessary to cross to that side of the room to take

down a volume, either of Grotius or of Pickering, and
his eye lingered for a moment on the little crowd
without. Mr. Grace's carriage was waiting, as long as
the police would let it stand; then it moved slowly
up and down the street, and waited again. A footman in livery behind, and another in front with
the coachman, attracted the attention of the news-
boys and other pirates of the street, and so quite.
a little crowd of loafers had assembled on the sidewalk.

But the horses pawed without avail, and the police
compelled even Mr. Grace's carriage to pass on once
and again; and once and again the group dispersed,
to form again when the carriage stopped again, before,
at six o'clock, the conference was over. The inner
office was opened to the sight of man again, and Mr.
Tangier led his important client even to the head of
the stairs.

Mr. Grace walked but slowly, and George and the
office-boy and the student and Mr. Heeren all thought
that he needed all the help Mr. Tangier could offer him,
and they did not wonder that both footmen.helped him
into the carriage. Indeed, I think no one of them
would have changed places with Mr. Grace.

George did wish that his pay might be raised from
three dollars to three and a half; the copying-clerk
wished that his salary, instead of fifty dollars a month,
was sixty; the student hoped that when the year
ended Mr. Heeren might make some offer of what
should happen when he entered at the bar; Mr. Heeren even had dreams that, if Mr. Tangier were obliged
to go to Europe in that delicate matter of the Jef-
freys' Trust, the whole office would be intrusted to

him. But neither George, nor the copying-clerk, nor the student, nor Mr. Heeren, wished to change places with Mr. Grace, as .Mr. Tangier helped him to the stairs; though Mr. Grace was known, of all men, to have the most beautiful house in the town, a charming family, and to be the lord of untold millions.

CHAPTER II.

LEAST of all did Mr. Tangier wish this.

Tired, — oh, so tired, — faint, without knowing what the word faint meant, Mr. Tangier turned back from the stairway, and met all the others with an anxious, manufactured smile.

"I am sorry to have kept you all so late," said he, as he put on his gloves to go, at last. He looked up to the office clock, as if he was personally guilty because it had so far passed five o'clock, which was the time when the door should have been locked behind them all. And he went downstairs and walked to the street-car which was to take him to his pretty home just out of town.

Oh, how tired he was! Not in his feet or legs, but in every part of him which perceived, or remembered, or thought, or hoped, or in any sort enjoyed. It would have been better for him, and he knew it would have been better for him, to walk the five miles which parted him from Glendean. But even for that he had not time. He knew that he had missed the car, which he relied upon, and that at best he should be late for his dinner.

Once in the car he had a faint, faint hope that no one would know him. He remembered that hero of Hawthorne's, who wore the black veil in all horse-cars of his day, so that people might not recognize him and speak to him. Poor, baited, and harried Mr. Tangier wished that he dared wear such a protecting veil. But that was not to be. One of his neighbors who had been away for months took the next seat, and saluted him at once. Poor Mr. Tangier knew that he was, himself, in for a conversation five miles long.

Once more he braced himself up. Indeed, he knew that "there was no act of parliament that he should be happy." He was glad to see Mr. Curtis looking so full in the face, — and with a good sunburnt color, — and he said so.

"You are a great stranger, Mr. Curtis. I am glad to see you looking so well."

But, alas, poor Mr. Curtis was not well, and never would be, and he knew it. He gave his hand cordially to the other, but said a little slowly, and with that wretched evidence that speaking occurred with pain and did not come easily, "I — look — better — than — I am. Paralysis, — you — know."

"Indeed, you do not show it," said poor Tangier, as cheerfully as he could.

"If — if — you saw me — saw me — get along without my left hand, or try — or try to, you would know," said Mr. Curtis, who seemed determined not to accept any of the commonplace conversations of every-day civility.

Mr. Tangier was courageous, and he could brace up to most duties of society. But five miles of symptoms, and one story of failure, was more than he dared to stand, and when the car stopped first he bade Mr. Curtis good-by, and left it hastily. He walked half across the town, and rang the bell at the door of his life-long friend, his classmate, and his physician, Morton. To his joy he found Morton in, in a dressing-jacket, with his feet on a foot-rest, and his back to the sunset, which glorified the bay. Morton did not even pretend to rise.

"How are you, old fellow!" cried he. "What luck to be in — there is your chair, and there is another for your feet. No man ever did anything worth doing, with his feet on the ground. So I will not stand up, even for you."

He put down the copy of the London "Truth," which he was looking at, and lay back in the easy-chair, the picture of repose.

Mr. Tangier felt the subtle influence of the place, and the easy manner of his host, as his host meant he should. He could not at once plunge into the story of his ailments and worries as he had meant to do. He sank into the easy-chair at which Morton pointed, and before he knew it he was sipping a cup of tea which some attendant had brought in. Before he knew it again, they were both talking Bulgarian politics, and then discussing Gladstone, and then Morton was describing Gambetta, and then they fell back on some old story of college times. The spells of the magician began to work, and when at seven o'clock Mrs. Morton came in, pretty and cheerful, and summoned them to dinner, Tangier found himself quite alert, ready to laugh with her, to give her his arm, and to lead her in. A long, merry, cheerful family dinner followed, and Mr. Tangier was really a new man when, two hours after, Mrs. Morton said, "We shall find it pleasanter in the red parlor," and led the way.

"You must excuse me," said Mr. Tangier. "I should have been at my house two hours ago. Mrs. Colquitt will scold me awfully, when I come. And now I want a word with your husband." So the two men went back to the doctor's comfortable library. They sat down as before; Mr. Tangier declined a cigar, and the doctor did not light one.

"I did not come to dine," said Tangier at once, "and I did not mean to stay ten minutes. I wanted to talk to you again about my sleep, or what you would call 'insomnia.' Since I saw you, I have had some new experience." And at some length he went into the details of his overworked life, his late meals, his failing appetite, and his sleepless nights.

He was a little annoyed that Dr. Morton asked no questions, and even affected to be a little bored.

When Mr. Tangier had wholly done, he said, "And that is about all."

"Yes," said Morton, "is it? I do not quite know why you want to tell it to me?"

"Who in the world should I tell it to? You do not suppose I talk my ailments to all the world — like poor Curtis."

"No," said Morton, "that is just what I do not suppose. So I do not know why you bring them here — why I must hear them."

"You!" cried the other; "because you are my medical adviser. I have come to you for advice. You must tell me how to get rid of these things."

"My dear fellow," said Morton, "do be serious. I am your friend; I am your very good friend; but I am not your physician."

"You, not my physician ! Why not ? When did that happen ? "

"I have not been your physician since — since — April 28," and he looked at his note-book. "You came on the 27th, for advice, much as you come now. I gave the best advice I could. You did not take it. That was the end. Simply, my dear fellow, I will not be responsible for a patient who does not give me his confidence."

"Confidence, my dear friend," said Tangier, amused at the other's manner, — "I have absolute confidence in you. Do you suppose there is another man in the country to whom I would have told what I have told to you ? "

"No ! perhaps not. But it is a confidence of lips. You do not obey me. I tell you that you are killing yourself ; you laugh, and say you know better. I tell you to change your manner of life. You go on just as you did before. If you were not a man of sense, .I should say you really believed that I had a bottle labelled 'Health' in yonder, and had only to give you five teaspoonfuls and you would be well. There is no such bottle. For my part, I will not have the disgrace of being the medical adviser to a man who will not obey me. Your case is not mine. You can go to any one else you like : I shall not be wounded."

Tangier was certainly staggered by the earnestness with which his friend spoke.

For two minutes neither spoke.

Then Tangier said, "You suggested my going to Europe."

"Yes ; if you would go to Spain, or Naxos, or Arch- angel, or somewhere where there are no mails, where your Mr. Heeren would not be sending immediate delivery letters, and cables a mile long, after you every day."

"I hate Europe as a medicine," said Tangier.

"I should think you would. There are as good Spains, and Naxoses, and Archangels, within sixty miles of you ; if only you cut the wire behind you, as they say Grant did once — or was it Sherman ? "

" That would be better," said the other. " Where shall it be ? You shall say."

" No," said Morton, " it shall not smell of this shop. You know that woman who said she thought when she was a child that asafœtida was the smell of doctors. One place is as good for you as another, so there is no door-bell, no mail, and no telegraph. Give such orders to your clerk as you know how to give. Go off for a month, and then come and see me again."

" Morton, you are a trump. Let me have to-morrow to give the orders, and the next day you shall see me no more ! "

And they parted.

CHAPTER III.

AND the next day Mr. Tangier gave the orders. "He gave them with a vengeance," as the copying-clerk said to George, almost in a whisper, so overcome with awe was he.

Mr. Tangier told Mr. Heeren that he was to be away for a month. "I am not going salmon fishing to Labrador, but it is just as if I were. Nothing is to be sent after me, and nobody. This is the 29th of May; on the 30th of June you will see me. We will write the necessary notes now, and to-night I shall bid you good-by. It will be your business to show that the office can do just as well without me as with me." This he said, with his old good-natured, open smile, which rejoiced Mr. Heeren more than anything he had seen on that care-worn face for six weeks before.

Then Mr. Tangier looked up a letter from Mrs. Dunster. It was an office letter, six months old. He had had to give some advice, as an old friend of her father's, about the probate of a will, and he had gladly given it. He remembered perfectly well that she had said, when she wrote to thank him, that if he ever wanted to run away from noise and smoke, he had better come to them, and hear the whippoorwills and bull-frogs. That was in late summer. There would be no bull-frogs now.

The letter proved to say still what it said before, and Mr. Tangier wrote this letter: —

DEAR MRS. DUNSTER, — The time has come. I shall take my carpet-bag to-morrow and go into retreat. Please find somebody who has a nice room for me, and you may as well not mention my name. Indeed, I should be glad if no one knew where to mail a letter to me.

Truly yours,

JEFFREY TANGIER.

Then Mr. Tangier put this letter in his pocket. He rang for the railway guide, and this lay on his desk when the copying-clerk came in to " take " the letters. Mr. Tangier and Mr. Heeren dictated one hundred and fourteen letters that day, explaining that he was called suddenly out of town. At lunch he disappeared, and for one month the office saw him no more.

" I will start to-morrow morning," said Mr. Tangier. He took his guide again, and began the difficult study of the minute and hour of his train. The university of the future will have foundations in college, to support teachers who shall understand time-tables, and show young men how to use them. Mr. Tangier had studied other things, and worked out only with difficulty the problem before him.

It was, in his case, specially complicated. He lived so far out of town that, as he well knew, he could more easily strike the local station of the Cattaraugus road than go into the city and start from the great central terminus. He knew perfectly well that to make his connections in the interior he must take the early train out of town. He did not know whether, or if, or how, the local station would accommodate him.

He began, as he always did, by study on the wrong side of the page. After he had made one or two memoranda, which he himself could not reconcile, he found he was reading down where he should be reading up, and that he must find another set of columns. Here time did go forward and not backward, as it had seemed before. And here, accordingly, he found, as he had feared, that the early train out of town ran as an express for thirty miles, and that he could not take it at his station.

His next affair then was to see what train, yet earlier, would take him up to Wentworth Junction — the Suez of his part of the world — where every traveller, from every quarter of that world, changed his train for another train, at certain hours preordained.

Clear it was, now, that other people lived who had his necessities. Early as was the early express, there was a local train still earlier. "These people understand their business," said Mr. Tangier, not displeased. "I am not the only man who has done this thing." Till this moment he had supposed he was, — so mad indeed, as it seemed to him, was the rising, almost with the sun, to go on this visit to an unknown region, to try this strange adventure with these unknown friends.

But he was determined. From the moment when he gave his word to Morton, this thing was sure. Midnight or sunrise, he would start when the fates directed. Nor did he even congratulate himself that they had decided on sunrise rather than midnight.

He hunted up a peculiar portmanteau, which still bore the custom-house permit of his last landing from

Europe, and which he had not seen since the day it took in the last waifs and strays from his state-room on the "Germanic." He opened it; and there still lay, in the bottom of it, the card of that Colorado cattle-man he used to walk the deck with. He remembered grimly how he had sunk half an hour in hunting among his papers for this man's address. Here it was.

He packed, or thought he packed. He wound up his watch, and it was after midnight. This was the beginning, then, of his obedience to Morton's instructions, and of securing regular sleep by beginning to undress at half-past nine. He knew he must be out of bed at quarter-past five. Five hours' sleep was to be the beginning of Morton's new regimen for sleeping.

But the machine did its duty. By that mysterious law, which nobody yet understands, he woke at quarter-past five, just so far as to pull out his watch from his pillow and to strike it. "Five and a quarter," said the faithful slave, just as the faithful machine made up of nerve, and sinew, and bone, had said; and in new wonder at that miracle of consent, Mr. Tangier kicked off the bed-clothes. He stood erect and said aloud,—

"The faithful Donjon clock had numbered two,
And Wallace tower had sworn the tale was true."

He staggered across to the pitcher and bowl. He sponged his head with the sharp, cold water which stood ready, and the happy moment of morning omnipotence began.

"Fortune favors the brave," he said, almost aloud, as he let the door swing behind him, and with his little hand-bag stepped out into the delicious morning air. He had let the housekeeper make him a cup of

coffee and a bit of toast, but he was rather a convert
to French fashions, and he had meant not to take his
proper breakfast until he arrived at Tenterdon.   Tenterdon was the oasis hidden away in the desert, yet
not so far from the ocean, where lived Mrs. Dunster,
who was the only person in the world who had his
secret.

"Fortune favors the brave," he said, for he really
felt as if this exquisite sweetness of perfume, this
softness yet exhilaration in the air, and the mist
just doubting whether it would stay or go, were all
one special gift, manufactured for him exclusively by
the good powers to whom the fortunes of his section
of the world were intrusted.   Then he saw a young
fellow who was hurrying to his street-car that he
might be at his post in time, and Mr. Tangier remembered that that young man rose at this hour every
morning.   Perhaps he thought the revelation of sun
and sky, and gracious mist, and fragrant air, was all
for him.   Perhaps it was.   Or, more probably, it was
for both of them, and for that woman yonder also,
who had been "watching" all night with poor Mrs.
Doubleday, and had now been relieved by the day
nurse.   Perhaps it was for all of them.

But Mr. Tangier met but few nurses relieved, or
clerks beginning.   He was just too early even for the
seven-o'clock people.   In the city where he was a
slave, the different work-people might have been divided in classes, as they began at seven o'clock, at
eight o'clock, at nine o'clock, or at ten.   He had always
been one of the nine-o'clock kind.   Now that he had
emancipated himself, he was in action even before the
seven-o'clocks, and those of them who lived in his

pretty Rosedean had to be on the alert at six, or a little after. It was not long after five o'clock now; and here was Mr. Tangier wondering, and philosophizing a little, on that daily waste of beauty and ecstasy of life which for Rosedean let the sun, and the sky, and the wind, and the mists, and the birds, and the trees set the scene every morning for a celebration which so few people of the human variety chose to look upon. All the more, however, did Mr. Tangier enjoy the spectacle, now that he was the principal actor.

Queer enough, — and he noted the queerness as he walked, and wondered that the long rays of the sun in the morning look as they do in the evening, — the thing he was reminded of most was, not another morning like this, but a simulated morning at the opera. He had to feel for the name of an exhilarated tenor, whom he remembered as the curtain rose for "Somnambula;" he remembered the way the stage was set for sunrise, and the gayety of the tenor as he stepped down from the back to the footlights, and sang, —

"Behold how brightly breaks the morning."

And again Mr. Tangier philosophized a little.

It was queer that he should have seen the sun rise at the theatre more often than he had seen it in the sky!

He had a walk of half an hour, and then he found that he had studied his Pathfinder so ill, and that he had allowed so extravagantly for one delay and another which had not taken place, that the station-house was not open. Nay! great advertisements of the trains made it clear that he need not go by that early "succursale," or train of supply, but that the great through express would, after all, pause on the wing, in its majestic flight, to clutch so worthy though so slight an atom as Mr. Tangier. Apparently he was to spend some thirty-five minutes sitting or standing on the steps of the station-house.

No! it was not so written. And Mr. Tangier, who was learning many lessons, now learned one which served him well through all his vacation. Clearly enough, this suburb was astir, though his lovely Rosedean was asleep. In three minutes all was changed. The ill-tempered station-master appeared, a minute late; it was because he was late that he was ill-natured. In a few minutes more, the first of the in-going trains appeared, and to feed it, men seemed to spring out of the ground, each with a tin lunch-pail in his hand. It passed, and Mr. Tangier was alone again, with the station-master.

And now it was, that he learned that that French cup of coffee, with its slice of toast, was but a faint stay for a man who walked in fresh morning air two miles, and had eighty more miles before him. So he asked, a little crestfallen, of a stray lad who appeared with a lunch-pail, whether there was any place where he could find breakfast.

"Porter's, of course," said the other, as he might have suggested the pump, had Mr. Tangier asked for water.

"Porter's!" He had hardly thought of the place since they drove across in triumph, to have their Sophomore class supper there!

Could it have looked quite as dingy and snuffy then?

No matter for looks. He was on the quest for adventures, as Amadis might have been, and here was adventure number one. This was his enchanted castle, and he passed in.

The damsel he discovered was not interesting to the eye, but when he asked for breakfast, his question was taken as the question of a fool might have been. Why else should they all be out of their beds, indeed, but to prepare breakfast for anybody who wanted it, — for him, if he chose to come, and for fifty others as good as he?

No one said this in words to Mr. Tangier, but this was the lesson he learned.

That is to say, it was not till one of the damsels he found, not very tidy of dress nor over-attractive to the eye, ordered him to a seat at a table where sat some others, among seven other tables, at each of which eight men were sitting, — it was not till then that it fairly dawned on him, on this morning, that his early rising was not a thing utterly exceptional and extraordinary.

But here were sixty other people, at an insignificant wayside inn, who had risen as early as he.

And, besides these, that morning train had taken into town five hundred others, many of whom had risen earlier.

In a minute more, he had another lesson taught him.

It was, that quite as good provision was made for these people's comfort as he was used to have for his own, though it came in different forms.

His plate was heavy, but it was clean.

His napkin was coarse, but it was clean.

The tumbler at his side was of pressed glass, but it was clean.

In thirty seconds the un-beautiful damsel had brought him a steak which was perfect, a baked potato which was perfect, two or three forms of bread which were perfect. She brought him a cup, which could have been fired from a cannon without being broken; but the coffee in it was better than had been given him at home, — better than Hyde's people had sent to him and Mr. Grace the day before.

The lesson which Mr. Tangier learned was, that he had better thank God that he was not alone in the world, but that he was one of the People, and to thank God also that the People had very much its own way.

He could not but remember, as the un-beautiful girl slammed his breakfast down on the table before him, that at Hyde's, where they would have served it elegantly in china, they would have served it cold, after he had waited twenty minutes. The first memorandum he was to make in his vacation note-book was to be: "The People will not stand nonsense."

CHAPTER IV.

NO, Mr. Tangier did not take a parlor-car. He always had ridden in one since they were invented, but now he was afraid that some one would recognize him, and he had not that convenient black veil which has already been alluded to. He took his seat beside a lonely woman in what is called a first-class car, and once more, as he found himself so comfortable there, he reflected, as he had done at breakfast, that the public in this country had found out very nearly what it wanted, and was quite sure in the long run to obtain it. He did not take his seat where there was an empty seat beside him, because he was haunted with the terror that some bummer would come along and cry out, enthusiastically, " Why, Tangier, are you here ? " and would sit down by him to entertain and to be entertained for seventy miles.

Yes, Mr. Tangier, you are very skilful, but all the same this world is a world of give and take, and you have your part to bear in it.

So soon as Mr. Tangier had read, from the first page to the eighth, and from the eighth back to the first, his copy of the " Iris," — which was the newspaper he bought simply because he never saw it when he was at home, — the woman by whom he sat, whom he had selected as his barrier against conversation, herself addressed him. He was caught in his own trap, but that was not the figure which occurred to him. He said to himself that it was like the ass speaking to Balaam, only in a topsy-turvy of his Scripture, the poor man felt as if he was the ass. "Can you tell me," said the woman, in a dialect which showed that she was born in Germany, "can you tell me if this car will go through to Milwaukee, or where shall I have to change ? "

Milwaukee !

It was more than a thousand miles away, if Mr. Tangier understood the geography of his country at all, and here was this poor woman who was to ride day and night till she came there.

And so the law of give and take asserted itself, and our friend, who just now wanted to be alone, and had tried to separate himself from his kind, forgot such wants, in his curiosity to know why this forlorn woman was going to a place she knew nothing about, in a train of which she knew nothing. Before he knew it, he was the questioner and she was answering. Gradually there unfolded all the romance about the sick husband, and the little ones left behind at their grandfather's in Nova Scotia; and then it proved, for the first time, that those two excellent little children who had met Mr. Tangier's approval already, because they sat so quietly on the seat in front of him, turning over the picture-books with which they were provided, belonged to the lone woman's caravan. She was leading them across this desert because the father had typhoid fever in Milwaukee, and she must go and nurse him.

So was it, that when the lightning express drew up for the first time at Wentworth, where Mr. Tangier was to leave it after his seventy miles' run, he had his hands full of telegrams to this man, and that, and another, by whose various offices he thought he could make her transfer simpler when she arrived at Milwaukee. He was not satisfied until he had provided her and the children with some extra refinements for the luncheons which, as he foresaw, they would have to devour before their thousand miles' ride was over.

The lightning train went on its way, and now he was left to inquire where he was, and what was to come next in the comparative loneliness of Wentworth Junction.

There were the various buggies, carryalls, and old-fashioned stage-coaches which were to be expected at such a place; but to none of them did he belong, as he knew, and none of them belonged to him. He placed himself in a favorable position to see and to be seen, and was accosted, as he expected, after a minute, by an overgrown boy who showed him a card on which his own name was written, and said, with some hesitation, "Be you this man?" Mr. Tangier said he was; and the boy signified by a gesture that he was the person who was to take him to his new home. Mr. Tangier had sent on by express the trunk which held his books and the most of those earthly possessions with which he was to solace himself at Tenterdon, so that a light carpet-bag made the sum of his impediments now. He was able, without delay, to join his guide in the carriage provided. Here, again, he found a woman sitting,—this time a young woman. She explained, briefly enough, that she was the niece of Mrs. Fairbanks, at whose house our friend had taken his quarters. It would appear that she had come over with the overgrown boy for the purpose of supplying any brains which might be needed in the enterprise, and from a certain fear that he had not at command any over-provision of intelligence.   As it happened, her service had not been needed; but Mr. Tangier knew enough of the exigencies of such an occasion to know that she had not been wrong in thinking that such exigencies might arise.

The country from Wentworth to Tenterdon is not, in itself, singularly picturesque.   But the wind was in the southwest, the trees were just beginning to grow green, the earlier wild cherries were just going out of blossom, the earlier peach-trees in an occasional farmer's orchard were just in their glory, a few straggling apple-blossoms were showing their color, there was no dust in the road, and to poor Mr. Tangier the whole was heaven.   He did not care to talk; he did not care to listen.   He did not object to talk, and he did not object to listen.   His companion was in much the same mood, apparently.   She was probably a good deal more afraid of him than he was of her.   Sometimes he asked a question about a bridge, or a pond, or a mill, and then she gave, sensibly enough, a bit of local history. Her voice had been spoiled in some public school, as far as a public school can spoil a voice, so that she talked on a strained, high, and generally unnatural key-note.   But Mr. Tangier knew men and women enough not to be surprised at this.   Indeed, in the luxury of freedom, leaving his prison cell now for the first time in eleven months, he would have talked good-naturedly to a chimpanzee, or to a gorilla, or, with equal good-nature, he would have let the chimpanzee or the gorilla alone.

The house proved to be a comfortable old palace,

of the days when some sort of business was profitable in Tenterdon which is not profitable now. Privateering, perhaps, or the East Indian trade, or the North-western trade, — *quien sabe?* as our Spanish friends say, and why should Mr. Tangier care ? Enough that in those prosperous days, some prosperous year had been made cheerful for Tenterdon, as the King Log or King Stork of the town, in that day, bade men cut pines and oaks on the Lebanon of the neighborhood, rough-hew them to their will, and build for him this comfortable home of six square rooms on each floor, with two or three more in an " L," and bade them make the whole to be three stories high. " Twenty-four large rooms, you see, Mr. Tangier," said the rather pensive Mrs. Fairbanks, who was to be the hostess of our friend, as she showed him to his own apartments, " besides the entry rooms, as we call them." The pensive air intimated, what Mrs. Fairbanks did not say, that the old Satrap who built the house had added at least ten rooms for the single purpose of making trouble for her. But she did not yet know Mr. Tangier well enough to launch on that broad subject, — the difficulty of dusting these various rooms in summer, and keeping them in order. For him, he hardly listened. There was a large room for him to " sit and write in," as she said. There was one equally large for him to sleep in. His trunk, with the essentials of his estate, real and personal, arrived before dinner-time, and Mr. Tangier had soon made those personal arrangements of the rooms by which he knew that he should be comfortable in this new castle.

For the afternoon of the day of his arrival — yes, and for most of the next day — the poor man had no wish to do a thing. He roused himself up to write Mr. Heeren a note about something which he had forgotten. Then, as soon as the mail-driver had passed, carrying the few letters of the office to Knox, which was the distributing office, Mr. Tangier remembered something much more important which had been forgotten. But these were only little gusts on the surface of the still sea of his day. The old Satrap who had built the castle had made no piazzas to it. But Mr. Tangier had discovered a lee side tó it, which had evidently been discovered by other explorers. For in this lee side of the old house was an iron staple driven, and not far away was a post driven, and, so soon as Rachel Fairbanks saw that Mr. Tangier had discovered it, she produced a Mexican hammock, which proved to fit the distance between the post and the staple. And to this hammock Mr. Tangier betook himself. On the ground under him there lay the "Philadelphia American," the London "Weekly Times," and the last "Revue des Deux Mondes;" and, even to himself, Mr. Tangier pretended he was reading. But when that night the Recording Angel posted in the Reading Ledger the amount which Mr. Tangier had really read that day,—lo! it was not so much as Jean Campbell had read in "Deestrict Number 10 School-house" hard by. Now Jean Campbell was only five years old, and was by no means sure of all her letters.

No; poor Mr. Tangier still felt as he felt that evening after drawing Mr. Grace's will. He felt a good deal as a bloom of iron feels after it has been pounded on the top and pounded on the bottom by a hammer weighing five hundred thousand million tons, and then has been pounded on the right side and pounded on the left, and then has had each corner turned up skilfully by the ingenious workman, so that it may be finished off by being pounded four times more.

But youth, and time, and the hour, and sunlight, and a southwest wind, and the good God who manages all these, in his love of men, will bring all things round if one will wait. And so it happened that on the evening of his second day in Tenterdon, — thanks also to good coffee, and a good omelet, and a good steak at breakfast, thanks to good roast mutton and a good apple pudding at dinner, thanks to a brisk horseback ride in the afternoon, thanks to a tea made up of a dozen achievements of Mrs. Fairbanks and of Rachel Fairbanks, for which no language known to Mr. Tangier had names, — thanks to all these, as he sat on the stoop of the castle, just as the sun went down, Mr. Tangier began to remember his duties to mankind.

He had not yet gone near to his kind correspondent, Mrs. Dunster, who had opened for him the gates of this paradise of rest; and she, sainted woman, had not come near him.

But he knew where she lived. The house had been pointed out to him by Rachel as they came from the station.

So Mr. Tangier determined that he would make his duty-call, and express his thanks in the gray twilight; and he sauntered along the pretty village street, and turned up the avenue, not too carefully tended, to her house. Just as he came to the door, Mrs. Dunster herself appeared, dressed for a walk, but she offered at once to turn back with him. On the instant, he felt that he should not have recognized her, but she knew him without difficulty. The truth probably was that she had been expecting him all day.

He declined her invitation to return, and said he would walk with her wherever she was going.

But she urged her proposal. "Indeed, it is of no sort of consequence," she said. "I was only going to our week-day meeting."

"And why should not I go to the week-day meeting?" said he, laughing. "Or is it one of those mysterious ' mothers' meetings' which excite men to such frenzies of curiosity because they are not permitted to attend?"

Mrs. Dunster had recovered herself by this time, and had sense enough to be ashamed of what she had said before. She mended it now as well as she could.

"There is every reason why you should go; only, to be frank with you, young men do not generally show much enthusiasm about attending prayer-meetings."

Mr. Tangier, just turning thirty, was not above the delicate flattery which classed him with young men. Perhaps he would have gone to the conference meeting simply from courtesy to Mrs. Dunster, who was his hostess in Tenterdon, — perhaps it would have been so. What is certain is, that he determined at that moment to go. He was with these people for a month; he would enter into their life, and live as they lived. This was the social institution provided for the occasion, and it should be his as well as theirs.

He did not pretend that he was in the habit of attending such meetings. He knew perfectly well that he heard the minister, every Sunday, make appointments for them, and that such appointments never stirred a fibre of his memory or took three words on the white paper of his tickler.

It was a pleasant walk to the vestry of the pretty little meeting-house. They loitered as they went. It was clear enough that there was no enthusiastic rush in the neighborhood of attendants thronging to the meeting. A boy, a little inefficient, was lighting some kerosene lamps which smoked, and which were, indeed, but a poor substitute for the splendor of the evening glow outside. There were but one or two people in the room. Mrs. Dunster introduced her companion to them, and they sat talking of trifles while a few more dropped in. At last the wheels of a wagon were heard rattling without, and in a moment Mr. Burdett, the minister who was to conduct the meeting, appeared. In a few minutes more he took his place at the reading-desk, asked God's blessing, and proposed a hymn. Mrs. Dunster played the tune at a wretched, wheezing little melodeon, and the people all sang, timidly at first, but with more spirit as they went on. Then he gave out another hymn, and another, and the singing was better with each hymn. Mr. Tangier himself had a good enough baritone voice, a good ear, and sang correctly. Mr. Burdett had a singularly rich and clear tenor. Women generally sing better than men, at such places, and, as each hymn was finished, they all passed to another with more spirit and more.

Then Mr. Burdett read two or three Psalms and a passage from the Gospel, sympathetically, and as if he loved it, and then led them all in prayer simple, natural, and true. He sat a moment with his head resting on his hand; and then, in the same simple way, as if he were in his own home talking to his wife and children of something which had interested him, spoke of the hopeful feeling which bubbled out from the words he had read, and drew the analogy between this feeling and the sense of joy which he had felt as he drove across, in the sunset, from his own home. It seemed that this home was at Warner, some five miles away. He spoke perhaps four or five minutes, not as if he were forced to, but as if he wanted to. Then he sat still. Every one sat still. Mr. Tangier was so unused to conference meetings that he did not know but people were expected to sit still. For his own part, he had been sitting still all day, and he would be glad to sit still all night.

But this was not the plan. After a minute or two of serene silence, Mr. Burdett rose and said, "Brother Beecham, will you lead in prayer?"

Brother Beecham rose, and offered what he would have called a prayer. But to Mr. Tangier it seemed as if there was but little heart in the words, as if he had himself heard them before, as if Brother Beecham had committed them to memory to use when he was asked to. In a word, poor Mr. Tangier was conscious that he was not praying, but criticising, and he was very glad when Mr. Beecham sat down. Then Mr. Burdett read another hymn, and they sang; he gave another, and they sang it better. Then, to Mr. Tangier's surprise, Mr. Beecham rose and delivered quite an address. It had nothing to do with hopefulness, — it was rather in a vein of despondency, with a tone of wrath. It was devoted, first to abusing the people of the village who had not come to the conference, and then to abusing those who did come. For Mr.

Beecham said that if those who came would speak, and make the meetings inter*est*ing, — and he put the accent on the second *e*, as if that had something to do with it, — the others would attend. For his part, he did not wonder that they stayed away.

Mr. Tangier had not had the slightest idea of joining in the conversation of the evening. He was a stranger, and it had not occurred to him that any man or woman was to talk, as a duty. But he did not mean to have the people round him abused. And so he said, very frankly and simply, that for his own part he had particularly enjoyed the silence; that he thought there was far too much talking in the world, of the machine kind; and that, especially in matters of religion, the less that was said of that sort the better. "I suppose we come here," said he very quietly, " to listen to God, and to know what He may have to say to us. Surely our friends the Quakers are right in thinking that we may hear Him better when there is no other talking."

Mr. Tangier did not mean to say anything. But he was wholly used to addressing assemblies much larger than Mr. Burdett's conference meeting, and he felt only more at ease the moment he was on his feet. As soon as he sat down, a lady behind him, with a rich, full contralto voice began to sing, —

"Lord, dismiss us with Thy blessing,"

and after this, whether Mr. Burdett wished it or not, he had to dismiss the little assembly.

Mr. Tangier and Mrs. Dunster had a word with him. He then released his horse, mounted his wagon, and drove to his home, and they walked slowly to hers.

CHAPTER V.

A S they came to the house, a wagon drove up behind them, and a hearty voice saluted them. It proved that the speaker was the doctor of the neighborhood, Dr. Tillinghast. He jumped from the carriage, evidently confident that the horse would stand, and joined the other two.

"Is this Mr. Tangier?" he said with the cordiality of a gentleman accustomed to meet all sorts and conditions of men. "I have just been calling on you at our good friend Mrs. Fairbanks's; Miss Rachel told me that I should find you here, so you must regard this as my call of hospitality. I come to offer you our all, — our meadows, our hills, our prospects, our wild-flowers, our distant beaches, and our neighboring river, with all the gayeties of Tenterdon society."

Mr. Tangier thanked him, in the same hearty way, and said that Mrs. Dunster had already told him that he was entitled to the freedom of the village. He also spoke of the pleasant talk he had had with this Mr. Burdett whom he had found at the church.

"At the church," said the doctor, with the slightest change in tone; "that is loyal in you, indeed. Frankly, Mr. Tangier, I divide our summer visitors into two classes: First, those who range themselves on the

side of order; next, those who range themselves nowhere, and thus belong, of necessity, to the party of
disorder."

Tangier laughed. "You remember," said he, "what
Byron makes the Devil say : —

'He who bows not to God, has bowed to me.'"

The doctor smiled his approval. "It is very good
gospel," said he, "whether it come from Byron, or the
Devil, or from both. Do not think that I am too
serious about it. Of course, when people come here
to play, they come to play. I understand that very
well. But here are Mrs. Dunster and I, and Rachel
Fairbanks, and Jane Campbell yonder, and five hundred other children of God, who are here all the time.
I can assure you that we watch pretty closely the
manners and customs of the polished people who come
to us from the scenes of high civilization. Your
friend Mrs. Fairbanks would call them 'the boarders.'
She divides the world into two classes : the people of
Tenterdon, and 'the boarders.' When I first heard
her I thought only of the 'Pirate's Own Book,' with
which I was familiar, and the thrilling cry of the sea-
fights, 'Boarders to repel boarders.' But if you are
skilful in dime literature, you know that there are
good ruffians as well as bad ruffians, just as there are
good giants and bad giants in the fairy tales. So
there are good boarders, like those who come to Tenterdon for the summer, and bad boarders, like those
in the 'Pirate's Own Book.'"

By this time they were all seated on Mrs. Dunster's
deep piazza. Somebody had brought out two or three
rugs, there was a moon, a quarter old, in the sky, and

there was no temptation to go in. After a little talk, Mr. Tangier recalled the doctor to this matter of the social order of such a scattered town, as it was affected by the annual inroad, for three or four months, of people who had nothing to do but to amuse themselves.

"To tell you the truth," said he, "I have thought of this, this evening, quite as much as I have thought of the Scripture lesson. I had around me one of the social institutions of Tenterdon. For the greatest of all possible subjects, for the one subject, indeed, which, rightly presented, interests everybody, there were nineteen people assembled on a pleasant evening, with a man of genius to talk to them, and with every association of the very best memories in their lives to bring them together. Of these nineteen people, well, I should say a dozen had passed that grand climacteric which Dr. Jackson says is the prime of life, — namely, sixty-three years, or thereabouts. Of the rest, two or three were boys and girls, who had come because the old people could not be trusted alone with the horses. So far as the meeting showed any social habit among the people of Tenterdon, it could not be considered as encouraging. Now, tell me what other social institutions are here, summer or winter, which bring these people together in larger places, or which show any heartier desire to know each other, to live in a common life, and to make these to be the best possible of homes."

Thus challenged, the doctor and Mrs. Dunster reviewed with some little care the history of the last year in Tenterdon. They told how many sleigh-rides had been arranged in winter, by which the young people went across to Wors-neck and had a dance there together. They told of the political caucus in the fall, when General Logan spoke to the whole county. They told of the cattle-show in the autumn; and this seemed to be, on the whole, the great social event of the year. Rather to Mr. Tangier's surprise, for his memories were of a different region and another form of social life, there was, really, no reference to those friendly visitings in which twenty or thirty people should come together to spend an evening, with the single exception of the monthly meeting of the ladies' missionary society, which Mrs. Dunster described with a good deal of spirit and humor.

There was a little lull after this somewhat scant programme. Then Mr. Tangier said, "Seriously, are these all the possibilities? When one remembers that as few people as these, when they gathered together at New Haven, had force enough to build up a commonwealth, to make its laws and so adjust its institutions that everything has worked well there for two hundred and fifty years, one feels as if five hundred people here might have better social institutions than these."

Dr. Tillinghast took him up with the same seriousness. "Yes," he said, " all things are possible where there is a leader. Where will you be Sunday afternoon? If you don't dislike a pleasant drive across the country, I will clear my docket in the morning, and in the afternoon I will take you across to Winthrop, and you shall hear their music there. Then you shall see what grows up on good ground when there has been good planting and good ploughing for half a century."

Sunday was fine, and the two started together, — two men who had just passed the flush of early manhood. Each, in his own place, was now beginning to feel that he had duties to society. They talked of everything as they rode, and they enjoyed everything. Most of all they enjoyed each other. The eight miles seemed only too short as they drove into Winthrop, which proved to be a little town dedicated to the manufacture of shoes, with rather a crude look of freshness in the great shops, scattered among the old houses of the days when farming still paid in that region.

"Mr. Dunlap lets me use his horse-shed," said Tillinghast; and they drove into one of a long series of sheds which the piety of former times had arranged for the horses of Sunday worshippers. Having cared for their beast, they walked across together to the town-hall, a new, unhandsome, brick building, spacious and convenient, to which the people of the village were already thronging.

Here they found perhaps a hundred and fifty people, chatting among the chairs and settees. In a minute there came in upon the platform the members of a large orchestra, with their instruments. In all, there were thirty-two pieces, and Mr. Tangier saw, a little to his surprise, that the different performers arranged themselves, and adjusted their instruments, with quite the artistic knowledge of the position, and consciousness of their own ability, which he might have expected had he seen Thomas's orchestra in New York. At once the assembly was seated and all conversation stopped. In a moment the leader of the orchestra tapped with his rod, a few strains were played upon one instrument, and then the whole assembly arose and sung as a choral:—

"A mighty fortress is our God,"

led by the director, whose superb orchestra rendered the tune.

Dr. Tillinghast had, with a good deal of skill, refrained from telling Mr. Tangier just what théy were to see and hear. The satisfaction of the afternoon, therefore, had to him all the elements of surprise. For two hours an orchestra, such as he had seldom heard, rendered with dignity and feeling some of the best music of the noblest composers. A modest little programme in his hand told him who these masters were when, as sometimes happened, he did not know. At the end of the service, and a majestic service it was, the conductor turned once more to the congregation, which rose again and sang a parting hymn as they had sung before. Some of the people went out, some stayed to chat with each other. Dr. Tillinghast and Mr. Tangier found their wagon and rode home.

"That is what is possible," said the doctor. "More than fifty years ago the musical society of this village was gathered and incorporated. That has probably helped in building up the taste of this town. But in our generation one modest man who knows the power of music has organized this grand orchestra. Nobody pays them, nobody pays him, except the good God. And I think He gives them satisfaction enough by way of present recompense. This man was the leader, whom you saw. If he had not been too modest you would have heard one of his own compositions. I dare say you have heard them in New York or in

Cincinnati. I wanted you to see this, so soon as you asked what was possible in a community of five hundred people."

Note. — I have here attempted to describe the interesting musical service which is carried on every Sunday afternoon in the town of Stoughton, in Norfolk County, in Massachusetts. My purpose would not have been advanced in the least, had I merely presented an imaginary picture. I have but described in this chapter, as well as I can, the service which the people of this town render regularly under the leadership of Mr. Edward Jones. — E. E. H.

CHAPTER VI.

MR. TANGIER did not find that he made more than a passing acquaintance with most of the people who were around him. His first personal contact with any of them was on a day when a sudden shower overtook him as he was returning from a long walk. He came, very much to his own satisfaction, to the little school-house of District No. 9. The house stood quite alone on the side of a rather dreary road, where it had been placed, in the canonical fashion of New England, in order that it might be as near as possible to the geographical centre of the district. Mr. Tangier arrived there, fortunately for him, just as the large drops were beginning to fall, and without much hesitation he opened the front door and found himself in a little hall, perhaps three feet square, where was another door which he knew would admit him to the school-room.

His own plan would have been to stay alone, and watch the rain in front of him, under this safe shelter; but the passing of any traveller, either on horseback, in a wagon, or on foot, was quite too much of an event not to have been noticed from the school windows. After a moment's pause the schoolmistress, who was never called by that name, but was always called the "teacher," came to the inner door, opened it, and asked him to walk in.

She was a tall, slight girl, not more than seventeen years of age. She blushed as she rendered the invitation, as she would have done had Mr. Tangier been cross-examining her as a witness upon the stand; but she passed bravely through the ordeal, and succeeded in offering her hospitality very simply. Mr. Tangier was not sorry to be asked. He said to himself that he should have a chance to see how much twenty years of Horace Mann and his disciples had affected the school system of his dear New England; and he would certainly be more comfortable sitting, as the shower went by, than he would be standing alone in the little entry-way.

The hospitalities were rendered a little more difficult because the "teacher" had no chair to offer, excepting that which she was in the habit of occupying herself. Mr. Tangier made the proper gentlemanly protests against depriving her of her seat; but so soon as he saw that it would really be a relief to her to have him do so, he took the chair, as Lord Stair entered the French king's carriage. He begged her not to change the exercises of the morning, in any sort, — assured her that he should like to see them. He nodded to a certain little Nellie Pingree, whose acquaintance he had already made in the neighborhood, took the spelling-book which Miss Gurtry offered him, and pretended to give attention to the recitation.

That particular class consisted of the typical "other little girl and I," which makes a prominent part in every district school. In point of fact, Mr. Tangier did not so much trouble himself to observe whether that little boy, and that girl with her finger in her mouth, could or could not spell "cool" and "pool."

He was more occupied in watching the aspect of the children, and the general make-up of the institution.

He knew already that he should see none of the larger boys there. They had quite too much estimate of their own worth, to go to school in the summer; and yet, be it observed, that same estimate would have compelled them to go to school in the winter. That is to say, they would have fought to·the death against any employer who refused them the necessary hours for the winter school. On the other hand, they would have absolutely disobeyed any employer who directed them to take six hours of his time in the summer, that they might go to the school-house. There was no distinction in this case between the teachers. This same slight, tall, blue-eyed Miss Gurtry "kept the school" in winter and in summer. It was simply a matter of conventional etiquette, belonging to the invisible distinction between a great boy and a little boy, and thus there was not a "great boy" of them all — that expression in this case meaning not a boy over eleven years of age — but would have preferred the hardest work in the hay-field, or the most disgraceful work in following after the raking-machine, when they had been cutting the rye, to the easy luxury of sitting under pretty Miss Gurtry's care for six hours of a sultry summer day. None of them would debase himself by going with the "little fellows."

But there were girls nearly as old as Miss Gurtry was herself. The population of the school, therefore, was, as it happened, eleven girls and six boys, and, of the boys, some were so small and so clad that it was difficult to distinguish them from their own sisters.

As for classification, as Mr. Tangier soon found out, there was little or none. The law of natural selection had brought together the boy and girl who were spelling "pool" and "cool." The teacher told him, with a good-natured laugh, as soon as she became well enough acquainted, that she had three other classes as large as that, and one class which was larger. But practically, for most of the studies, she was obliged to engage each scholar, as it were, hand to hand; and thus the scholars all had the full benefit of her personal assistance and advice. Mr. Tangier came into the building with a simple curiosity about a system which has extended itself, nobody knows how, over the training of more than three million people in New England. He had a theoretical respect for the principle by which the children of these three million people receive some sort of training, in some sort of literature, for at least twenty-five weeks in each year. To tell the whole truth, he supposed that this training was of a very negligent and shabby sort, and when he saw the young woman who gave him his chair, it was with a simple feeling of pity that, where a world was out of joint, she should be set to put it right, even in one of its least important corners.   -

But as the shower went on, possibly in the course of an hour, she called up to her eight or ten different pupils, now fashioned in classes of two, and now quite alone; and with her kindly, simple, pretty way, made to each of them the lesson of the next hour clear and interesting. Mr. Tangier found himself engaged, before long, in some quite labored speculations as to methods of instruction; and he began to wonder how it was that a girl, not much more than half his own age, should be handling, with so delicate a touch, the machinery of life of infinite beings, so wisely and successfully as he saw she did. He pretended that he was not watching her, for he saw in a moment that so long as he did watch her she was ill at ease. He walked to the wall, therefore, and affected to be interested in the geography of the States west of the Rocky Mountains. Then he read, or pretended to read, the Constitution of the United States, which was framed in a broadside and hung on the other side of the room. But really, all the time, he was wondering to think how it was, by what law of natural selection or other selection, that a person so competent to deal with these little half savages had drifted into the place where he found this young woman. He said to himself that his first letter to Morton, instead of being a description of morning sunrise or of the glow of sunset, would be an enthusiastic rhapsody on a subject for which he had supposed he cared so little as the working of the common-school system of America.

He was fairly sorry when a scream from one of the children announced that the lower arc of a rainbow could be seen from the eastern window. The teacher permitted the children all to run to the door to look out on the beautiful spectacle, and poor Mr. Tangier had no longer an excuse for staying to watch the performances.

He then made his good-byes very cordially, asked if he might not come in and examine the school again (laughing as he did so), nodded to his new acquaintances among the children, and renewed his walk.

CHAPTER VII.

ON his return home, after the adventure at the school-house, Mr. Tangier found that a new arrival had disturbed the usual stillness and serenity of Mrs. Fairbanks's establishment. A party had arrived from New Hamburg. The existence of this party had been frequently alluded to by Mrs. Fairbanks. Mr. Tangier had observed that she spoke of it as one might speak of a bale of cotton, or of a barrel of molasses, which an agent had shipped, regarding whose quality the consignee was comparatively indifferent. A party was, to Mrs. Fairbanks, a party. It occupied such and such rooms; and thus it left such and such other rooms to be divided between the woman who had written from Omaha, and that Mrs. Jones or Mrs. Smith who had written from Washington, and the people who had the L chambers last year, who were not sure whether they should come or not this year. "It all depends," said Mrs. Fairbanks, as she reviewed the position to Mr. Tangier one morning as he sat at breakfast, "it all depends on whether their Uncle Silas dies or not. If he should die, — well, they would never come here again. They would go to Newport. For they would divide his property with that Mr. Clam, — I dare say you know him, an insurance man in Chicago, — and they would not come to a place like this. But if he does not die, — and die pretty soon, — they will take the second-story L chambers again."

And as Mrs. Fairbanks studied her "Deaths" every day, when the paper came, it was with a special interest in the death or life of the uncle.

How little did he or his physician know how his ups and downs affected the interests of this unknown corner of the world!

Mr. Tangier found the new party at tea. He was introduced by name to Mrs. Hasey, the older lady, — to Mrs. Floxam, whom he soon fixed, and fixed correctly, as Mrs. Hasey's niece, — to two tall and hungry girls, — and to two short boys, equally hungry, who, fortunately for his peace, said nothing, but ate the more. This was Mrs. Fairbanks's affair, not his. And he was so far a philanthropist, that he was quite willing to do his duty in passing the syrup backward and forward. Mrs. Fairbanks, watchful at her post, observed this philanthropy, and at the next meal placed these young people together, with syrup pitchers of their own. "I do not mean to have you do the work of my table-girl, Mr. Tangier."

If the children were silent, the cause soon appeared. If Mrs. Floxam seemed a little weighed down, the cause soon appeared. Mrs. Hasey, cheerful, smooth of face, and unconscious of fatigue, bore no sign of the six hundred and seventy-seven miles which they had passed over since they left New Hamburg, say thirty-one hours before. The pillow of the sleeper had left no wrinkle on her face, the motion of the train had not affected her appetite. She wore the same sunny smile with which she may have looked on a Commencement at William and Mary, when, as a girl of twelve, she had first graced a public pageant, and when she first smiled her commendatious upon the graduates of the day. She was not at the head of the table, and there was nothing arrogant in her manner. But, from the beginning, she was as perfectly at home here as she would have been at any table of her own (if, poor soul! she had had such a table in many years). It may be said, in passing, had she been at a Royal party at Windsor, she would have assumed the same cordial expression of interest in all people present; or had she been asked to try pot-luck in the seediest and poorest tenement-house iu the city of New York, she would there have borne herself with equal ease and good-nature.

The busiuess of eating and drinking had scarcely been undertaken, when she addressed herself to Mr. Tangier. She did not affect to have known him before, but she spoke to him as if they had travelled on the highway of life together for twenty years. Still, her first question acknowledged her ignorance. It was to ask him whether he were any relative of a gentleman named Tunis, whom she had known in the city of Fredericksburg, in Virginia.

. Mr. Tangier was amused, but he did not yet feel intimate enough to laugh. He said, which was true enough, that he knew that there was such a name as Tunis, but he did not think that he had any relatives of that name. It was possible, he said, however, that they might have crossed together in the "Mayflower," or the "Lion."

Mrs. Hasey took up the word "Lion," and said at once, "Ah, then we are relatives ourselves, Mr. Tangier, at least, so far as the "Lion" goes; for I am quite sure that my people came over in the 'Lion,' or if my people did n't, my husband's did, and that is very much the same."

Mr. Tangier laughed this time, and was amused, but was willing enough to enter into the intimacy which was proposed, and took her on her own easy terms.

"I made quite a study once," he said, "of the people on board the 'Lion.' I think Roger Williams was on the 'Lion,' and I once tried to write a little essay on the talk that he and the other passengers had. I did a little to work up their characters and notions from what came of them afterwards. But he is a skilful artist who can make those hard old fellows live and move and have any being, and I was willing enough to put the whole into the fire."

"Ah, then," said Mrs. Hasey, "you are one of the literary gentlemen. We had an author here last year, and my daughter there used to help him reading his proofs. I forget what he was making. Was it a dictionary, Mary, or a volume of sonnets?"

Mary set her right as to the dictionary and the volume of sonnets. In point of fact, it was neither. It was an abridged history of the United States, for the use of schools. They all laughed at the nice old lady for her indifference to the subject, and some one told the story of the other old lady who arrived at Mrs. Hayward's house, and said she should like the novel which she had left unfinished the year before. When she was asked what the novel was, she did not remember its name, and she did not know what the story was about; but she did remember that the back was of the same color as the paint on the banisters as she went up to bed. So one of the young ladies went up to the library, took the color of the banister in her eye as she went, and matching the novel, brought it triumphantly downstairs.

Mr. Tangier said that this showed the disadvantage of being color-blind. He said it would be very hard for a man who had read half through Bancroft's history to find himself going on with Gibbon's "Decline and Fall," merely because he could not tell the difference between purple and green in the cambric binding.

"As to that," said Mrs. Hasey, "I do not know myself how they remember anything about either.

"I should think, Mr. Tunis," she continued, in the inexhaustible flow of her good spirits, good-temper, and general friendliness, "I should think that you would move your hammock, and swing it so that you might look down the road and see the passing."

Mr. Tangier started, without meaning to. It was so clearly his own business where he should or should not take his afternoon nap, or whether he should take it at all, that it had not occurred to him that his place for it was to be discussed in the daily caucus of breakfast, dinner, or supper. But he was good-natured, and was amused. He said only that he found the staples driven where they were; that when a man went to a hammock he was not in a mood for reforms, and that he had left them as he found them.

"Oh, yes, Mr. Tunis, I understand all that. But this nice boy that brought us over, I am sure he is handy with tools. I saw how he knocked the stone out of his horse's hoof. He will change them for you, if you ask him. I will speak to him when he brings my trunk upstairs."

Here Mr. Tangier proved rebellious. And he said, simply, that he would give his own directions when he made up his mind where the hammock should swing. The old lady listened, not at all displeased.

"I beg your pardon, indeed I do, my dear Mr. Tunis. You must not be offended with an old woman like me. My brother John always told me that my advice-mill was always going. Don't you mind it. Let me talk, and do not listen if you do not care to."

"I have had one little tiff with Mrs. Fairweather already," she said, laughing good-naturedly, — for she was the essence of good-nature. "I advised her to hang her clothes on the sunny side of the house; but somehow she did not like that. But we have quite made it up. And you and I must be friends, Mr. Tunis, because we are to sit together. I am sure we are to be friends." And so in fact they were.

Poor Mrs. Floxam, beat out and reduced to her first elements by her six or eight hundred miles of travel, withdrew as soon as she might, after she had taken a cup of tea, and hardly appeared again in the conclaves of the house for the next three days. At the end of half an hour of toast, and biscuits, and Indian-cakes, and buckwheat-cakes, varied with clam-fritters and chicken-croquettes, and finished by tipsy-cake, the hungry girls and hungry boys so far ceased temporarily from hunger that they slipped from their seats, and went off together on a walk in search of the beach. To his equal amusement and amazement, Mr. Tangier found himself sitting on the front stoop of the house with old Mrs. Hasey, and listening to her views on the difference between Pennsylvania and New York, New York and Connecticut, Connecticut and Rhode Island, as she had gathered them from the ride of the last day and a half, of which nine hours had been spent in the seclusion of her own sleeping-car berth.

Mr. Tangier remembered that agricultural correspondent of the London "Times," who enlightened "Times" reading Europe by a general review of American agriculture, after he had passed for four hours along the Shore Line Road, from Harlem to Providence.

Why did Mr. Tangier sit there and listen to the old lady's chattering? He could have gone to the side piazza. He could have sat on the open veranda which was his own, where no one could interfere, for it opened from his own room. To this question he gave a good deal of attention, as he put it to himself, three hours afterward, when he was undressing for bed. Why had he spent these three hours listening to the chatter of an old woman?

First, perhaps, because she was a lady through and through; for a lady may have the passion for talking, and yet shall not cease to be a lady.

Second, because she never spoke one unkind word of anybody. Things and institutions she might disapprove of; but if she disapproved of people, the disapproval was buried as a deep secret in her own heart.

Third, because it was clear that talking was simply life to her — or life was talking. You sat by her and enjoyed the constant stream as you enjoy the fall of a pretty cascade in the flow of a forest brook. Very likely you do not look at the cascade all the time. Very likely your thoughts are far away, a-flood or a-field. You are fighting with Zulus in Africa, while the stream babbles on and the water falls; or you are striking whales with Gardner in the Arctic; or you are drawing forth "cheers from the opposition," as you electrify Parliament in your discussion of the Land-league. And still the cascade talks to you; nay, it improves your speech by its talk to you. If the cascade stopped a moment, why, the Land-league speech would stop as well.

These were the accounts Mr. Tangier gave to himself of his listening, or of his sitting there as if listening. So far as they went they were true accounts. But in this particular case there was something more.

The week which he had spent in the absolute serenity of Mrs. Fairbanks's house, and its almost absolute stillness, had about exhausted his newly-discovered joy in such silence as existed before chaos began. For five or six evenings Mr. Tangier had sat on this stoop and looked on this sky; in which evenings, from one half-hour to another, no creak of a wheel, no cry of a distant goose, no stroke of a bell or whistle of an engine would break the stillness. Least of all would there sound any whisper of human intelligence.

At first, as his friend Dr. Morton expected, this silence was absolute bliss to that poor tired brain. To live, to breathe, to see, to enjoy, — all these were possible, with the omission of to listen, to think, and to reply. Nature, silence, God, had done their perfect work for the poor man as these days of silence went by. But it is not ordered that such days shall last forever, nor is it best that they should.

"Man is a gregarious animal."

Mr. Tangier was not to forget the sounds of the English language, nor the moods and tenses of its verbs, nor the construction of its sentences, because he had taken his vacation.

And that kind divinity which was delicately carving for him those pretty figures in the ends of his life, which for himself he had shaped rather as a bungler does, had now devised this simple plan. This good-natured, simple-minded old lady, who was a lady indeed, who envied nobody and despised nobody, and would not pain a fly, was moved up by the pawns to the square next Mr. Tangier's square on the chessboard. It was quite clear that their lives would never conflict. She could not conflict with anybody. She was like a bishop white, who cannot touch the pawn who is safely on the black square. But from her square to Mr. Tangier's square the sound of the steady flow of the ripple could pass across; and he, hardly knowing himself how much he needed such a soothing mixture, had been tranquillized by it as these three hours went by.

CHAPTER VIII.

MR. TANGIER found unending interest in his walks. The country all around Tenterdon is one of those regions where the New Englander found little occasion to stay, after the foresight of the National government gave to him, elsewhere, a farm of the best of land if he would only go and ask for it. Over the old grass-lands and corn-fields here, had grown new forests. If the old tenant had not been gone many years, the aspect of the approach of these forests was pathetic. Even before the trig chestnut fences rotted, by which it had been his pride to protect his land, inquiring seeds of birch and pine had flown over and settled, and the next spring they had germinated. With another year more of such discoverers passed the frontier, and some of them came farther on the fated field. Meanwhile, the last year's invaders were bigger and bigger. Not many years of such invasion covered the whole of the acres, where so much labor had dragged away the stones for walls almost cyclopean. While this process was going on, when yet one side of the field, once mowing-land or corn-land, maintained the pretences of a worn-out pasture, the advances which the forest made upon it worked like the stealthy approaches of an assailing army.

Once and again Mr. Tangier came upon a little cellar which showed where the Burge house, or the Winter barn, or the Comegys place had stood. And there were two or three of these deserted mansions still standing, — the windows gone, a wretched bit of stove-funnel, with the absolutely useless parts of a few boots, remaining in them, perhaps ; and, as Mr. Tangier found once and again, enough roof for a shelter if a summer shower came on. For one considerable section of the town, he found that such were almost the only houses remaining. The old roads had sunk into being mere wood-roads, of the very worst. Nobody repaired them in summer, because the snow of winter would make them into the most convenient of highways, precisely fit for their only purpose, — the dragging of wood out from the forests for market.

There was, however, in this precinct one inhabited house. It was very much inhabited. It stood in a picturesque position, where it had a wide outlook on the distant sea, with a nearer prospect of one of the pretty ponds which give life to the woodland scenery anywhere. Mr. Tangier did not understand its internal plan. But it was so small, and the windows were so few, that it seemed clear enough that there were but few rooms within. Still, it had so many inhabitants on the outside, — if the extravagance of the expression may be pardoned, — that you wondered what became of them all when they chose to inhabit it indeed. Groups of black children of all sizes, and of the capacities belonging to such sizes, were invariably lounging about the house when Mr. Tangier passed it, or were sunning themselves upon the ground. He met people whom he supposed to be the fathers and mothers of these children, and with them he always, of course, passed the civilities of travellers who meet, as they met, in the wilderness. There were explanations made by Mrs. Fairbanks, which made it probable that a grandmother and a great-grandmother lived with the several families and parts of families which made up this establishment at Joe Turner's. Further inquiry made it certain that Joe Turner had been shot in Florida in the war. But his name clung to the establishment, because Joe was, on the whole, the person of most capacity who had held this fort within the memory of man.

With this rantipole crew Mr. Tangier had established friendly relations. He had picked up one of the boys at the post-office one day, and had taken the boy sailing with him, to help him about his fish, if he took any. This boy became afterward a sort of retainer. Mr. Tangier wanted to carry his intimacy with the family rather further, and the next time he wrote to New York he sent an order to Scribner's for half-a-dozen toy-books, to be of the most gorgeous colors, with which he meant to open his intercourse with some of the younger brats when he next passed Turner's in a walk.

It was therefore with a certain personal interest that he started from bed one night, waked suddenly from the profoundest sleep by the cry below in the roadway, twice repeated, "Joe Turner's afire!" He started from bed, flung up his curtain, and could see above the trees of the orchard a lurid red light flashing up and coloring the clouds. He was dressed in a very few minutes, sprang over the rail which cut off Turner's little water-washed roadway from the main road, and ran up the hill to the scene of the disaster. One or two other loafers from the village were before him, and from the sounds behind he knew that one or two followed him.

It was scarce half a mile away, and a few minutes brought him there; but the mischief was already irreparable. There had not been a gallon of water within a quarter-mile of the house. Turner's had never known any such luxury as a well, and for a century every drop of water used there had been painfully carried up in buckets from the pond below. So soon as the smell of smoke in the roof had been perceived, "Sabriny" had dragged her babies and children from their lairs. "Orson, he run and told Quintus to go fetch somebody to help grandma; Typhosy, she waked the old woman up, and drefful hard to wake her it was, too; I got her mother out o' bed, and Cesar — woll, the fust thing I see o' Cesar he went up on the roof, with a blanket an' an axe, a tryin' to see where the fire was. And I sez, 'Cesar,' sez I, 'you can't do nothing up there Cesar,' sez I; and jost that minute the ladder sort o' lurched, sea-fashion like, an' Cesar he tumbled right down on the axe, and he cut hisself, — see there, Mr. Tangier, — but he larfed, an' I larfed too, Mr. Tangier, 'cos they was n't no need cryin' anyway."

This was the rather lucid account of the fire which Mr. Tangier received from Mrs. Wotch, who had never spoken to him before, but who regarded him as a friend because he had taken her boy when he went for bluefish.

It was a ghastly, melancholy sight, as they stood and saw the torrent of fire rise into the sky from those miserable walls. Why they stood, it was hard to say. What there was within, to burn with that lurid flame, Mr. Tangier wondered. Again he was reminded of effects on the stage. The figures of the children running to and fro between him and the red glow were like little devils he had seen in the strontian-made hells of the opera. On one side, almost as if it were the chariot of Ahriman in some spectacle, was "grandma" seated with "ole Aunt Eunice," — whoever she might be, — on Virgil's ox-cart, which, with more speed than could have been expected, had been brought to the scene of action. Virgil lived on the other side of the pond. He was by far the most substantial of that community, half black, half Indian, to which the Joe Turner colony belonged in line of race. So soon as he had seen the light, he had remembered Aunt Eunice and grandma, and had fastened his oxen into his wood-cart, throwing in some cotton quilts for their comfort at midnight. From his side he arrived, as Mr. Tangier and the village people arrived from the other. And as they all stood and watched the flame, the patient oxen wondered, and the two old women, more pleased with the excitement than distressed by any fancied loss, pointed out the rise or fall of the unsteady flames, and gave such accounts of it as suggested themselves.

"There goes Jabe's gun," as a sudden discharge intimated that the wretched duck-gun had been heated hot enough to fire its wad. "Them's Sabriny's beds," when a shower of sparks seemed to show that the straw had taken fire. But such comments were silenced by Sabriny herself. She had been counting up her jewels, who, one might fear, had never been counted before. With one shrill cry she silenced all other discussion.

"Ware's Nathan?"

Clearly Nathan was not present; yet he had been there two minutes before.

Ten seconds was enough for the whole of the imaginative party. Each person had put himself in Nathan's place in fancy, and Sabriny expressed the feeling of all, when, in a cry of agony, she announced:

"He's gone for his chicks."

All parties changed their places. It seemed there was a wretched shed on the other side the cabin, scarce big enough for Joe Turner's cow of other days, for which Joe Turner had built it. Standing outside the rest, it had not burned at the same moment. But on the outside the flame had already run along the shingles, and the top of the little roof was of a blaze.

Into this appendix to a hovel it was supposed Nathan had gone. The wretched Sabriny soon fancied she saw his form, and screamed to him.

At the moment she did so, Mr. Tangier jumped in at the window of the shed and disappeared.

CHAPTER IX.

MR. TANGIER arrived suddenly in chaos.
The stillness of the whole scene but a minute before, as the flames and smoke rose into the sky, and the family looked on, almost without a word, had seemed strange to him. With his plunge through the window he had entered a very different world.

At the bottom of this world, as a critic on Dante might say, was a dirty, deep pit, five or six feet beneath the surface of the world without, to which Nathan usually descended by a ladder from the cabin itself, which stood upon the surer level of mankind. Upon this rickety ladder Mr. Tangier fell heavily as he sprang through the window. The crazy thing broke with his weight, and he came heavily down on his side in the filthy hay and straw, which was heaped up as the first foundation of the hens' palace. It was pitch-dark; for the wall of the house on that side had not given way, and the door by which Nathan had entered, by a bit of forethought, was so made as to swing to, after it had been opened, which prevented visits from the poultry into the kitchen or sitting-room from that entrance.

Nathan was himself wallowing in the muck-heap, doing unequal battle with a cockerel which he had seized. The hens were yelling in mad flight above, unintelligent as hens always are; for they are the most stupid animals yet discovered. A few minutes, however, were enough for them. The open window which Mr. Tangier had destroyed gave them means of escape, which they had not before. Nathan had sense enough to perceive this, and let the rooster follow them, releasing him at last from the stout hold he had kept upon his legs.

It was not so easy for Mr. Tangier and Nathan to follow, and withdraw from the place of battle.

The hen-house, like everything else in Sabriny Wotch's way, was used now for a different purpose from that for which it had been made. It may be added that it was as nearly unfit for the purpose of a hen-house as it could be. Nathan had himself made the ladder by which, on necessity, he could descend into it from the low doorway. A larger doorway, which opened from the side, was closed at night against the attacks of foxes or fox-like men, and was made fast, as Nathan hastily explained to Mr. Tangier, by what he called a "timber" pushed against it on the outside. It opened on the level of the average world, and was six or seven feet above them as they stood, or reclined, and rapidly discussed the position.

Mr. Tangier would have made light of the difference of level, — did make light of it at first. But on the first effort he made to raise himself by his hands from the hole in which he and Nathan were immured, he found to his disgust — not to say his dismay — that he had sprained his wrist. The fingers of the hand refused to clasp on the stone of the cellar wall as he bade them; and the arm itself, from elbow to shoulder, was so strained that he found it hard to lift it as high as his head.

Here they were, then, safe enough for the minute, but knowing, both of them, that they were not safe for two minutes. He would have been a bold man who would have sought to pass through the burning cabin. They had, however, no chance for such desperate courage, for the fall of the ladder had made retreat through the door impossible. The window which had let out the fowls was high above their heads, but it seemed the only feasible escape. For a little light boy, and a strong and athletic man, it appeared at the first an easy escape. But one and another effort showed the man that he was not strong, and showed him, also, that fear was not giving his companion wings. On the other hand, the lad was ineffably stupid in the presence of danger, and had already begun to cry.

Once and again with his left hand Mr. Tangier set up against the wall the short remaining bit of the ladder, lifted the boy upon it, and instructed him as to the best way of clambering to the sill beam of the shed above them, from which he could easily swing himself out of the window. Once and again the fallacious stick rolled away under the boy, and he fell heavily back in the mud-heap. Mr. Tangier, in the grim presence of danger, could not help remembering John Bunyan, and the long-continued and useless labors of the man at the house of the Interpreter. He was himself well aware that he could probably save himself only by using the counsels which he gave the boy. But he had not entered the shed so abruptly simply to get out of it. And the closer the danger, the clearer was his duty.

"Is n't there a barrel, Nathan? is n't there any old box here? What do you keep the corn in?"

"Ain't no corn. Warn't never no corn. Never feed 'em with corn. Ain't got none," sobbed and slobbered the boy.

"Don't cry, Nathan, don't cry; there is no good in crying. Don't you think of anything like an old rake, or a pitchfork?" — for all was still black darkness.

"Ain't no pitchfork. Never was none. Dan Haggerty, he stole the rake; come 'n' got it day I was at the March meetin', 'n' never fotched it back agin — never had no rake agin!" Thus the boy blubbered, as Mr. Tangier, with little help from him, again braced the bit of stick which seemed his only resource, placed Nathan's foot upon it, and bade him catch by the fowls' roosting-rail, and swing himself toward the window. The feeble rail broke under the boy's weight, and he fell, much as Mr. Tangier had done, and blubbered more lustily than before.

At this moment a sudden lurid light relieved them from their darkness. But the relief was scarcely encouraging. It simply showed Mr. Tangier for the first time where he was. It explained to him his strange failure thus far, which had seemed, indeed, like the powerlessness of a dream. He was in an oblong hole, roughly walled with stones, which had, however, been laid so carefully that in the darkness they had given no hold to feet or fingers. The bottom of this hole was the abyss of rotten muck which he and Nathan had been sounding. Above it was the shed, which the blaze of the roof enabled him for the first time to see.

He saw also, however, — and in an instant acted on the sight, — a bit of board above his head which had made a part of an old floor. With the bit of ladder left to him he was able to start this from the stones into which it was built. By word and example he showed the boy how to pull with him upon his lever, and in an instant more the floor board fell. They set it against the wall so that it gave a foothold for Nathan, and Mr. Tangier lifted him so that he might scramble up to the sill of the shed. But at that moment all their devices were made unnecessary, as the side door rolled open, and screams from without announced the anxiety of their liberators. In half a minute more, Nathan and Sabriny were blubbering in each other's arms; Mr. Tangier was thanking his rescuers, and receiving their voluble excuses for their delay.

The truth was, that the moment after he had dashed in at the window, all the able-bodied people around him had understood his danger. But they had lost time, as people in panic will, in relieving him. " Remphan, he hollered, and Jabe, he hollered, and I told 'em both to fetch the ladder ; and Jabe, he said the ladder was behind them barberry-bushes, and we went to the barberry-bushes, and they wornt no ladder there. An' it wornt by the ox-cart nither. 'N' then Jabe, he says, ' Run like hokey 'n' open the side door. They 'll be burned to death, sure !' says he. My ! was n't I frightened wen I see the roof blazing ! "

CHAPTER X.

MR. TANGIER came down to breakfast next morning with his hand tightly bandaged by Mrs. Fairbanks's care, and a perceptible odor of hamamelis. He accepted quietly the sympathies of all parties, and resigned himself, as a philosopher should do, to the discussion held in caucus as to what should have been done and what should not have been by all parties on this occasion.

"When I heard that it was a hen-house that was on fire," said Mrs. Hasey, "I knew that you would have very hard times. I have always found that hens were very stupid creatures. Indeed, Mr. Tunis, if you remember, they seem to have no brains. I have studied hens a great deal. There used to be hens at the place where I boarded when I was at Yonkers, and I always felt sure of their phrenology, as I scanned those hens. They have no brains, indeed, Mr. Tunis; they have no brains."

Mrs. Floxam was not a person who took, by any means, the optimistic or good-natured views of her aunt. Perhaps one ought to speak of Mrs. Floxam with more tenderness than most people did speak of her, for she was certainly a most unfortunate person. She was her own tormentor, or, as Swedenborg says so wisely and well, "she carried hell about with her wherever she went." Such a person ought to be pitied;

but such a person is not apt to be pitied in this world, which is made up of people of different motives, and people, indeed, who are very apt to speak what they think at the moment, without giving that consideration to their words which a true religion or even a profound philosophy would warrant.

Mrs. Floxam, then, was one of those persons who, perhaps from having had misfortune in early life, perhaps from the first theology of her early life, perhaps from the unsympathetic friends in early life (who shall say for what perhaps?) always ran across the current of thought or life that was near her.

A very accurate use of language has called such people "cross."

Whatever they say always crosses the remark of the person before. Whatever they think, they are sure to think that all that is around them is wrong. Thus, if the day should be sunny, they are eager to say that a rainy day was desirable. If the day should be rainy, such people are eager to say that the weather is always bad.

It is because they thus cross the regular drift of the river of life that such people are called cross people. Mrs. Floxam was certainly cross.

She had fallen, by this time, into the habit which some such people do fall into, of generally paying no attention to the conversation which was around her. This was her method of showing the perfect scorn with which she regarded all her neighbors, and her indifference to their affairs. But as it would happen, that after the conversation had well begun, she would be so much interested in it that in spite of herself she wanted to understand what people were talking about, she would interrupt the regular flow of the talk to ask what the nominative case was, and who were the subjects of discord.

To Mr. Tangier this lady was a new study, and rather an amusing one. But he was quite indifferent to her patronage, and, as it happened, he had never seen a person who had set herself so distinctly against the current life, or Providence, or fate, or history. It fairly amused him to see how much inconvenience she brought upon herself by the steady determination to look darkly on the flow of things. It so happened that in early life, in some transactions in which her husband engaged, she had been a visitor for a fortnight in the palace of the Mexican governor of the city of Coahuila, where was maintained a good deal of the state of old Spain, where a good many servants were in attendance, and where the etiquettes had still a certain European method. Mrs. Floxam was never tired of alluding to these days; and she spoke of them so much and so often, that one might readily have imagined that the greater part of her life had been spent at the court of Madrid, and that it was by a mere accident, say from a little curious experiment on pastoral follies, that she had ventured upon the town of Tenterdon for the weeks that she was here. If any question of manners or decorum turned up, Mrs. Floxam instantly was listening, and contrasted the behavior of the people around her with that to which she had been accustomed when she was the guest of Governor Cervantes. If the company were divided in opinion on any subject of ethics, or even of politics, it always proved that Governor Cervantes had uttered some oracle on this subject which ought to decide it for each and all. Indeed, the younger persons of the assembly, till they became used to Mrs. Floxam, held themselves in perpetual self-contempt — or she meant that they should — because they had never basked under the sunlight of Governor Cervantes's favor.

It was only after people had been in the same house with her three days that Governor Cervantes became an amusing shadow of a shade, and they began to watch to know at what moment he would speak out of the darkness to illustrate and improve the present time. To Mrs. Hasey's phrenological speculations Mr. Tangier answered good-naturedly that the hens the night before had shown a certain amount of practical ability which neither he nor Nathan had at command. They had got out of a hole which he and the boy had found it more difficult to escape from. "I dare say," said the old lady, "if running away is to be done, hens will run away fast enough. I am seventy years old, Mr. Tunis, and since I was a girl of six there have not been many years in which I have not had to run after one or more hens, and sometimes have known that the dinner I was to eat depended on my success in overtaking them. Yes, if flying away is the first end of two-legged creatures, the hens certainly have the advantage of us. But which of my old friends the Greeks was it, who said that you and I were hens without feathers? Mr. Tunis, that was your misfortune that you could not mount on wings, as you should have done."

Mrs. Fairbanks interposed, and said that she had been so anxious about Mr. Tangier's hand that she had not asked what became of poor Nathan, for whom so much risk had been run. Mr. Tangier laughed.

"When I left him," he said, "he was quite as cheerful as he had been depressed when we were down in the dirty straw. I scarcely remember to have seen a more sudden contrast."

"Ah!" said Mrs. Hasey, "I know you well; I do not doubt you gave him reasons for being jolly. A boy like that is quite indifferent whether there is a house over his head or not. If he has a quarter of a dollar in his hand with which he can go to meet the other boys, his cup is full."

By this time Mrs. Floxam had aroused to the consciousness that some event had taken place the night before which was possibly worthy of the attention even of the guest of General Cervantes. Till this time she had been engaged in declining hot Indian cakes; refusing the fricasseed chicken which was offered her, saying that she never ate cold mutton; asking if there was any dry toast on the table, and finding that there was none, giving an order for it. She had sent away the egg which she broke, because it was not boiled enough, and had asked Mrs. Fairbanks to give her another cup of coffee, without sugar. Having thus done all she could to make the people around her uncomfortable, she roused up now to the conversation before her, and asked little Flossy, who sat by her side, who it was that they were talking about. She asked this with a certain contemptuous air, which implied that of course they were persons who would not have been received at the court of Coahuila. The little girl explained that there had been a fire at Sabrina's house, and that Mr. Tangier had had a fall there which was the reason his hand was lame.

"But I thought somebody said something about hens," said Mrs. Floxam, contemptuously, as always.

"Yes, my dear," said inextinguishable Mrs. Hasey; "I said that hens were always stupid, and Mr. Tunis said that they had sense enough to fly, and I said that they were always good for getting out of the way when they were wanted. But I have known a good many people of whom this could be said."

"When I was living with my husband in the city of Coahuila," Mrs. Floxam said, "we were dining one day with General Cervantes, who was the governor for life of that province, and at dinner-table we had a Spanish dish, of which he told me the tradition had been brought from Castile by his own grandfather. I have never seen it again, and I doubt very much whether it could be made with our poultry. They dressed it with tomatoes, Mrs. Fairbanks, and with rice. If you like I will write out to one of the Mexican ladies. Perhaps you will like to try it some day here."

Mrs. Fairbanks said that she was always glad of a new receipt in her cook-book, and that if Mrs. Floxam would have the goodness to write for the formula, she would make some experiments with it. Why Mrs. Floxam had made the suggestion, it is rather hard to say; for with the immediate desire of contradicting Mrs. Fairbanks, she said, without the least pettishness, that she did not think that anybody in Tenterdon would understand the delicacies or intricacies of Spanish cooking; that since she had lived in Coahuila she had never found any food that agreed with her, and that she was quite sure that Mrs. Fairbanks would fail if she tried the experiment she proposed. Indeed, she

thought the breed of hens in Mexico was quite different from that in New England. She had more than
once said so to General Cervantes himself, and General Cervantes had expressed the same opinion.

This view of General Cervantes she laid down
with a certain decision which seemed to announce
that this subject was exhausted, as they say in the
French chambers.

Mrs. Hasey, after this interlude, returned to her
sympathetic talk with Mr. Tangier. She offered to
cut up his meat for him, and he permitted her to do
so, as his right hand was entirely disabled.

"Now, my dear Mr. Tunis, you must let me read
you your newspaper to-day. We have got you on the
invalid list, and we mean to pet you." "Why, my
dear Mrs. Hasey," said Mr. Tangier, laughing, "I
have sprained my wrist, but I have not sprained my
eyes. Reading my newspaper is the one thing that is
left to me. What I am in doubt about is how I am to
write my letters." Then he added that that was exactly what would please his friend Dr. Morton, who
had charged him not to write, during the whole of
the visit to Tenterdon, any more than should be
absolutely necessary to keep the supplies of human
life a-going.

"He did say that I might draw a check, if I was at
the last gasp for a bit of bread or a cup of coffee;
but beyond this I was to write nothing at all. As
I lay awake last night with the pain of this hand, I
began to think that the powers which rule my life
had leagued themselves with Morton, so as to make
perfectly sure that his directions are accomplished.
Any way, it is quite clear that I shall not draw any

checks for the next month, and I shall be living on the charity of you who are around me here."

"What do you say about charity?" said Mrs. Floxam, rousing herself to the great controversy with life again. "General Cervantes used to say, and my husband agreed with him entirely, that what we call charity is a miserable gift, which merely makes the poor poorer, and makes no one any richer. In fact, General Cervantes thought, and my husband thought too, and I am sure I thought, that beggars are only so many plunderers of the community, and that if we gave less to them there would be fewer of them. Is not that so, Mr. Tangier?"

Mr. Tangier did not know Mrs. Floxam so well as he came to know her before this month was over, and was a little amazed at finding the greatest question of social economy flashed upon a breakfast-table, to be decided in face of an absolute decision by an infallible oracle. But he always took things good-naturedly. Mrs. Floxam, as has been said, amused him already; and in reply to her he said, "I was not talking of the general questions of charity, Mrs. Floxam. I am ashamed to say I was thinking of myself. I had not come upon the high planes which General Cervantes lived upon. No; my business in Tenterdon, I believe, is to get rid of the great subjects, and, indeed, of the little ones as far as I can. And I have made a beginning by disabling my arm, by scratching my nose, and by making a fool of myself generally, as far as I can find out. But all the same I find I can eat Mrs. Fairbanks's omelette and drink her coffee. I think I can ride horseback, and I am by no means sure that I cannot steer a boat. Mrs. Hasey and I have a good many questions to settle with regard to the Greeks, and Romans, and Polynesians, and the rest of the world, and so I think I shall not give up the world in despair quite yet."

Mrs. Floxam retired into her silence and brooded, it is to be supposed, upon that seventh paradise in which she had lived in Coahuila, intimating for a moment in her manner, as she had before, that the world of Tenterdon was nothing to her thought, or that of General Cervantes.

The irrepressible Mrs. Hasey began again: "I was quite wrong, I see, Mr. Tunis. What I meant to say was that I should be very glad to write for you if my writing were not so very old-fashioned that you would be only ashamed of it. And my spelling is not quite perfect. Indeed, in my days of girlhood, you know, while we were expected to write a little, people did n't mind very much if we spelled very badly. I was very much amused the other day when I found in one of Mr. Hale's books that even Mrs. Washington, Martha Washington (Lady Washington, we called her when I was a girl), did not spell with perfect accuracy. I thought I should hold her up as a great example of mine, and, indeed, as my instructor, when I next saw the schoolmistress. There are some poor little grandchildren at Patterson made to learn, I don't know how many lines of words, and spell them in some new fashion which I did not in the least understand, every day of their lives. And it seems now that the mother of her country, Martha Washington, spelled 'lie' with a 'y' and 'middling' with one 'd.' I was very much comforted when I heard of this."

"Who are you talking about?" said Mrs. Floxam.

"Did I hear some one speak of Martha Washington?" Mrs. Hasey said, still as good-naturedly as ever, "Yes; it appears that Martha Washington was not perfect in her spelling, and I take great comfort in that."

"General Cervantes used to say, when I lived with my husband in Coahuila, that he thought the character of Washington had been very much overrated, and that, as for his generalship — "

Here the prompter's bell may as well ring, and the curtain may fall on this scene. But the reader who is interested in Mr. Tangier will remember that some such conversation as this passed at every breakfast, at every dinner, and at every supper, while he remained the guest of the anxious but hospitable Mrs. Fairbanks.

CHAPTER XI.

IT was very soon clear that Mr. Tangier's arm and wrist needed more skilful care than Mrs. Fairbanks's tender and womanly attentions. She had sent a boy, indeed, for the doctor as soon as she had bandaged it in the morning, and Mr. Tangier himself was not sorry when he saw the doctor's well-known horse and wagon driving up.

The two gentlemen had become very fond of each other; and whatever happened to the other patients that morning, it was foreordained that Mr. Tangier should have an agreeable call of an hour and a half from a man whose insight and foresight he already respected sincerely. The doctor did not give any encouraging prospect for a speedy use of the wrist or arm in any very vigorous athletic exercises. Indeed, for the simple matters of dressing and undressing himself, Mr. Tangier had already found that he must have the assistance of Silas; and he needed no doctor, as has been seen, to tell him that he could not write, even if it were to draw a check for his board bill.

But the two soon passed beyond the talk of the patient and doctor into the wider talk which had once and again engaged them, as to the condition of the neighborhood in which they were.

Here was this curious yearly flood, from regions entirely unlike Tenterdon, of people who had little enough sympathy with the dwellers in Tenterdon, very little knowledge of their tastes or of their lives, and who, excepting that they brought a certain amount of money which they paid in return for the eggs, milk, bread, and other human necessities, might be said to have no dealings with them, more than if they had been Samaritans.

On the other hand, here was this rather quaint and old-fashioned population with a certain self-respect which involved pride in their home. Yes; without it they would most certainly have left it and gone to the more engaging fields and pastures of the West. They had a certain dignity which belongs to people who own land, and gives to Real Estate, with a large "R" and a large "E," the right to be spelled with two large letters. Here were these people who saw the annual flood of summer visitors pour in with a certain satisfaction and a certain wonder. In the autumn, they saw it pour out with much greater satisfaction, for they dropped back upon their old habits. They had not to hold themselves on their dignity against a certain patronizing habit of the new-comers. And they had in their pockets the silver, and possibly the gold, which the new-comers had left behind them.

"It reminds me," said Tangier, "of that queer story in the 'Arabian Nights,' which I have quoted from a good deal, of the palace by the seaside, to which there came the forty people on wings, who stayed forty or seventy days (I forget what oriental number), and then were forced by their fate to gather themselves up and go off for a time, leaving that poor fellow stranded there alone."

"Only the poor fellow, as you call him," said the doctor,—"I am the poor fellow you see in the parable, — was by no means very sorry to be left alone, although he hoped that his agreeable companions would come again.   In the real story, which is not the story of the 'Arabian Nights,' he girds himself for the winter; he repairs his damages; he builds his bay-window here and his new piazza there; he paints his house and his blinds; he rakes up his avenue, and wonders by what means he may entice in a few more of these flying houries whom he calls boarders, when the next year comes."

"I am glad you take it like a philosopher," said Mr. Tangier.   "We are both philosophers, and I should say that the business of the time was to see how this flood (for we may as well change our figure) can do something real to fertilize the land over which it flows."

The doctor laughed.   "Very much obliged to you," he said.   "I have always heard that the earth which slips into the Missouri River makes the Mississippi water itself the most palatable water in the world. And the people in the low countries there, think that it is a very fountain of health and long life. Let us try, while we are here about it, to see that the returning flood may carry something away from the land which will be of permanent benefit to itself and to others."

"I beg your pardon; I beg your pardon, my dear fellow," said Tangier.   "My metaphor misled me, and I was painfully conscious of this when I was half through what I said.   You know what Heine says: 'Save me from the devil and the metaphor.'   And Heine is perfectly right.   Half the follies of human

argument come from the people who let their meta-
phors run away with them. What I mean is what
you mean. It is absurd that two sets of people who
are really cousins of each other should lead two lives
as different from each other as this summer life is
from this winter life."

The doctor said in reply, that he had once seen a
very striking letter from that gentleman to whom this
country is so largely indebted, Mr. Frederick Olmsted,
who said in it, that much as he had done for the rural-
izing of the great cities in the establishment of the
great parks which owe their plans to him, he felt that
the other work of urbanizing the country was a work
no less important.

"It seems to me that it is a work which has already
begun, and that it is a very easy work. Think of the
admirable instructions given to the whole country, —
think of the admirable impulse which is given by
the universal habit of reading, and by the universal
facilities of the post. I look with reverence on this
broken-winded fellow who goes through here with
his spavined horse, and his almost unpainted carriage,
every day with the mails. He takes on all the aspect of Hogarth's angel descending on the pool of
Bethesda. He has no wings which other people see,
but all the same he is an angel. He is a messenger
of light and truth; and if he brings with him a good
many circulars of quack doctors, they go to their own
places and are forgotten. But the light is never extinguished, and the truth is never made dumb." "You
are quite right," said Tangier, " that is what one has
on one's side; " and then he added very seriously,
"the Almighty is always on one's side, and, as that

Italian used to say, 'Time is with us.' I am immensely interested in all that I see here of the determination of the best people to do the best with what there is, and their refusal to be ground down by the scorn of such fools as my friend Mrs. Floxam here. I am interested in seeing how such things are regarded by the dwellers on the soil. At the same time, I hate to see any aspect of conflict between the new-comers and my friend who drove me over the other day. I am glad to see that he is no longer afraid of me. And on the other hand, from the very first I formed a certain respect for him.

"I told you how the district scnool impressed me. Now, there is a thing born from the nature of the case. There is a thing in which the good sense of these people has had its own way. There is no nonsense about it. But the first thing I shall hear will be that, in a stupid desire to imitate the mistake which the great cities have made, these people will be wanting to extend their school and keep it open ten months in the year.

"The truth is, that the exact merit of the thing is that it grew out of the conditions of the country.

"These children go to school in the summer enough to show them what school life is, what books are, and to give them a very good entrance into the mysteries of letters and of figures. Just when they begin to lag a little in their attention, the curtain falls and they are turned out into the open air.

"They begin to learn what God Almighty has done for them in his wisdom and in his providence. They know the difference between a horse and a cow; they know the difference between an eagle and a dove; they know the difference between salt marsh and fresh meadow. This is more than any of the children know whom I have the pleasure of hiring as office boys. These boys run free, their lungs open, their legs and arms are educated, their hands are trained. A boy can drive a nail: as likely as not he can shoe a horse; certainly he can saddle one and can harness one.

"When the snow begins to fall, things at home become a little more quiet, and of a sudden, thanks to the wisdom of the fathers, as I say, for two hundred and fifty years, the school-house opens again. All these boys and girls gather there. They make the pleasant and friendly acquaintances which they ought to make thore. They are brought together in the healthiest form of society, with the common interest which their books give to them. They go to work on these books with an eagerness and a relish which your boy in a New York high school does not conceive of, and your girl in a Chicago school never dreamed of. In the eleven or twelve weeks of the winter school they learn as much as would be learned in any of these grand, highly-polished city establishments in six or eight months. What is more, they learn it in the right way. They learn it each as a separate human being; while in your magnificent graded system, which I hear a great deal about, they learn very much as a shoe-last learns, which is made into its shape with one hundred and forty-seven other shoe-lasts which are manufactured in the same hour.

"Then, so soon as they are well started upon this, the school closes, you say. The school-houses close, but the school does not close. The books exist; the taste for study exists; the mutual sympathies exist; and all along, in the different homes of those children, if the children are good for anything, they are learning the winter through. They are there continuing the training which they began under the direction of the teacher. I say if the children are good for anything. If the children are good for nothing, I see no great use of attempting to polish base metal, or to carve any stone which will not keep the carving."

Tangier had become quite eloquent as he made this address. But Dr. Tillinghast did not laugh at his eloquence; he was interested in the views he took, which were the views he had stated himself hundreds of times to different people, who, however, seldom listened to him, as in this world people seldom do listen to anybody. "Every word you say is gospel truth," he said in reply, "and the analogies of the school-house seem to me to be the analogies to build upon. That is the reason I wanted to take you over to hear that magnificent music which we heard in the town-hall yonder. That man had relied upon the intelligence and enthusiasm of his neighbors. He had used that intelligence and enthusiasm to a purpose, and it proved he had not relied in vain. In your modern system of bargain and sale, every one of those performers would have had to sign a long written contract. The man who banged four times on the top of a kettle-drum would have signed one in which that man should bind himself to be present at such and such rehearsals, and at such and such performances, and by which it could be shown, if anybody cared to show it, that each bang on the kettle-drum was for two cents and a quarter, or fifteen cents and a half. In place of all that miserable mercantile haggling over the details of music, you are able to rely here on the generosity, and courage, and public spirit of the people. Every one plays, as the boy played in the story about Mendelssohn. He played his trombone because the great master wanted to have the trombone played. Every one that you heard on the platform the other day played in that way. Now, if you are talking of harmony, if you are talking of real music, if you are talking of that which is agreeable to God and man, as a child of God, that is what you want. You do not want fourteen cents' worth of music served out to you because you have bought a ticket which is worth fourteen cents. You want the exuberant and harmonious union of five people, or of fifty people, who have come together because they love music, and, so far at least, love God and man. They are doing their best to express that love."

Tangier assented sympathetically, and said: "You played your best card first. You showed me the best possible illustration which I could have had of the common life of an ideal community. I always said that if I went out as a missionary, I would not begin by telling the people what was the last sweet improvement, either on Calvin's doctrine or on the doctrine of Pelagius. I would begin by bringing together those who wanted to sing old-fashioned psalm tunes, and they should sing old-fashioned psalm tunes together till they found out what the word 'together' meant. When they had found out that, we would see what they could do with that great discovery."

"I understand you," said the doctor; "and if you and I carry out our views, I think it must be upon those lines that we are to work. Old Ramsdell and the deacon will quarrel till the crack of doom about the flow of the water over the dam up at Cropsy's, yonder. But for all that, old Ramsdell's father and the deacon's grandfather marched shoulder to shoulder the day the English frigate was aground off the rips, and one of them rammed down the cartridge while the other touched off the cannon. The deacon and Ramsdell would do the same thing to-morrow, if there were any public exigency worthy of the occasion. And you have only to show them that there is a public exigency, demanding a public library, or demanding such a musical institute as they have in the factory town yonder, or demanding any improvement in the lyceum, or demanding any improvement in the ornament of the square, and you will find that those two men, though they will hardly speak to each other on the street, are willing to work together in the common cause.

"In fact, this is a Commonwealth, and the genius of the Commonwealth impressed itself upon all New Englanders very early in the matter. Touch them on the side of their public spirit, and there is a good deal more to rely upon than appears upon the surface. But you must be sure that it is the public that demands it. You must be sure that Ramsdell, as an individual, is not to be benefited more than any other individual. The deacon must be quite sure that Mrs. Fairbanks does not want to sell a lot of land from her orchard, or that I am not interested in having a shorter way when I go over to my patients at the Mill Village. It is for the public that these people will pay, that they will work, as for the public they have been willing in old times to die. And their one weak point is that they are apt to suspect a cat under the meal, and to be afraid that there is a job hidden away somewhere."

CHAPTER XII.

MR. TANGIER found no fun in sailing, now that his hand was disabled. He could not throw a line for bluefish. He started to ride on horseback one day, and Dr. Tillinghast arrived just as he was scrambling on his horse from the old horse-block. The doctor scolded him quite as he deserved, much as Morton had done when he sent him to Tenterdon. Very unwillingly, Tangier scrambled back off his horse. But such rebuffs as this awaited him every day.

They probably threw him back more than anything else would have done, on his long conferences with Mrs. Dunster, and the doctor, and Mr. Burdett, on social improvement. Mrs. Dunster had now some nieces staying with her, and one night there was almost a formal conclave on the great problem of Tenterdon's society. Mrs. Dunster told what she called her North Somerset story. Some one had asked the teacher of the academy in North Somerset why she dropped a term, and spent her time in Boston instead. She laughed and said, "Spend your winter in North Somerset, and you will know. In Boston, I have a free library to read in what I choose. I have free galleries to visit when I choose. I can hear a concert of the best instrumental music for quarter of a dollar. And every evening, if I choose, I can go to hear Huxley, or Wallace, or Dawson, or whoever happens to be lecturing, or I can listen to Phillips Brooks, or Freeman Clarke, and I am welcome."

Mr. Tangier listened to this story half amused, and much edified.

So, with more formality than was at all worth while, Mr. Tangier went into rather grave social discussions about wealth in common and the commonwealth. He had been a good deal interested by this story of the schoolmistress, and he said, what was true enough, that she was gladly availing herself of the resources which the whole community in that city received from the wealthy people who had gone before. If Mr. Joshua Bates chose to buy for her the books for her to read, why should the girl go back to North Somerset and buy her own? If Mr. Higginson chose to provide for her the best music in the world, why should she go back to North Somerset and play upon a badly-tuned piano? Mr. Tangier said that she was using the common wealth which the public spirit of this generation and of other generations had provided for her. And it was very natural that she should like that common wealth better than she should the separated property of such a town as he supposed North Somerset was.

"Yes, and this is all very grand, if you will permit me to say so," said May Remington, one of the nice nieces who has been mentioned. "And I do not doubt that the young lady, who I dare say was a very nice young lady, used all these pleasures and was glad to use them. But, if you will permit me, I will tell you another thing which she liked, which was called, as I suppose, the accumulated wit of the day. I liked it too. She liked to be able to walk on a dry sidewalk, and she liked to be able to get into a street-car and go where she chose, and pay five cents for it. So far as I know, the main difficulty of our life here in Tenterdon, which I believe Mr. Tangier thinks needs improving, is that half the year we cannot go anywhere without putting on India-rubber boots. Then our skirts are so draggled that we catch cold as soon as we get home. And if we want to ride anywhere we must coax Jonas, or Silas, or John, or whoever it may be, to harness the horse. He will be cross. He will say the horse has a shoe off. And it makes such a fuss that it ends in our staying at home. There, in a word, is the reason why your country is less social than your great city; and is the reason why your schoolmistress, who likes society as well as you like it, and as well as I like it, — this is why she preferred to spend six months where she could get society, to spending them where she was obliged to read Shakspeare and Milton at home. Shakspeare and Milton were very good and great men; but I do not myself believe that the learned men who advise me to enter into companionship with these leaders of the past sit more than four hours a day reading Shakspeare, or more than three hours a day reading Milton."

Mr. Tangier was interested and amused at once by this frank statement of Miss May. He acknowledged that he had not thought of that, and he said to her, "Then I suppose, in our reconstruction of society, you would begin by laying a railroad track for street-cars. That is not generally supposed to be the first effort of civilization. The theory in New York is that it is the last decline of a degenerate age."

"You might do a worse thing," said Miss May, "but I do not want to have a street railroad. What I want is what I believe the people of Provincetown did. They had some money, — some surplus revenue, I think it was called, — and they had a town-meeting to see how they would spend it. It was agreed that a plank sidewalk, from one end of the town to the other, was the best thing they could spend it upon, and upon that they spent it."

"They were quite right," said the doctor. "After all, civilization begins with the making of roads. That is an old hobby of mine. If you trace back the germ of civilization, you will find that it is not in the school-house, as some people say. It is not even in the blacksmith-shop, as other people say. It is not even in the building of a meeting-house, as the eulogists of our old Puritan forefathers are apt to say. Civilization really begins when a set of men make a road through a swamp or a trail through a forest. Civilization means society, and society means the way by which I go from one man's lair to another."

"Of course," said Miss May, "you should see how everybody waits at the window and is ready, if by great good luck Mrs. Fairbanks here has the sewing-circle at her house, and has intimated up the road that the 'Barge' will pass along between two and three o'clock, because the mud is so bad at the Willows. People do not want to sit still and crochet, when they can come to Mrs. Fairbanks's and hear her read Browning. But, on the other hand, they do not want to put on India-rubber boots, and if the expression were proper I should add, — they do not want to sit four hours with wet feet or ankles."

"Not much," said the good-natured doctor, "if they have ever heard one of my first-class scoldings." And it would seem from the glances between him and Miss May that she knew what he meant.

"I see truth, and infinite truth, in every moment," cried Mr. Tangier. "Why will no one take up Miss Remington's parable? What she tells me explains things untold by Carey, or Say, or Foxwell, — why the pressure is on cities, and why the country is abandoned."

"You shall not laugh at me, Mr. Tangier."

"I laugh at you? I beg your pardon. I am seriously in earnest. I believe you have hit on the central thing. We are social beings. We go where we can easily have society. There is the whole of it. If sidewalks give society, we go where there are sidewalks. If a street-car gives it, hurrah for the street-car!"

"And are the New York aldermen," asked Mrs. Fairbanks, thoughtfully, "are they apostles of the new civilization?"

"Unconscious apostles, yes; for even Satan serves the servants of the Lord. I had no qualms of conscience when I last took a Broadway car."

"I can assure you," said Miss May, "that many a nice girl goes to New York or to Boston for a long visit, with this for one of her chief satisfactions, — that now she can take her exercise; that from February to May she will not be blocked up in the house."

"And for Tenterdon," said Mr. Tangier, "the prophet is to be not so much one in camel-skin, eating locusts and honey; he is rather to be James Haraden with his grays. I wish the oldest one were not sprained. But perhaps the 'Bedouin Liniment' will cure him. I read the bill yesterday, — it cures everything except thunder-humor and blind staggers."

Then the talk fell on details of what had been done in a social way in Tenterdon, and what had failed. Mostly it turned on questions of rooms for concerts, halls for dancing. There was no whisper, as Mr. Tangier observed, of social inequalities or religious discords. But the practical obstacles to bringing fifty people together in one place were represented as enormous.

This is a good enough specimen of the talk which occupied the meeting at Mrs. Dunster's; and some of the results of the talk will appear as our story goes on.

They all agreed that it would be quite possible to bring the people of Tenterdon together sometimes, so that they should know each others' faces, if there were a convenient place where they might meet. And the doctor was rather tempted to "switch off" here into learned discussions about the word "synagogue," and the Roman and Greek places of meeting, and the importance that these places of meeting had on the growth of civilization. But they all laughed at his learning, and told him that the essential thing was to find in Tenterdon some spreading oak beneath which it should be quite warm in winter and quite cool in summer, and where they could have the fifth symphony of Beethoven, or the play of Harry the Fifth, or a spelling-bee, or anything else that they wanted to have, without either freezing to death or roasting.

Then came an examination which to Mr. Tangier was very curious, as to the several resources of the town for such things. He asked his friends if there were any traditions of other days where people had met, when they had, perhaps, a victory to celebrate, or to sew for soldiers, or on any other public occasion.

Then it appeared that the old stage-house, as everybody called it, had been the scene of all these gatherings. And it came out, almost by accident, that, with the decline of the old stage-coach system, the society of the town really declined also. For this old stage-house was a place where, from east to west, and from north to south, the stage-coaches of that day stopped, their horses were watered, or perhaps their horses were changed. The passengers breakfasted, or dined, or took their supper, or bought a lunch. There was some excitement at the place, some reason for the people coming together there. The post-office was there; the blacksmith's shop was there. What was more to the point, there were large rooms in the stage-house. One dance-room Mrs. Dunster remembered as being a room in which sixty couples could form in the Virginia Reel, and this showed that it must have been a place of considerable size.

But with the railroad all this had come to an end. The stage-house was left half or quarter of a mile out of the way. The last use it had been put to was to make it a sort of barrack-house for some laborers whom the Government employed when they were building the breakwater, and now it was really used for nothing. Mr. Tangier had noticed it in his rides as a forlorn, broken-down sort of a place, with many signs hanging out, indicating that it was for sale if anybody wanted to buy it, and with an occasional hole through a window. But most of the windows were boarded up, for fear of an attack from wayward boys.

CHAPTER XIII.

MR. TANGIER'S mind rested on the stage-house. He spent one or two days in inquiries as to the ownership of the house, as to the feasibility of restoring it into a sort of central place for the hospitalities of the town; and these inquiries ended in his obtaining permission to make use of the old dining-hall and the old dancing-room for any purpose which he might have in mind. He accordingly, with the assistance of Mrs. Fairbanks, issued a joking invitation to the heads in the "social movement," as he insisted on calling it, to meet him for a picnic lunch one day at the stage-house, and examine what were its possibilities. He sent in advance his old friend Warner, and his protégé Nathan, to get the doors open and to do some preliminary sweeping, and at least clean up chairs enough for them to sit upon, and a table on which Mrs. Fairbanks could give them a cup of coffee and something to eat.

For Mr. Tangier was master of the great central law of hospitality,—that hospitality means more than salt, perhaps more than bread and butter; it means the fit refreshment of the bodily frame, and the refreshment together. People must have something to eat or drink together, if anything is to succeed in this world.

A very jolly and merry party he brought together. It was on a Saturday, so that his little schoolmistress could come over from her district, and he had collected almost all the other teachers too. They came, somewhat on their dignity, doubtful what they were to come for, and very much afraid lest they should commit themselves. This is the fashion of their craft. But, before the hour was over, they were jolly, and as sociable as any one else was; and they really knew the town and the people of the town better than any one else did, excepting always the doctor and the minister. This is to be observed in general of the district schoolmistress in New England, or the keeper of any public school, that, if you talk of general service to the public, these young people are the most valuable public servants that you have, and do most to bring together the different classes of society and to keep open the lines of social promotion. Mr. Tangier, with his right arm still in the sling, and Mrs. Dunster, welcomed their guests very cordially, and it proved that the party, with the additions which have been named, and some others, was quite large. They met in the old office, or bar-room, of the hotel, into which various chairs, some with three legs and some with four, had been brought. There were different settees, which had remained from old times, and the table in question, spread with a white cloth, had its coffee and chocolate ready for the welcome of those who had come from a distance. When it seemed that almost every one was present, Mr. Tangier himself led the way to the old dancing-room.

Here they all sat down at the little picnic which Mrs. Fairbanks had provided. A very jolly feast it made. "When hunger and thirst were fully satisfied," Mr. Tangier proposed that they should summon the elect, whoever the elect were, and interest everybody in the project of re-establishing the old hotel as a central point for the gatherings of the neighborhood. Different people contributed different suggestions, and it ended in an agreement that the clans should be rallied for the next Saturday. Saturday was the day determined upon, because Saturday was the day when all the teachers could be present; and there was a certain tradition of a half-holiday, which gave them the help of the bigger boys and the young men.

Fortunately, also, they were at the time between planting and hoeing, which in the country is traditional as a time when people may go a-visiting, or may attend to their amusements. Mr. Tangier and the doctor and and Mrs. Dunster acted as hosts. In the week which had passed, Mr. Tangier had been in personal relations with the present proprietors of the hotel. They were glad to have even a nibble of a tenant, although he gave them no definite promises for the future. It was agreed, in New England fashion, that he was to have the occupancy of the house for the next two months, "if they could n't do nothing better with it," and that they should give him fair notice if they could do anything better with it. A very low rent, almost nominal, was fixed for these two months, with the understanding that this was to make no precedent for the future. In fact, both parties had come together, as men of New England blood like to come together, in a certain vague determination on both sides that they would do "about what was right," though neither side knew exactly what, in future, he might wish to do.

To the satisfaction, and even to the surprise, of the head centres of the "movement," the attendance of boys and young men was a good deal larger than they had dared expect. But each of the teachers had two or three loyal supporters among the older of her winter scholars; and it had been enough to intimate to them that there was a project for some union festivities, or union meetings, at the hotel, to induce them to be willing to lend a hand. And their assistance proved very effective. Among them was a certain young fellow by the name of Pingree, who was, however, always called Silas, who had taken the precaution to bring with him his box of carpenter's tools, and who proved, as the vernacular says, "awful handy" with tools, and whose tools were, indeed, freely used by all the young men. They had all been trained to the work of a farm, which implies a handy use of all carpenter materials.

As before, Mr. Tangier led the way to the great dancing-room of old times. In those days it had opened by large doors upon an outer piazza, to which, strange to say, people had been able to ride up and enter the ball-room directly, without the intervention of any anterooms. These great double doors had been long since disused, excepting when, in the spring and autumn, they were opened that the place might be made a sort of storage room for the sleighs, which were only used for a few months in winter. Half a dozen sleighs of every pattern, therefore, and every conceivable sort of lumber were in the room, and the object of the present gathering was to clear it out, and prepare it, as it could best be prepared, for the purposes which were intended. It would be hard to say what was not to be found there. As they worked, they came upon four little pulpits, which had been used in some traditional time by a lodge of Masons which had occupied the room.

While the ladies were encouraging the young men, and the young men were laughing, lifting, and piling the various affairs which had been stored away nobody knew how long, Mrs. Fairbanks, to her great delight, came upon a roll which evidently was faded bunting, in which her experienced eye discovered more than flags. She called upon John Whitcomb, whose ready knife cut the old strings. The roll was developed on the floor, and it proved to have various mottoes, — "Honor the Brave," "Welcome Home," "Newburne and Washington," "Olustee," "Cross-Creek," and others which were almost Greek to the young people. "Alas and alas!" said Mrs Hasey, "that you should not remember the names of the battles in which your own fathers lost their lives, perhaps. But I ought to rejoice, I suppose, that in these days of peace we forget that there was any war." Mrs. Fairbanks was well pleased. She said that this bunting and those mottoes marked the time when the room was last used, as she supposed, for any public festival. And she herself remembered that, as a little girl, she was not permitted to come. But when their company came back from the war, she knew that there was a welcome and reception there, and a great feast given, and these were the memorials of that day. Mr. Tangier took up the tattered rags with a certain reverence. "We will connect ourselves with the past," he said, "We will use these flags as a part of our decorations. Let us hope that our boys may be as brave, and our girls as willing, as were the boys and girls of that generation."

Silas pulled out the nails which were the only locks on the great doors. He repaired some broken boards in the piazza. He set up a "joist" as a temporary pillar where one of the Doric columns of the piazza had fallen out, and then, having opened the folding-doors, called upon willing hands to pull out one, two, three, and the rest of the sleighs which had been waiting for the next winter. Meanwhile, some of the young men discovered what would be needed most, and had made some birch brooms which would be sufficient for the severest sweeping. The boys, at the direction of the women, had lifted seats here and chairs there. Hot water and sand had been brought, and the old pulpits had been scrubbed and washed, and by the aid of half a dozen centres of action, as the hours flew merrily by, the room began to assume the aspect of a place which could be possibly inhabited.

Mr. Tangier had set some of the smaller boys to work, to creep in behind the rubbish and go around on the outside of the building, so as to tell him how many panes of glass were cracked, and how many were broken, in the enormous windows which had formerly lighted it. Some of these windows were covered with boards, and some were so left that they could still admit light. Different boys brought in their returns, now marked on a shingle, now marked on a slate, and now in the less reliable form of their own memories. But he wished to give his orders in a more thorough way. Still he was fettered by his lameness, as always, and looked around rather wistfully to see what arrangement of paper or pen might be made from any old pack to serve his purpose. May Remington caught his eye, and what was almost a frown upon his face, — a frown born from the sense of incapacity, which is so annoying to a strong and active man. When the girl asked what she could do, he smiled again, and confessed that the sense of powerlessness annoyed him, and that he wanted to write down the information which these boys were bringing to him.

"I suppose if I were a shepherd on the plains of Arabia, I could remember for seventeen years how many lights are wanted which are eight by ten, and how many which are fourteen by twelve. But being nothing but a lawyer, I am used to having such things on paper."

"If that is all," said the girl, "come back with me into the parlor, and make me your secretary." Then she called the boys, one after another, and made them follow her.

Mr. Tangier followed willingly enough, too, but wondered how the writing was to be done. But almost before he could express his wonder, the girl had taken from her own hand-bag a little portfolio, small enough to go into it, had opened the spring ink-, stand which belonged to her portfolio, and then, in the same good-natured way, said, "Now begin, Mr. Tangier; you have rubbed the lamp, and the genie is ready."

Mr. Tangier was pleased — as well he might have

been — with the genie of the lamp. She took at once the idea of what he wanted, and she and he together soon brought the somewhat wild statements of the boys into something like system. Fitz-James and Cephas had to be sent back once or twice for the revision of statements which were quite incredible. But after a little it was quite clear that they would need so many new panes, and that it would be well that they should have ten or twelve new sashes. Miss Remington's ready calculation gave the size of the sashes, and a measurement, undertaken by Silas Pingree, confirmed the accuracy of her arithmetic. Mr. Tangier was now engaged in what he liked. There was something tangible and visible to be done, and he saw no reason why he should not do it. He sent for Mr. Burdett, who appeared in a minute with his staff, — two or three bright and ready boys.

"You look like the Earl of Southampton and his train in 'Kenilworth,'" said Tangier, in open admiration. "Which of these boys is to be William Shakspeare?"

"I dare not say. We think, now, that we will all be good ship-carpenters, and build better sloops than the 'Mayflower.' But we shall see what we shall see. Thank you for seeing that we live on the feudal principle. These boys are my staff, — I am chief of staff, — and there are three or four others as good as they. Are there not, Fred?"

"Five more," said Fred, blushing proudly enough, "five more, sir, but off on duty."

Mr. Tangier was well pleased. Every such intimation that these young people were recognizing the great law of "Together" pleased him, and gave him new hope. "I sent for you, Burdett, to show you these figures, which my good genius here has made for me. Is there any reason in the world why we should not go ahead, now and here? No powers of good can wish to prolong the reign of smashed windows, as it seems to me."

Mr. Burdett looked at the figures. He explained them to the boys at the right hand and at the left, as he did so, as if they were his comrades rather than his followers. "The sooner the better, if we are sure of going on."

"Of course we are sure of going on. That is, I am sure of going on. I am not used to taking hold of things that fail. Burdett, no ship can be launched till the whole ship is built. It does not answer to build the forecastle and launch that, hoping that the forecastle may make a voyage which will pay for the stern. Unless you build the whole vessel, you fail." He saw the boys were listening amused, and he went on to them : —

"That seems to you very simple, boys. But it is a great truth, which the world often forgets. Many an enterprise fails because people start when they are only half ready." Then, turning to Mr. Burdett, "I do not see why I should not do this now. Really, we need for our launch very little. Tell me, who was that tall, wide-awake fellow, whose eye-teeth were so perfectly cut, whom you stopped to talk to, the day we rode to Goodwin?"

Mr. Burdett did not remember at first; but when the wide-awake fellow's wagon was described, his span of white horses, and his ladder in the wagon, he stood revealed at once as Scott Meakin, the master carpenter of Goodwin. The day they had met him, he was going to Clavers to shingle a barn.

"The same, the same," said the now impetuous Mr. Tangier. "Now, what reason is there, human or divine, why this Scott Meakin shall not be called into the social reformation, and made to put in new sashes, of which Miss Remington has so clear an idea? Let him bring with him some glazier, half as clever as he, Galileo Silex — or whatever his godfather may have called him."

"Of course," said Mr. Burdett, laughing, "there is no reason why he should not come, if you are willing to pay him."

"'Of course,' do you say, — innocent dove that you are, fresh from the study of the Chaldee Polyglot! 'Of course!' There may be many reasons, my dear Miss Remington, my dear young friends of the staff — pardon me if I am compelled to show to you some of the wisdom of this world in contrast, alas! with this heavenly ignorance of our dear friend Mr. Burdett."

He was laughing, and they were all laughing now.

"You see, dear Miss Remington, there may well be another joiner, or carpenter, or house-builder, or architect — perhaps seven inches nearer to us than Scott Marden, or whatever. Or this other man may have put in the sashes originally, or his father may. Or he may vote the same ticket with the man who owns the hotel, my friend Frink, or belong to the same lodge. And our friend Scott may vote another ticket, and belong to no lodge. Many, many are the reasons, my dear dominie, why Scott Meakin may be the wrong man. But I like his looks, and know he will do our work well, if I may send to him."

Mr. Burdett was not shaken. There was no rival joiner; Scott Meakin was the only man any one in the neighborhood would dream of sending to in such an exigency.

"Then," said Mr. Tangier, "we will go and see him to-morrow."

"Why not write to him now?" said May Remington, perfectly simply.

Mr. Tangier was surprised this time. But he was pleased. He was both pleased and surprised that a young girl, whom he had only seen as a summer vacationer, should know how much might hinge on twenty-four hours. He was pleased, if not surprised, that both she and Mr. Burdett were entering with such perfect cordiality into his plans. But he answered, with mock melancholy, "First, Miss Remington, because I have no hand to write with; second, because I have no paper; third, because there is never an envelope."

"You do not say because there is no ink, or no pen; for both are on the table. Here is the paper, now; here is the envelope," she said quickly, as she produced both, "and here is the hand." She paused just a moment, blushed a little at her own courage, and then said, "'How shall we ever reorganize society' — I think that is your grand phrase — if everybody does not 'lend a hand'? That is our modest phrase."

The girl had not the least idea how her simplicity and courage together affected him. That any one felt as he felt, that there was something worth doing, that he was not on a quixotic enterprise, in which other people humored him, and that this bright young woman saw its possibilities, — all this encouraged him. More than this, he knew, as a man of affairs, that the saving of a day, even in such a petty affair, might mean the saving of a week.

"I cannot so much as sign my name," said he. "But you and I can make Scott What's-his-name come over. Let us write as you say. Burdett, you and the boys may go back to your sweeping. Miss Remington and I will put in the windows."

And he dictated his letter, and watched with pleasure the easy, quick movement of her hand, and her round, pretty, large, and legible handwriting. He went into every detail with the builder, told him where he would be, and asked for an early interview. When the letter seemed finished he looked it over, made no correction, thanked her, and said : —

"We may as well tell him to bring over a paper-hanger. Those' walls look like Noah's ark."

And at this moment a knot of young men came to ask the two to join the others in the dining-room.

This invitation surprised Mr. Tangier. With all his high notions about hospitality, he had still regarded this assembly as a party for work, and it had not occurred to him that it could be made a festival. But as he came into the old dining-hall, and found there all the arrangements for a hearty meal, it was explained to him that some of the young men of the Knights Templars had taken the entertainment in hand at their meeting the night before. They had been asked to the working-bee, and this seemed a good way, and a good place, to help. So they had hastily arranged the feast. Their only anxiety had been to keep all the preparations secret from Mr. Tangier, Mr. Burdett, Mrs. Fairbanks, and Mrs. Dunster.

And in their secret they had wholly succeeded.

CHAPTER XIV.

NOTHING could have met Mr. Tangier's wishes so completely as did this unexpected picnic provided by the young men. It had annoyed him, in all his stay at Tenterdon, that he was not making the acquaintance of men of his own age, and men five, ten, and fifteen years younger. He fancied that they were shy of him; and yet he was always cordial in his approaches, without being too cordial. The truth is that the young men were at work. They had their own companions; they had no need of his society. And on the one hand, they were too proud to put themselves upon a man, who, they thought, might not want to know them; on the other hand, they were too modest to suppose that a stranger, coming, as was said, for his health, needed other society than he found in his books or in his immediate neighbors. Thus it happened to Mr. Tangier, as it often happens to a man staying in such a place, that he knew a dozen of the women where he knew one of the men.

He began his talk with Drummond, — who, though not the president of the company who were their host, seemed to be the acting man, — by saying that he was glad that anything had called together so many of the neighbors, and that he thought it gave a good omen for the usefulness of the hall which they were trying to refit. Drummond answered very cordially that, so far as the Temple went, they would be very glad if the hall could be put into good order. There had been traditions that it had been used for some such purpose; he hardly knew why that use had been given up. As matters stood, they would be as glad as anybody if they could have the use of it for some of their meetings; and he expressed, very frankly and simply, his pleasure that there was any movement in that direction.

He showed so much real interest in this that Mr. Tangier ventured to put to him some of the questions which they had not solved in their caucus on Mrs. Dunster's piazza. He asked him, first of all, why it was that the men seemed to herd together so much as they did, and the women also. "Of course this is not natural," said Mr. Tangier, good-naturedly. "The boys and girls go together to the same school; men are going to marry women eventually. Why is it that, in the intimacies of young people, the young men are all in one set of clubs and the young women are all in another, and that there seems to be a sort of hitch when any effort is made to bring them together."

Drummond laughed at first, and then looked very serious. He said, "I hardly know whether you will agree with me, but I am apt to think that the girls themselves are partly to blame in this. I hardly ever read a story in a magazine which pretends to explain country life in America, but it seems to me to make the matter rather worse than it was before. If you will think of it, Mr. Tangier, you will see that a very large number of our young men go from the country at once to the active life of the world. They go to the West, or they go to New York or the other large cities, and there are comparatively few of us left here at home. I had the curiosity once to make a little census of the matter, and even I was surprised to see how many families there were here in Tenterdon in which two or three girls were left, while all the boys over fifteen had gone to the West, or to Boston, or to Lowell, or to New York.

"But this is not the whole. Take the people in this room. There is hardly a young lady in this room but, after she had gone through with our district school work, was sent to the high school at Woodstock, or some female college, maybe, or in some other way had a year or two added to the schooling she received here. On the other hand, we boys (I am one of them, though I am twenty-five years of age) went to work at once on the farm, or over in the mills, lucky if we could spell English, or could write a hand that did not disgrace us. Really, Mr. Tangier, when our own sisters come home from the high school, or academy, or college, or what not, we are by no means sure that we can talk with them about the great things they have been reading. I cannot read French; my sister Mary can. I can play a few chords on a melodeon, but I cannot pretend to talk of musical criticism with her. I am glad enough to read my 'Tribune' when it comes in the evening, but I don't know anything about the books that she has been reading at school. And I am, in short, but a very indifferent companion for her in such things as those. On the other hand, she finds half a dozen old neighbors among the girls who are glad to keep up their French, or are glad to be reading some new book together. They come together, with or without form, at their little meetings, and naturally talk about the things that interest them.

"For me, on my part, for these fellows around us here, we do not need their society; we have society enough of our own. This temperance business, which calls us together in this Temple, or any work there is to be done in politics in the town, the engine company, — all such things give us association with good fellows who cannot play the piano, who cannot talk French. But it is enough for me, and it is enough for these young men whom you see here.

"When I read in the magazines and in the newspapers that the higher education of woman is the necessity of our time, I sometimes wish that some sensible man or woman would write a paper to show that the higher education of woman is doing a great deal to separate the sexes from reasonable and good-natured intercourse with each other. That paper might do some good at your Vassars and your Wellesleys." As he spoke, Drummond beckoned to another man named McVicar, who was dispensing the ice-cream, and said to him, "Leave your ice-cream to Ben and John, McVicar, and hear what treason I am talking to Mr. Tangier."

McVicar fell into the same strain with Drummond, and as the three men pretended to be eating their ice-cream, Mr. Tangier, finding he had their confidence entirely, told them what had passed in one or another of the caucuses of which the reader has some account. McVicar laughed at the difficulties which the ladies had brought forward, approved of the doctor's rather straightforward views, and said: "I do not think we need discuss the theory of the matter much, Mr. Tangier. That girl was right, whoever she was, — you did not name her, — who spoke of the street-car as the centre of social order. Now, we do not need a street-car here, but a great deal could be done by a plank sidewalk. I should really think, myself, that far better than a cartload of resolutions on the subject of reorganization of society would be a plank sidewalk laid from — well, say from the water-tank above Clements's — it is not more than a mile and a half — as far as the group of houses at the crossings. Begin at the beginning is a good rule, Mr. Tangier. If we had a walk, over which people could go in such weather as is here nine days out of ten, people would seek each other a great deal more than they do, and would not live in the isolation of their houses."

So the Templars came out on precisely the same socialistic doctrines with the people who discussed social order at Mrs. Dunster's.

CHAPTER XV.

WHEN Mr. Tangier came down to breakfast the next morning, he knew that the plans which had been blocked out at the meeting of the day before, would have to pass the criticism of the little caucus which met three times a day at Mrs. Fairbanks's table. He was in no doubt, of course, of the views which the two leaders of conversation would take. Good Mrs. Hasey would approve of everything through and through, and from her store of epigram and memory would have valuable illustrations which would show the certainty of success, even in the smallest detail that was proposed. On the other hand, Mrs. Floxam would disapprove, first of the plan, and then of every incident which had any connection with it. Her relations with General Cervantes were such that she would know that failure brooded over the enterprise from the very beginning.

Still, Mr. Tangier, who was, like all the rest of us, susceptible to the fears of his kind, entered on the discussion with a certain feeling of curiosity. A long experience, indeed, never made him able to foresee the particular lines of opposition which one of these ladies would take, or of assent which would be represented by the other.

"Well, Mr. Tangier, you stayed so late on the hill that we had no chance to hear from you about the meeting after I came away. Of course the girls have told us what they did, and they seem to have had hard enough work. That was to be expected. But I told them that I should not feel that I understood anything about it till I had an official report from you."

This was the welcome which was given him by Mrs. Hasey, as he took his seat by her at the table. Before he could reply, Mrs. Floxam said: "I felt really sorry when I found you had taken so much pains about it, Mr. Tangier. If I had known what it was that you were planning and talking about, I could have told you that my husband knew all about such things, and that he used to say that it was utterly in vain to start anything of the kind. Indeed, when we were in Mexico, where for some time we had an opportunity of knowing how they manage things in their way, he often talked about it. I remember at the palace, one day, something was said about the reason why Spaniards never would live in the country. My husband himself was a country boy, and he had to move from the country to New York just as soon as his father would let him go. He said so to General Cervantes, and General Cervantes said he was quite right; that it was wholly impossible in the surroundings of agricultural life for a man to cultivate any of the powers which are necessary for business; and that he always chose upon his own staff men who had had a large experience with other men and women, such as you could not have if you were taking care of sheep or were out on a ranch after cattle."

Mr. Tangier had never heard Mrs. Floxam make quite so long a speech, and he was amazed to find that the good fellows he had been talking with the afternoon before were set down as a sort of rancheros, merely because they had not had the advantage which Mrs. Floxam had had, of living in a fourth-rate New York hotel. He was not much in the habit of answering Mrs. Floxam. After a day's experience, he had found that little came of that. He had also learned that it was quite as well to leave her to the free graces of Mrs. Hasey; and he did so now.

Mrs. Hasey, however, was quite too good-natured ever to pretend to answer anybody. Quite as if nothing had been said, she said: "You had a good time, they tell me. If you had told me that there was to be something to eat, I am not sure but I should have stayed longer, when, in fact, I came home in the carry-all. But, really, when you spoke to me, I did feel that I was nothing but an old woman and should be of no use to anybody. So there is to be a plank sidewalk, they tell me."

Mr. Tangier said that the plank sidewalk seemed to meet general approval when it was proposed; that he had never seen the need of it himself, and that there had been very little rain since he had been in Tenterdon. He said that the general verdict of the young people, and of the older people, seemed to be that there was disposition enough for meeting together for social purposes, if only they could come and go.

"If there is any way of wasting money more absurd than another, it is the trying to make any sort of road out of wood." This was Mrs. Floxam's interpolation at this time. "Do you not know that the great fire in Chicago was all due to the fact that they had paved the streets with wood and covered them with asphalt?

The moment that wretched cow kicked over the kerosene lamp, it ran out upon the asphalt, and that street was in a blaze, and all the other streets were in a blaze, merely because they had paved them with wood. I thought everybody knew that, Mr. Tangier."

This was quite a direct challenge, and Mr. Tangier was about to take it up, when a lady from Chicago, on the other side of the table, went into the battle bravely on her own account, and explained that a street paved with wood would no more carry a fire from one end to another than if it had been paved with iron. Mrs. Floxam was not in the least disconcerted.

"All I can say," said she, "is that when we were living in the city of Saltillo some of those ignorant Mexicans tried to lay a walk with their own foolishly-hewed boards, and it did not answer at all. I remember perfectly that General Cervantes was dining with my husband, and he said that he had seen such walks tried in many cities and that they had always failed."

After this the conversation went on to other details. Mrs. Hasey expressed her regret that she had come away so early, and confessed again that if she had known there was to be a picnic she would probably have stayed; but she said she knew perfectly well what Mrs. Fairbanks had arranged for dinner, and that she was not certain whether there would be any cold lunch at the old tavern.

"As to that," said Mrs. Floxam, "if there is anything that it is imprudent to eat, it is one of those cold collations. You never know who provides them; you are never sure but what there is poison in the tin cans. They always make you eat ice-cream, and you do not know where the ice-cream comes from. I have made it a rule, and my husband did before me, never to eat anything at any such place."

Mrs. Hasey said: "Ah, well; that is very well for you; but for common people like myself I find it a good rule to eat whenever God will give me anything to eat, even if I go round to five meals in a day." Then the good-natured old lady began again with Mr. Tangier and his plans.

"I do not want to advise, Mr. Tangier, you know. I never do give any advice" (and here the old lady laughed good-naturedly); "but I am a good deal of the kind of an old friend of mine who was at a very grand woman's rights convention."

"Pray, what was that? as the fox said," said Mr. Tangier.

"Why, they had a grand meeting in some very high-strung circle, to know what was the matter with the health of the girls. It was generally agreed that the girls studied too much and exercised too little. Then one old lady said it would be better if they swept more, and told great stories about the value of sweeping in opening the chest."

"I suppose," said May Remington, "that she said that the breathing in of the dust was very good for the lungs; did n't she?"

"I dare say she did. There is no end of the nonsense that old women will speak on such occasions, or young women either, for that matter. But after the sweeping-woman had done, another woman prophesied to show that they had better wash clothes for exercise."

"Oh, dear!" said the same Miss Remington. "I thought the divine law was that we were to wash on Monday, but on no other day in the week. Is there a new gospel by which we are to have six·washing-days, or possibly even seven ? "

"You must go to the next woman's rights convention, my dear, and ask your own questions. Don't ask me. I prophesy, as you know, on my own account. After the washerwoman had done, there was a moment's pause, and my old friend Miss Katherine Flint, who had never spoken in meeting before, and I think never has since, rose in the back seats and said, ' Why don't you let them dance ? ' And with that there came a solemn stillness over the great assembly."

Mr. Tangier was not displeased with the story. He said however, that if the tavern was ever once whitewashed and the windows put into it, he would, for his part, be very silent as to the uses which were made of the old hall. That must be on the conscience of the people who used it from day to day. He was simply going to try to provide the place of union, and in that place they must work out their own salvation.

"That will never do," said Mrs. Floxam. "If you let people undertake to carry on their own plans, they will bring very low people in, indeed, and these very low people will decide. We had a good deal of experience of that when I lived in Mexico; I recollect that — "

And here May Remington fairly cut her off, and would not let the Mexican contingent be brought into the conversation.

"I am glad you say that, Mr. Tangier. I had a little of Mrs. Floxam's fear that we were all to be tied up and worked by a charter and under a constitution. Now, I hate constitutions; and if I were to tell you the truth, I should tell you that women do not work very well under constitutions. Constitutions are masculine in their make-up, and girls and women have very much of a disposition to do as they choose on each particular occasion, without consulting the fathers, or, indeed, taking anybody's advice about it.

"I am rather apt to think that if a lot of girls get together in your hall and want to dance, there will be some way found to dance, if only there is any music; and as for that, I am not sure but I will contribute three jew's-harps for that precise purpose to be hung up on the wall." Mr. Tangier said that the matter of music had occupied his own mind. He hated melodeons 'so that he had been tempted, against his own principle, to put in letters of gold over the door, "No melodeons admitted here." But he supposed that he must not interfere so far as that.

The girls assented to this notion of his, and said that it was bad enough that there should be a melodeon in the vestry of the church. They said they would consult with each other about it. They seemed to think that there was an old piano in the Gingerly House, which was locked up by the Gingerlys, who were all in Italy. They seemed to think that a letter, if it could be properly addressed, either to Genoa, or Mentone, or wherever the place was, might obtain permission for the borrowing of this piano. "Only then, Mr. Tangier, the summer will all be gone before the letter will come." Mr. Tangier said he did not think the piano the most difficult part of the matter. "But we will advance step by step," said he, "and accordingly see what we can do."

CHAPTER XVI.

STEP by step they did advance. The great social movement, as they called it in joke, had its ups and its downs. Sometimes there was a very bad hitch, of the nature of which Mrs. Floxam was always eager to prophesy whenever it came up in the conversation. Sometimes there was an immense tide-wave in its favor, and by the end of the day things were advanced as nobody had ventured to dream they would advance. The providential carpenter took a cordial interest in the whole plan, which was necessary. For if such a man as that had chosen to say it was a "bad job," that it was all nonsense, and that it was a mere whim on Mr. Tangier's part, even though it would have put money in his pocket to attend to the thing, he would have delayed and waited and taken care that the sashes did not arrive from town in time, and would have had it in his power to throw the whole thing over, perhaps to another summer, perhaps to another year. But in point of fact Meakin took an interest, first in Mr. Tangier and then in his plan, from the very beginning. So to speak, he lent himself to the social revolution. And instead of sending an incompetent journeyman to see to it, he came himself, and made excellent suggestions. Mr. Tangier so wished that he could have Scott Meakin in town with him, to take oversight of the houses of his clients, which it was his business to keep decent and in repair. In short, Scott Meakin was that sort of intelligent supervisor of a neighborhood, who exercises the same general detail over its homes as a good old country doctor exercises over its health. Scott Meakin knew what house ought to be lifted up and have another story put under it. He also knew what house was rotten in its timber, and ought not to have ten cents spent upon it for repairs. Scott Meakin detested what he called a "bad job." And you might send to him as often as you chose to carry out some plan of your own which did not come in with his general idea of the fitness of things, and Scott Meakin would always be engaged somewhere else. On the other hand, if what you proposed to him was something he had planned himself, as he had been passing by some day, Scott Meakin would gladly come to the rescue. Before you were well awake the next morning, he and a dozen of his men would be on hand, and your innovation in your own house would have been carried out better than you had planned it yourself, simply because he considered it a good job and a thing which ought to be done.

In such hands, the old stage-house began to assume quite another aspect in a very few days. As has been said, it was a little off the high-road proper, but every loafer in the town made it his business to go round and see how the improvements went on. Before a fortnight was well over, every individual in the town thought he had suggested the greater part of these improvements himself, and began to think that the social revolution was a matter which he had himself suggested the day he was walking here or there, as the case might be; and thus without any-body's effort there was enlisted a general sympathy in the plan.

As for the plank sidewalk, Mrs. Floxam's views were in an indirect way sustained, although she never knew this. It was a discovery of the little school-mistress, which she mentioned rather timidly to Mrs. Dunster one day, out of which came the particular enterprise by which the sidewalk was undertaken and in the end completed. The little schoolmistress had been picked up one day by Scott Meakin, as he was driving an empty lumber-wagon back from the old tavern to his home; and she had ventured to tell him what all the women said, which was, that the great difficulty of Tenterdon was the difficulty in going from place to place in the winter rains, and in the spring when the frost was coming out of the ground. In short, the sidewalk question occupied her mind quite as much as it did that of Miss May Remington. She asked Scott why it was not the business of the town to provide for the people to walk quite as much as it was for them to ride, and said that she never had any horse and never expected to have any horse. It seemed to her rather mean that all the money which the town spent should be spent for the benefit of people like Scott Meakin, who drove a span, and that she and her school-children should have to take their chances in the middle of the road.

Scott Meakin told her that he could recollect a town meeting in which there had been a proposition made by somebody that there should be a sidewalk laid, and he told her also that it met with the objection which all such plans meet. That is to say, the people from a distance who were not going to walk on the sidewalk did not choose to be taxed for the benefit of those who were. "And that is just what you would find now," said he, "if you tried to do anything about this in town meeting. Those folks over in the north district have no idea of putting down a sidewalk for you and Mrs. Fairbanks and the doctor here. They would make no end of fun about it. They would propose sidewalks in every precinct of the town, and after ten or fifteen minutes' fooling, the whole thing would be thrown out."

The girl asked how much such a sidewalk would cost as had been talked about, more than a mile long, — nearly a mile and a half, indeed.

Meakin made a calculation unnecessarily accurate. But she was used to such sums in the Emerson's Arithmetic, and followed him, not without interest, taking, indeed, some ideas for her next blackboard lesson with the older boys at school. When he came out on his results, however, for a sidewalk three feet wide, made of plank an inch and a half thick and supported thus and so, she did not wonder that no conceivable town meeting in Tenterdon could be made to vote such a convenience for her and the other people of her own sex who had no votes to bring. She did not say to Scott Meakin that she thought he was proposing accommodations much better than were necessary. But, like the sensible girl she was, she recollected all his figures, and when he left her at the school-house, she jotted them down on a bit of paper for fear anybody should tell her afterwards, as men will tell women, that she knew nothing about the subject.

When recess came the next day, Miss Gurtry took

James Hodgdon with her, and they walked back into the pasture, and across by Wilfred's ten-acre lot, till they came to a little steam saw-mill, which had been established on the edge of the woods by a Maine man only two years before. Miss Gurtry told the boy, as they went, that she was going to talk with the Maine man about the sidewalk. She saw a little smoke curl above the woods as they approached, so that she was well pleased to find that he was on duty in his rather lonely place, and he was equally pleased to find that he had a visitor, even though that visitor brought him no promise of an order.

His speculation was sufficiently modest. It was long, long ago, since there had been a saw-mill within ten miles. In the mean while there had grown up some wretched second growth, which was really not worth hauling to any mill that anybody knew anything about. The arrival of this enterprising fellow, therefore, with this little establishment, had enabled everybody who wanted a little lumber and was not very particular as to the quality, to haul his own logs in winter and carry back just what he wanted for his own purposes. The Maine man lived by himself, with a boy he had picked up from some poor-house; and in a pioneer fashion, although he were close to crowded towns, he would make for a year or two a decent living, when he would carry his machinery to some other such forgotten forest, and glean what was left again. Miss Gurtry had stumbled on him in one of her walks after wild-flowers, so that they did not have to begin on the formalities of personal acquaintance. "We have come over to talk about stuff for a sidewalk, Mr. Rostock," said she. "A sidewalk!" said he, in surprise; "I do not deal in flagging-stones." This was his little joke. "No," she said, she was not grand enough for flagging-stones; but she had noticed that he was feeding his fire with the slabs from the logs, and that made her think there was not a large market for them. "No, Miss Gurtry," said he; "no market at all. When I went to school, the benches was made of slabs with the smooth side up; but you school-marms are quite too grand for us now. That was the only market we ever had for our slabs, and now we have to put them into the fire." So the girl told him, very frankly, that if he would put the lowest possible figure on the slabs which he had, piled up everywhere around him, she thought it not impossible that she might find him a customer. He promised that he and the poor-house boy should count them before night, and bring over to her some estimate of the number of feet he could provide; and then said, very frankly, that he did not want to be hard on anybody, and should like to oblige the neighborhood, if he could, so that he would fix his price for the slabs at the very lowest. So, in fact, the good fellow did; and when he came over, after school was done in the afternoon, with his estimates, Miss Gurtry was not dissatisfied with the results of her morning expedition.

CHAPTER XVII.

THE saw-mill man was as good as his word, and better. Had Miss Gurtry known it, her visit to him and his poor-house boy, when she went with her Squire, was a step not unimportant in what May Remington called "the social revolution." The lumber-man was used to life in the woods in Maine. But life in the woods there meant a dozen good fellows at your side, a game of cards at night, no end of fun as you cooked the breakfast in the morning. There was no lack of society in the Maine forest. Now, life here in the parish woodlands of Tenterdon, by the side of Casey brook, with nobody but the poor-house boy, who was as stupid as he was good-natured, was very lonely, though it was not three miles from Tenterdon steeple. The saw-mill man would not confess it to himself, but he was sadly bored; and the visit from Miss Gurtry and her companion was acceptable from points of view much more elevated than the business contract he made with her. He was now taken in as a partner in the commonwealth. He had some one to talk to, to whom he talked his best. And when the school-boy who came with her went up with the poor-house boy to look at a certain woodchuck's hole, not far away, he watched this companionship with real satisfaction.

He appeared at the school-house that evening, according to his promise, and he was now a different man externally. An old chest — "chist" in the vernacular — had been hauled out and had given up its buried contents. He was arrayed in them, — arrayed, that is, in "store-clothes" made by a ready-made clothier some ten years before, sent then to Vienna where they had not met a market, returned to America, and shipped as damaged to Ellsworth. Here the saw-mill man had bought them, and in them he had appeared on occasions of ceremony ever since.

He was, as has been said, much better than his word. He had in his hand what he called a "kind o' cradle," which he had hewn out with his ax, and which, with some pride, he explained to Miss Gurtry. He said that it would be easy to lay two slabs parallel with each other, — as it were a sort of foot railroad, and so he called it, — to support them in beds made in cross-ties, which he called "cradles," and so give to people walking abreast the privilege of dry foothold, though all the space between them was wet.

"En I thort, Miss Gurtry, that ef your boys here keered much abyout the walk, they might chop out such cradles as this b'tween schools. Seems to me, you know, that ef the boys make the walk, they will ollers keep it right. En ef they ain't interested in it, why, it won't last long, you know."

He laid down an important law as he said this, and he did not hesitate to do so in presence and in hearing of the boys, who were themselves explaining to each other the plan of the cradle. As the reader has been told, these were the little boys of the neighborhood, the bigger boys despising a summer school, as they might despise a pinafore or petticoats. But the little boys also were trusted with axes or hatchets, and they knew very well that, trusted or not, they would be able to bring them to school for the service proposed. They also knew that the big boys would gladly lend a hand in such an enterprise as this, however doubtful they might be of combinations for learning arithmetic or spelling.

And the result of Mr. Rostock's visit was that Miss Gurtry, partly from her own scanty stores, and partly from various quarter-dollars brought in by the boys from home, was able to order six hundred running feet of slabs "ter take 'em as they might come; but that it would be handier if the mill cut them into lengths such as the boys could handle." Mr. Rostock also agreed to cut a sufficient number of cross-ties from the thicker slabs, which could be hewn into such cradles as he suggested. All that Miss Gurtry had left to do was to obtain nails and spikes enough for three hundred feet of sidewalk; and all that the boys had to do was to beg, borrow, or "convey" the axes and hatchets necessary at their houses, and to persuade the bigger boys to come and help them in the morning and at night. Of course the enterprise was no secret. It was very popular so soon as the plans were adjusted. Fathers were found who permitted their "teams" to haul the slabs from the mill to the school-house. Miss Gurtry had offers of more nails than she could use; nay, hardly a little boy came in the morning who had not gleaned nails, as he said, with parental consent, from the family store. And so it happened that, before the caucus at Mrs. Dunster's knew anything about it, a girl who thought herself the most insignificant person in the town solved the central and crucial question in the new organization of society. For this bit of sidewalk was a concrete and visible fact. Such a fact always affects a New England community more even than a deduction of the severest logic or metaphysics. If, by good fortune, you can present both in such a community, you are omnipotent there.

While Mrs. Floxam still said, on occasion, that a sidewalk was useless and impossible, that country people were fools and could do nothing, a clean, not "impracticable," sidewalk existed on the main road; far distant from any house, but along a bit of lowland certain to be muddy if there were mud anywhere. It was a visible gospel of good sense and neatness. It did not go to the school-house. The school-house was on a narrow side road which ran uphill from the main road and was never muddy. But it was a daily relief, three days out of four in the year, to all the girls of the school and to every woman whose exigencies took her on foot that way. Six days of the joint work of the scholars and their big brothers finished it; and it was the admiration of the neighborhood, and topic of general daily congratulation after the third of the six days.

CHAPTER XVIII.

IT seemed worth while to go into this detail as to the most unimportant part of the physical enterprise by which the social economies of Tenterdon were to be changed, because, as it proved, the example or challenge set by the school district, which was the most insignificant in the town, compelled the rest of the town, however indifferent it might be, to attend to its share of the duty. Miss Gurtry's sidewalk was at a considerable distance from the old tavern, which was now under the charge of the carpenters and other workmen. But the fact that, with so small a force as she had at command, she had done what various town-meetings had refused to do, was, as has been said, a visible fact which all men apprehended; and it was clear to all eyes and to all hearts that the rest of the town would be disgraced if this challenge were not at once taken up. When there was talk, on the part of the more cautious and conservative, of having an article put into the warrant for the next town-meeting, the women, who were the most interested, ridiculed any such delay. The town-meeting would not take place till the next March. Before that time who should say how many people might have caught their death of cold? No! Miss Gurtry had shown how the sidewalk should be made, and made it should be, and made at once. If the men

had any improvements to make on Miss Gurtry's
methods, let them show what they would be, but let
nobody say that the "Centre" could not have a sidewalk, when Miss Gurtry had succeeded so well in her
outlying region.

There were many searchings of spirit as to whose
business it was to go forward in this affair. But these
were all solved by the prompt declaration of the
Knights Templars that they proposed to undertake
this sidewalk, and that any man might do his own
share about his own house if he chose to. Only they
wanted to be notified who would and who would not
help, where they would help, and how they would
help. It is the fashion of New England that no one
likes to be dragooned or driven to his duty. And the
number of different ways in which persons thus challenged by the Knights Templars showed how they
could help without helping as other people did, would
stagger the belief of the average reader; nor shall he
be indulged by a calendar of them. Suffice it to say
that the Knights, or Drummond, who was their spokes-
man, found that they had all the help that they knew
how to handle, all the tools they knew how to handle,
all the nails they knew how to handle, and it seemed
that there would be but little difficulty in collecting
the money which was needed. When it came to the
question of money, the ladies' society of the church
proved to have in its treasury a considerable sum,
from which it was proposed that an appropriation
of fifteen dollars should be made. But the men refused this. They said that that money must be used
for purposes more distinctly ecclesiastical or sacred.
But some one intimated that if it was considered de-

sirable to take up a collection in church for this special purpose, such a collection should be permitted. To this collection Mr. Burdett gave a ready assent, and it was determined it should be taken up accordingly.

As the little cluster of visitors met at Mrs. Dunster's house one evening, when the stroke of the adze and the sound of the hammer could be distinctly heard, as a knot of spirited young fellows were at work on the sidewalk, Mr. Tangier said that there was so hearty a spirit of co-operation in the matter that he could not but wonder why it had not been done long before. How should it be that an improvement which everybody recognized as necessary should have "hung fire," to use the vernacular, so long, when it was so easily done now that it was proposed?

"I do not know what the wiseacres will say," said Mrs. Dunster, "but if I understand the people among whom I live and of whom I am, nobody likes to be ordered to do anything in such a community as ours."

"That is true enough," said the doctor. "More than this, you may say perfectly safely that people do not like to work for a mere abstract idea, for a reform stated on paper; that is, the greater part of them do not like it. There are also a few poor *doctrinaires* or theorists who prefer the paper theory to the concrete fact. But take the Yankee by and large, and he wants to see the thing that he is to do. He is much more certain to do it if it has been tried in another place, particularly if it has been tried in another place in New England; and then, if he has seen it with his own eyes, or if his father has seen it, or his brother has seen it, he is determined that he will have it himself. But the parable, and better than the parable, the concrete experiment, is a great help. You were more helped by Miss Gurtry and her lumberman than you know."

"I wish," said Miss May, "that any of the rest of you in all your grand social economies and politics had any eyes for the romance of this situation."

"Romance?" said Mr. Tangier. "Pray tell me what is the romance in two-inch nails, or what is the romance in the swinging of an adze?"

"That depends on who drives the nails, and that depends on who swings the adze," said Miss May. "But if any of you pundits had half an eye, you would see that Mr. Drummond, as you call him, the Knight Templar man, is very, very, very fond of your pretty Miss Gurtry. And if she were not a woman, and it were not disloyal to her, I would add that the pretty Miss Gurtry likes Mr. Drummond just the least bit in the world, although neither of them dare say so to the other."

"I own myself a fool," said Mr. Tangier. "I own that studies of social economy have blinded my eyes to what was before them. Now that you tell me that this is so, I am willing to take it on your authority. But as you are so learned, would you go a little farther, and would you tell me why in the world, if Mr. Drummond likes Miss Gurtry, he does not tell her so, and why he should not tell her so?"

Miss May laughed very heartily. "I should think you had never seen a novel in your life, Mr. Tangier. And sometimes I think that you are all so busy with your beginning of the term and the end of the term, with the coming in of the court and the drawing up of lists of the jury, that you cannot be made to take the least interest in a good novel, whether it is displayed under your eye or whether Mr. Howells writes it. For my part, I am not very sorry that we women are shut off to the enjoyment of the realities of life, and that you men have to pick up the cobble-stones and crack them, if you cannot see what, as I say, any blind calender with half an eye could see."

"I have acknowledged my imbecility," said Mr. Tangier, "and I acknowledge it again; but I wish you would tell me why in the world, if Mr. Drummond likes Miss Gurtry, he should not tell her so? Is it foreordained by any Capulet or any Montague, or any other old man in silks and satins, that the house of Drummond shall not tell the house of Gurtry how fond we are?"

Miss May still laughed very heartily. "That is not foreordained at all. There is no house of Drummond, and there is no house of Gurtry. On the other hand, Mr. Drummond is a stranger in the town, who came to us, well, from somewhere up in Vermont, I suppose; that is the reason he is so tall, and his hair is so black, and his face is so brown, and, if you please, he is so handsome. It is a little bit of the Norman blood that you Vermonters have; and your pretty Miss Gurtry, as you call her — "

"It was not I who called her pretty," said Mr. Tangier. "It was Miss May Remington who called her pretty."

"Very good," said Miss May, still laughing; "my pretty Miss Gurtry, if I called her so. She comes to us, well, I think from Ohio. I do not know why the Western girls come East. I believe it is because there is not "culchaw" enough at the West to go

around. Anyway, she comes from Ohio and she keeps
this school, and there is not another Gurtry in the
county; and, so far as I know, there is not another
Drummond in the county. There is no Capulet and
no Montague."

CHAPTER XIX.

"WHAT I think," said Mr. Tangier, "is that we ought to go on and see how the carpenters are going on."

"We all know," said Miss May.

"We know, in a fashion. But we really know nothing till we have seen with our eyes and heard with our ears. It will be a pity every time you dance in a German in the new hall if your eye rests on a cornice you dislike, and you have to say, 'I could have had that all right, but that I was lazy.'"

"Yes," said Miss May; "and I see deeply into the mind of the counsellor who proposes this. It would also be a pity if Mr. Drummond and Miss Gurtry did not have an opportunity to meet each other. Was that what you had on your mind, Mr. Senior Counsel?"

Mr. Tangier laughed, but would confess nothing. He insisted, all the same, that all the conspirators, as he always called the heads of the social regeneration, should meet at the old stage-house the next day. He asked Mrs. Dunster to lend her carry-all for the more distant members; but he said he would bring Drummond and the other men, without horse-power. It was known that Mrs. Fairbanks would send them over something for a picnic tea, and it was thought that the new cooking-stove could be put in order in time to heat some water. "It will be, therefore," cried May Remington, "the beginning of the social regeneration. Social regeneration in the midst of shavings. Mr. Tangier, you are more right than I supposed."

Mr. Tangier asked her to come down from her station so far as to write a note for him to Drummond, whose daily work was at the Crossing, and another to the doctor. The doctor would pass early in the morning, and would like to know then what was on the cards for the day.

When she had written these notes he bade her say at the bottom: "JEFFREY TANGIER, his mark," and then with his left hand he made a cross on each of them.

"That is all very well for a joke," said he. "But, Miss May, would you mind writing another for me to my partner, Mr. Heeren?"

"Mind? I shall be most glad to. You do not know yet what a pleasure it is for a girl fresh from school to find herself of any use to anybody."

He replied, as indeed he had to, that she was of great use to him.

"Indeed, Mr. Tangier," said she, a little amazed, "I was not asking for a compliment. I ought to have been more on my guard. But — no — I was thinking of a scene I saw in a visit I have been making at Warwick. There was a cross brute of a man there, who abused his wife, and his children, too, whenever he happened to be at home. Fortunately, this was not often. But one evening when we had some music at our house, he chose to come over. And what he said — which I remembered — he said it to his own pretty wife, too, and he made her cry — was that she could not do a thing for which anybody would pay her five dollars a week. He said that if she advertised for work in the 'New York World' under the 'Wants,' and told all she could do, nobody would hire her for five dollars a week. She tried to laugh, but the tears came into her eyes. And then he thought he would make the rest of us cry, so he said that the same might be said of all the women in the room. My nice Mrs. Curwen was even with him. She said: 'When you have a woman on your list, Mr. Fonblanque, who will do for my baby what your wife has done for yours in the last fortnight, send her round to me and I will pay her twenty dollars a week.'"

"Good for Mrs. Curwen," said Tangier. "Try to introduce me to her the first time I go to Boston."

"Yes. Wasn't it good? All the same, Charlotte and I went off to bed, asking what we could do that would appear to advantage in the 'Wants,' column. I do not mean teaching. Teaching is, after all, handing along the same state of ignorance and of information. I mean work — what I heard the doctor call 'subduing the world.'"

"Very good," said Tangier. "And I hope you and your Miss Charlotte did not make the common mistake of young ladies — or, for that matter, old women, too."

"What is that?"

"It is to speak of this difficulty as if it belonged to your sex. The truth is that it belongs to everybody born into the world. It is only lately that women have begun to talk about it; that is all. But, in truth, every boy who leaves college finds it just as hard to find the right niche as every girl who leaves

Wellesley or Vassar. Only, by misfortune, there are women's journals and 'departments' in newspapers, in which women can groan about these things, while there is no journal open to Brother Smith, who finds that the high school has taught him the wrong way to calculate interest, or to Tom Jones, who does not know the difference between white lead and barytes."

"You do me good, Mr. Tangier. I wish I thought the boys one half as discontented as I am sometimes. And what am I to say to Mr. Cross-Brute the first time I meet him ? "

"If I tell the truth," said he, " seriously enough now, you call it a compliment. So I will not say that you write a better hand than he does, unless he is an exceptional man, and that you translated that scrap I gave you in Grimm so that one might have thought that Grimm wrote English. Really, you know, I suppose, that your Mr. Cross-Brute, without knowing it, has opened up the general question of the New Education."

"I do not know what you mean," said Mrs. Dunster.

"Yes, you do, only I put it badly. In the Old Education, so far as a college went, a man was taught to understand the language of his time. To tell the truth, he was not taught much more. But when he left college, if he met a man of letters, he could talk of literature; if he met an electrician, he could ask a question and understand the answer; if he met Baron Humboldt, he could learn from him of botany and zoölogy, and if he met Metternich or Baron Bunsen, he could learn about European politics. But now he may be thoroughly up on one of these things, but he has not so much as the elements of the others. The New

Education is on the lookout for his bread and butter. It says: 'I will make you a statesman. I will make you an electrician. I will make you a botanist. I will make you a Latinist. But you must choose.' I suppose the man has his reward. But those of us who remember Mr. Irving or Mr. Everctt, or the tales of Mr. Webster — well — no matter."

"I see what you mean," said Mrs. Dunster, "and it is rather an encouragement."

"It reminds me," said May Remington, " of what dear Dr. Gray said. You know I saw him at Princeton. He said it was very good fun to be seventy-five — that you did not have to know everything and to have an opinion on all subjects."

"Precisely. Now, why a girl of eighteen or a boy of twenty should know everything, or have an opinion on all subjects, I do not know. I used to think," Mr. Tangier went on, " but I express myself with terror lest I be sent home, — I used to think that a woman wanted to lend a hand everywhere, as your nice magazine says, Mrs. Dunster. I used to think that the mother Elizabeth was the type of womanhood. She put her hand in her bag when anything was wanted and that thing came out."

"I remember her," said Miss May, " and I adore her. I see what you mean. The gimlet was perhaps a bad gimlet, but it was a gimlet. The smelling-salts were perhaps bad smelling-salts, but they were smelling-salts. Yet, well — Lucy says something the same thing to Harry, I believe, and Lucy was not ashamed. But I — "

"You are the creature of your age," said Mrs. Dunster, "and cannot live without eating out your own heart. Perhaps a happier age will come in the next generation — "

"When I shall look out and not in," said the girl, triumphantly. "Let us hope so. But we do not get on with the conspiracy."

No. They did not. For at that moment an elegant equipage appeared, and a footman in livery brought round the cards of Mrs. Somebody and Miss Thing-um-bob, grand people who were staying at the Surf House, at the sands, — the nearest watering-place proper. Mr. Tangier immediately vanished — no one knew where. But the next afternoon, as had been planned, the conspirators met at the stage-house.

It had no new name as yet — indeed, one of the "objects of the meeting" was to devise a name. It is rather curious that the passion of people of Teutonic blood for "meetings" is so strong that they will "get up" a "meeting" without knowing very definitely why they do it; and, after they have met, different people will inquire what is the "object of the meeting." Different men will say that they cannot preside, because they do not know the "object of the meeting." But, somewhat as a botanical party on new ground finds a Shortia, or perhaps a Longea, which nobody expected, the meeting, having met, discovers an object.

In this case, Miss May Remington had in mind one object — Mr. Drummond, perhaps none, but that he was asked. Mr. Tangier had always the general object of waking up Tenterdon, if he could — or what they called the reorganization of society.

He arrived first with his faithful Squire Nathan. For, ever since the fire, Nathan had attached himself.

somewhat like a boy Friday, to the fortunes of Mr. Tangier, and wherever he went, was not far away. Mr. Tangier was amused by his loyalty. He said that it was a survival of feudalism, which had little else to boast of in Tenterdon, and he encouraged it, just as he had brought with him "Quentin Durward" for his reading. On this occasion he had called the boy, who was loitering by the well at Mrs. Fairbanks's, and had talked with him all the way. The new sidewalk, glorious in a freshness not yet stained with rust, was finished almost all the way.

Drummond appeared, immediately after, with another of the young men of the fishing-gang to which they belonged. He and Tangier were now quite intimate.

"I was afraid you might not get away," said Mr. Tangier to him as he gave him his hand, and as Drummond introduced Knapp, his companion. "But the wind has hauled into the northwest."

"Yes," said Drummond. "There is no chance for a haul after this, I suppose, till it comes round. But, to tell you the truth, I would have come any way, even if the boats went off without me. Knapp would have hauled double for me."

Knapp laughed, and said that, since the repairs had begun on the stage-house, they could not always rely on Drummond in the boats. "They" were a crew of young fellows, mostly belonging to the neighborhood, who had established a sort of camp on the sea-shore, where they watched for the signals made on the different heights which showed whether there were or were not a run of fish, so that it would be worth while to go out in the boats with the long seine.

Mr. Tangier said that he hoped the results of the new conspiracy would be important enough to justify the occasional loss of a Spanish mackerel or of a bluefish.

At this moment the carry-all from Mrs. Dunster's came up with pretty Miss Gurtry, with Miss May Remington, with Mrs. Dunster and old Mrs. Hasey. Tangier took care to hear a carpenter call him upstairs, so that Mr. Drummond might have the pleasure of giving Miss Gurtry his hand. Miss Remington had already sprung out on the other side, and was holding the horse's head so as to keep herself out of the way. Mrs. Fairbanks took Mrs. Hasey into the reception-room, as they began to call the old bar-room of the stage-house, and Mr. Drummond had to decide which of the young ladies needed him most. Of course he decided against his own wishes, and went to the horse's head.

"No, Mr. Drummond," said Miss Remington, "you are very kind, but you must leave me to my own affair. Peg, as we call her, understands me, and I understand her. I will just lead her into the shed, and I will join you and Miss Gurtry in a moment. I have been telling Miss Gurtry that I want her to look at the frieze which Mr. Tangier has ordered from some of the swell paper-men in New York. I think it is absurd myself, but Miss Gurtry's eye is rather better than mine."

And with this the crafty girl took herself and her horse away, and Mr. Drummond and Miss Gurtry were left together exactly as she had intended.

It was long, indeed, that afternoon, before, in the intricacies of the house, inspecting of the various rooms, of staircases taken away and ladders for climbing, one of these societies of ladies found the other. This was not, indeed, so strange, since Miss May Remington was determined that she would not interrupt the *tête-à-tête* between Mr. Drummond and Miss Gurtry; since Mrs. Fairbanks was equally determined that Mrs. Hasey should not interrupt it; and since Mr. Tangier had planned the whole expedition in order that these two young people might be together. How little Mr. Drummond or Miss Gurtry knew that the stars in their courses were fighting for them, and how annoyed one of them at least would have been, could she have suspected that her most private affairs were thus a matter of interest to other people!

Mr. Drummond was so shy that he blushed, and knew he blushed, as he said to Miss Gurtry: "I am amused to see how much there is to be decided before we can clean up an old tavern. All this about tints which harmonize and tints which do not harmonize is a very new affair to a fisherman like me."

Miss Gurtry made courage enough to say: "You have not been a fisherman so long, Mr. Drummond, that you have lost all knowledge of the inside of a house, I suppose. Indeed, they tell me that the housekeeping is very good down on the beach."

"Who tells you so?" said Mr. Drummond, a little surprised. "I did not know that the fame of our life had extended so far up as your school-house, which I think we must now call the centre of the world, since the side-walk victory."

His surprise gave her a little courage, and she said: "Oh, you think that, because we are an interior district, we know nothing about shad and bluefish and mackerel! I assure you that we get a sniff of the sea-air sometimes, and there is one of your boys, who is now on a visit with one of my boys, and therefore is sent to my school. I believe they thought that it was necessary that he should have mountain air." The girl spoke now as if she felt a little more at ease, that she was speaking of what was really her own affair.

"I remember," said Mr. Drummond, "and really the boy tells you the truth; the doctor thought, and I guess thought truly, that being wet through five times a day was of no great advantage to Jotham. Country air is a very good thing when it is accompanied with clothing reasonably dry and a first-rate education. Do you know, Miss Gurtry, I also am one of the great army of schoolmasters? I kept school when I was five years younger than I am."

The girl did not tell him that one of the big boys who had helped in making the sidewalk — and, in fact, had done the most work that any of them had done — had talked to her well into the middle of the night, one evening, of his enthusiasm for Mr. Drummond, and the help that Mr. Drummond had given him in school and out of school; and had spoken of Mr. Drummond as one of General Grant's aids might have spoken of him, with that enthusiasm which is itself the best education, and worth a hundred times all the in-struction that can be given by all the cyclopædia-bred men in the world. She did not dare tell Mr. Drummond how much she knew of him through the eager and en-thusiastic gossip of this boy. All that she did say was: "Oh, yes, almost everybody is a teacher sooner or later!

People teach till they find they can do something better, or what they think is something better."

"Yes," said Drummond; "in the gang down on the beach we were talking of it the other night. I found that half the boys (as we call each other, for we are really all men) had sooner or later been in one district school or another. Sometimes I think it is better so, and sometimes I suppose that it leaves the training of the little ones to be all a matter of choice." Then, with a gulp of great courage, he said: "I wish I could have gone to your school, Miss Gurtry." And he pretended to laugh.

"You would not say so if you had seen it," said she. "I was more ashamed than I can tell the other day, when your friend Mr. Tangier came in to escape a wetting. It sometimes seems absurd to call it a school. But I can tell you, indeed, Mr. Drummond, there is nothing we do not teach there, from the art of washing the hands with ivory soap round to words in three syllables. Really, this business of the sidewalk came in quite naturally as a part of the very various exercises of the school."

"You are not graded yet," he said, and he laughed; for the grading of the schools had been a matter of town politics of the most intense interest. Montagues and Capulets had, indeed, quarrelled on the question whether the school should be graded or no.

Ah, me! it did not matter what these young people talked about with each other. Miss May Remington had seen with a very keen eye when she had noticed Mr. Drummond's bearing with the pretty schoolmistress, as she called her, on the last picnic party which they had had at the old stage-house. Mr. Drummond regretted, in all this talk in the question about friezes and the decision about staircases, that he could in no way appear at what he supposed was his best to Miss Gurtry. And the poor fellow supposed, of course, that he was making blunders all the time and was appearing at his worst. In fact, he was a manly, intelligent fellow, who had his own canoe to paddle and was paddling it; who knew that he ought to be of some use in the world and was of much more use than he thought he was; and the first moment when he was unconscious he was singularly attractive: first, from the directness of speech with which he always addressed himself to the subject in hand; and second, from the indifference to himself, which you could not but notice, in his way of handling that subject, whatever it might be.

CHAPTER XX.

WHEN Miss May Remington was sure that Mr. Drummond and the schoolmistress were alone together in the shaving-piled room where they were talking, she was well pleased with her work, and she said so.

She was with Mr. Tangier and Mrs. Dunster in another room, where the shavings had been roughly swept up on one side. "Mr. Tangier and Mrs. Dunster," she said, as she seated herself on a tool-box, "we have not lived in vain."

Mr. Tangier pretended not to understand her. "They have done something since I was here; but I hoped things would be more cleared up."

"They! Mr. Tangier, you do not deceive me! What is a week, more or less, in the opening of your Palace of Delight here, when compared with the joy or wretchedness in life of two human beings who are now downstairs? If Mrs. Dunster with her gray horse Tom, and I by my occasional words of wisdom, and you by your ready assent to plans which you only partly approved and only partly comprehended, — if we three have achieved this, why, let us die happy."

"As to that," said Mr. Tangier, laughing, "I had much rather live happy." And Mrs. Dunster agreed with him. Then he went on to say that he could not see why all this working was needed. He had not seen, since the beginning, why, if Mr. Drummond liked Miss Gurtry, he should not go and tell her so.

"And I suppose," said Miss May, indignantly, "I suppose if Miss Gurtry is conscious some morning that she remembers with pleasure something said to her, and would like to go on with the friendly intimacy, she is to go and tell him so! Really, Mr. Tangier, the profession of a great conveyancer — are you a conveyancer? — leaves some great gaps of — I will not say ignorance! Pray, is Miss Gurtry to dismiss school early, and walk down to the beach and climb up the steps to the fish-houses, and say, 'Which is Mr. Drummond's house?' And, when poor Drummond has come out, all dazed and wondering, is she to say, 'I thought I would like to tell you something I thought of after you went away'? Really, Mr. Tangier, if you expect that, you expect much more than you will have."

"This is to be said," said Mrs. Dunster. "If there were no such difficulties, we should have no novels. What is it all but the fanning of the spark till the fire flames?"

"Or the rubbing the match," said Mr. Tangier. "We do not have tinder-boxes now, and we know but little of sparks. But say 'match.' Perhaps you do not rub it hard enough; then it goes out. Perhaps you rub too hard; then it breaks and a bit of fire drops to the floor, and you put your foot on it, and that is all. Perhaps it just lights, and you hold it, in terror — oh, how still! — afraid you shall blow out the blue flame; then — joy of joys! — it burns. Then you turn on the gas —"

"And the rush of air is so great it blows out the match!" cried Miss May, delighted.

"Not at all! You waited till the first rush was gone! You touched the gas, and all was light where it was dark, and happiness where it was doubt."

"Now you talk like a reasonable being, Mr. Tangier, and not like a conveyancer."

"I am not a conveyancer, and never was."·

"It makes no difference. You are something, and I do not know what a conveyancer is. Anyway, you talk sense now. And I beg you to observe that the interview downstairs is not a thing which happens every day in the lines of fishermen, or in the lines of schoolmistresses. For me, I am neither; I can teach nothing, because I know nothing, and I am sea-sick in a boat, so I cannot fish. But all the same, Mr. Tangier, I see the advantage of mixing people together."

Mr. Tangier said that an amusing report of Tom Hughes tells the difficulties they had in the Working-men's College, in London, in making government clerks in the post-office meet cordially with the makers of delicate astronomical instruments. The officer of the Queen considered that his rank was higher than that of the man who had no commission.

"Fountain of honor! Yes," said the bright girl, thinking, "I think that helps us about the theory. Now, if we can all see that we are the King's Daughters, and the King's Sons too, — that we take our honors direct, — perhaps we shall all get over Mr. Hughes's troubles." And she pointed to the little bit of purple ribbon which marked her as a King's Daughter.

"Precisely," said Mrs. Dunster. "And if you will both come down from the heights a little, you will see that this is what our sidewalk and our 'Palace of Delight' here are for. Accept the meeting downstairs as a good omen. You want a name for your palace, Mr. Tangier. Call it 'The Happy Meeting.'"

"As to that," said he, "the old Yankee word, 'Meeting-house,' was a much better word than the purists knew who threw it out. I suppose the word 'together' is the centre of Christianity. 'Synagogue' meant meeting-house, and I do not know why the grand people try to discard so good a word."

"This place will always be called 'The Old Stage-house,'" said Miss May. "You cannot change names by votes. But if it is a meeting-house, really and truly, that is what it is for."

Then they went off, talking about Mr. Walter Besant and the way in which his "Impossible Story" of "All Sorts and Conditions of Men" had proved itself possible, and had worked out the palace which he dedicated the other day. "Only," said Mr. Tangier, sadly, "this I have seen. I have seen a lobster on the beach with almost no shell, who made for himself an excellent shell. But I never saw a lobster-shell, however perfect, which made of itself a living lobster."

"Nor did I," said May Remington, sadly, too. "But is n't this perhaps because the lobster-shells you and I see have been boiled, Mr. Tangier? They are red and not black."

"I see what you mean," said he. "Let us hope that there is a live lobster somewhere, and that he will not be afraid of a live shell."

And then they went downstairs again, into all the rooms but one. They changed the order that had been given about double doors in the reading-room. They ordered the east window in the reception-room to be cut down and changed into a door out upon the west piazza. Many other like details did they attend to. But they did not interfere with the interview, though it was somewhat prolonged, between Miss Gurtry and Mr. Drummond.

CHAPTER XXI.

AT this moment, however, the afternoon was broken, and if Miss May Remington had any slight hopes of observing the results of her stratagems for other people's comforts, she was disappointed. The clatter of a light wagon at the door called some one to the window, who announced a telegraph boy. The well-known yellow envelope in his hand was token who he was before he spoke.

"I am the one who is in no danger," said Mr. Tangier, as the boy came upstairs to them, in answer to Mrs. Fairbanks's call. "Heeren knows far too much to send one of those things at my head."

But the boy called for "Mr. Tan-geér" as he entered the room, and demanded a dollar as his compensation for coming from Knox. Mrs. Fairbanks paid the dollar and bade the boy wait, while poor Mr. Tangier, with a troubled look on his face, took his fatal yellow sheet to the window.

Mr. Heeren announced, with regret, even in his telegraphic brevity, that Mr. Grace was failing rapidly, and that there was every reason why Mr. Tangier should see him at once, if this were possible. Mr. Tangier read, read again, looked at his watch, passed the despatch to the sympathizing Mrs. Dunster, and asked the boy for a blank. The boy, of course, had none, such being the order, apparently, of the Western Union.

Miss Remington opened her bag and produced one. At his request, she wrote for Mr. Tangier, whose hand was still disabled: —

" All right.   I will come on the express to-night. — T."

"Mr. Drummond and the rest will expect you at their collation, Mrs. Dunster," he said.   "But I must go home, at least for a day.   Miss Remington, I wonder if you could not drive me over to Mrs. Fairbanks's and do some writing for me.   Nathan shall take me to the express, and then you can come back to them." And then he smiled for the first time and said, "You will not mind missing the feast."

But Miss May had already disappeared.   She picked up a boy on her way to the horse-shed, and in a minute more they had brought the carriage round to the door. She and Mr. Tangier were soon in Mrs. Fairbanks's "little room," as it was always called.

Mr. Tangier dictated some careful and quite extensive orders to Scott Meakin.   He wrote a note to the man who represented the owners of the stage-house, and made him a definite offer for the rent of that building for five years, giving him one week for an answer. He wrote a note of farewell to the doctor, and another to Mr. Burdett.   That is to say, Miss Remington wrote these notes.   They were even signed with his name, "by R.," as he instructed her.   All this she did promptly, and without curiosity or surprise.   Then she said, "I am sorry that you write as if you were not coming back soon."

"On the contrary," said he, "I hope I may be back

on Monday. But who knows? I do not choose to leave this thing, or, indeed, anything, dependent on such a trifle as a clot of blood, harder or softer, in the nape of my neck. And I am quite too much interested in our 'Palace of Delight' to let the experiment hinge on the accident of my life." All this he said quite seriously. The girl had seen the serious phase in him often, indeed. But she liked this frankness in speaking of death more than anything she had seen. Then he crossed the room and shut the door. "Miss May," he said, "they take up the contribution at church next Sunday for the sidewalk. I do not want the thing to be botched. On the other hand, I do not want to be known as its chief promoter. You will find in my pocket-book nearly thirty dollars, in money of all sorts, which I have been collecting and reserving for use in this contribution. Manage, somehow, that a dozen different people put this money into the contribution boxes, and do not let any one of them know that any one else has such a charge."

"I see, I understand, and I obey," said the girl, amused by his complete comprehension of the position, and well pleased to find that he trusted her good sense for such a commission. She understood this man better from the half-hour which she thus spent on this work, than she did from the weeks in which they had met, almost every day, since her arrival. So soon as she had taken the money, he called to Nathan and set him to packing his portmanteau. Nathan proved but a dull valet, however. Miss Remington had not been sent away, and when she saw the boy vainly trying to make Creasy's "Fifteen Battles" break a portable inkstand which he was crowding into the wrong compartment, she begged leave to come to the rescue. "I do it for my father every time he goes on circuit. Nathan, you can be eating your supper and harnessing Dan. I am sure I can do it, Mr. Tangier, if you will tell me what you want." Then she begged pardon very nicely and said, "I do so hate to see a thing done wrong."

He did not need any apology. He also hated to see things done wrong, and was chafing all the time for his "imbecile inability," as he called it.

So he and Nathan were on time when the express stopped at Knox, and at eleven o'clock that night he was in his own bed again, courting such sleep as the starched bandage on his right arm would allow him.

The next morning at ten o'clock he presented himself, by appointment made already by Mr. Heeren, at the house of his dying client Mr. Grace. In a drawing-room he found Dr. Morton with two other physicians whom he knew well. The three admitted him, as a confidential person, to the close of their consultation.

"Yes, I am glad you are here," said Morton. "Practically, it is all over. But his mind is as clear as a bell, and if you want or he wants to make any farther arrangements, now is your time. He expects you, and the sooner you begin, why, the sooner you will be done. Poor fellow! He slept so little yesterday that we would have given him a sedative to-day, but for you." And so Mr. Tangier went upstairs.

"It is much as I told you, Mr. Tangier," said the sick man, even cheerfully, as the lawyer took his seat by the bedside. "You will excuse my hand. I do not move easily. Yes; if you remember, I said I had not many weeks. And now I am so sorry to call you back from your holiday."

Mr. Tangier, in a word or two, implied that he was sorry for the cause, but that really he should have come before but for his accident.

"Your arm hurt! Indeed, I did not notice. We sick people are so selfish. All the same, I can tell you what I want. Since I have been lying here, I have thought of several things which slipped my mind that day. If you will put them on paper this morning, I can execute the thing at noon; and then," with a lovely smile he said this, "I shall be quite through."

The tears were in Mr. Tangier's eyes, but he tried to smile also. The dying man called his attention to a porcelain slate on the bedquilt, and bade him read the memoranda on it. They were bequests, — some of large sums, some of little tokens of personal affection, — he explained, with perfect simplicity and ease. Mr. Tangier read them, received the other's explanation, and said, "This is very simple; is this all?"

"Not at all," said Mr. Grace. "For this I would not have telegraphed you. Mr. Heeren would have done this, or my executors, indeed, would respect that slate. But, as I said to you, I am in doubt about that larger gift, which a man, as prosperous and as happy as I, owes to the country which has given him his property, or to the church which has tried to teach him how to live. Fix the amount at two hundred thousand dollars, Mr. Tangier. That is the meaning of that separate memorandum. Easy enough to write that. But, as your friend Lord Lytton says, 'What shall he do with it?' You know I doubted before. I am somewhat doubtful still."

"You spoke of leaving a large discretion to your executors," said the other.

"Yes. But, as I lie here, this seems to me mean, not to say foolish. If I do not know what I want, how in the world should they know?"

"You spoke of the University for Moral Science."

"Yes," said Mr. Grace, doubtfully and inquiringly, and then was silent.

"You spoke of a Home for Old Married Couples."

"Yes," said Mr. Grace, perhaps with a little more interest, but again there was silence.

"We talked of Travelling Scholarships for graduates."

"Yes," said Mr. Grace, quite indifferent now. And after a moment he added: "And I said, of all these, that they were things other people would think of, and that each of them was outside my life and me."

"You said," said Mr. Tangier, "that you looked back happily and with interest to your native place, Steuben's Ford. You said that you knew it would always be a cheerful, healthy country town, and never rattling, prosperous place of manufacture. You said that you wanted to be remembered there, and, in the will I drew, there is a gift of ten thousand dollars for the foundation of a library there."

"Yes," said the other, not indifferent this time, but with a sort of eager sympathy. It may be said that it was Mr. Tangier's readiness of interest, by which he recollected each little detail of his clients' affairs, and put himself eagerly in the places they were in, — that it was this which made him the favorite he was among the men who consulted him.

"Mr. Grace," said he now, "perhaps I shall surprise you. But I also have thought much of your will since I was in the country.

"I have seen a country village, much like what you describe your Steuben's Ford in its make-up. I have seen all sorts of people, — good, bad, and neither. The thing they want most is better acquaintance with each other, — more easy intimacy and society. A dozen times I have said to myself, 'If Mr. Grace has no other plans, I will advise him to make a larger bequest to his old home.'"

"Two hundred thousand dollars," said the other, this time with some surprise. "Another academy?"

"Hardly that," said Mr. Tangier. "You think, and I think, that money enough is spent on children already. If I were you, I would give this money for 'all sorts and conditions of men'; the same sorts and conditions for whom you pray every Sunday. I would enlarge the library bequest to fifty thousand dollars. I would direct the trustees to connect with the library, rooms for concerts, reading-rooms, chess and checker rooms, — theatres, if they choose, — places where all sorts and conditions of men can meet each other. I would have tennis courts and croquet grounds and archery grounds in the garden around the hall. I would permit the trustees to spend money for musical instruments, if the people would make a band. I would keep a greenhouse by the library for the common good. If necessary, I would found prizes to interest the children in gardening. In a word, I would do what I could to make Steuben's Ford as pleasant a place to live in, — well, as there is in this world."

"Mr. Tangier, I thank you a thousand times.

Please open my desk. No, not that; the small desk, between the windows. Look in. No; the upper part. See a file there marked 'Gansevoort,' is it not?"

Mr. Tangier found the file, as the accurate merchant directed.

"Take those papers and you will find some hints in the same line. I am so glad to see that a man of your sense has come at this same point. They are going to give me some beef-tea and champagne now. But if you will have this ready at one, I will be ready. You have made me more happy than you can think. I cannot thank you enough for coming home from your holiday."

And so the courteous prince smiled again. As Mr. Tangier rose from his chair, Mr. Grace said, "I think you may as well say three instead of two."

"You mean three hundred thousand," said Mr. Tangier.

"Precisely," said Mr. Grace.

Mr. Tangier called in the nurse from the next room, and went downstairs. Here he called his short-hand writer, who was waiting, and sat down with him in that same parlor where the physicians had consulted. The elegance of the furniture seemed ghastly, as it had seemed before, now that they were almost in presence of death. Mr. Tangier pulled aside the lace curtains and raised the shade, bade the young man draw up an elegant blue satin ottoman to the light, and sit upon it while he wrote. He opened the file of papers to which Mr. Grace had referred him, and in a very few minutes found that his client had anticipated him in some of the very plans which he had been forming, and in the experiences which he had passed through at Tenterdon.

In a few compact and intelligible sentences the codicil was drawn on the lines indicated in the largest paper in his hand, and hinted at in his own suggestions to Mr. Grace. A board of seven trustees was appointed, one of whom was to be chosen, once in five years, by the people of the town; one was the minister of the old church; one was the judge of probate of the county; and the others were named by the testator. This board was to appoint the successors to these four on their death or resignation. The objects of the trust were briefly but sufficiently stated. They were to maintain a building near the middle of the town, sufficient for a library, for concerts and other entertainments, with rooms for pictures, reading, conversation, and improving social gatherings; they were to maintain a public garden and greenhouse, and, in general, to provide measures for making life attractive and happy to the people and to strangers among them. In the execution of their trust they were to make no distinction of race, class, calling, or birth. Mr. Tangier borrowed, as he had before done, the language of Mr. Besant, and directed that the Library Hall, as it was called, should be arranged for the benefit of "all sorts and conditions of men."

The clerk withdrew, with instructions to bring two copies of the will at one o'clock. Mr. Tangier did not even leave the house. He spread a newspaper on the satin of the sofa nearest the window, lest his boots might soil it, stretched himself at length, and took from the clerk's bag a book which contained the printed evidence on both sides in a patent case in which he was retained. He knew very well that no one would seek him in Mr. Grace's palace. Of what might happen in his own office he was not so certain. Lying thus, he read for three hours.

At one the codicil was ready. Mr. Tangier read it and read it again with diligent criticism.

At quarter-past one, Dr. Morton came by appointment and went upstairs. In a few minutes more a servant called Mr. Tangier, and he went again into the sick man's room, this time followed by the clerk, who went as a witness.

Mr. Grace seemed as cheerful as he had been in the morning, light-hearted, indeed, that this affair was off his mind. Mr. Tangier read to him, slowly, first the private articles, which he had copied from the slate, and then the longer and more important article, which in this form Mr. Grace now heard for the first time. He approved of the draft, and called to the bedside Dr. Morton and the clerk.

"Gentlemen," he said, "this bequest, which Mr. Tangier puts in form for me, is no new thing to me. He will show you a paper in which I sketched some plans for it some time ago. But I like his phrase. It is for my birthplace, Steuben's Ford. We shall build what we call a Library Hall there, for 'all sorts and conditions of men.' I have made a self-perpetuating board of trustees, but three of them are to be the judge of probate, the minister, and one person chosen, every five years, by the town. I mean that they shall spend the income of three hundred thousand dollars. With this money they ought to be able to heat and warm their building, to maintain the garden and green-house, to keep open rooms fit for pictures, for reading the magazines, and other social purposes, and do something toward providing books and musical instruments. I say this, gentlemen, that you may see I know what I am doing. Take the paper to the window and see how well Mr. Tangier has drawn it."

Then, as they withdrew, he asked Mr. Tangier about the accident which had disabled him, and about Tenterdon.

The others brought back the document and placed it quietly in Mr. Tangier's hand. He indicated the places where it was to be signed. Mr. Grace wrote his name firmly, and the two others added theirs as witnesses. Again he smiled cheerfully, and this time he said he would not trouble them longer. But Dr. Morton stayed with him. As for Mr. Tangier, he never saw his old friend again, excepting when his body lay the next week in its coffin.

CHAPTER XXII.

THUS ended Mr. Tangier's first vacation in Tenterdon; and thus, just as the world was in its first beauty, was he shipped back upon his work in his office, with a hand which would not hold a pen, with the arrears of a month's business, and with every one in the office, down to the errand boy, curious to know when he could be spared for his vacation. No; he did not go back to Tenterdon on Monday, as he had dreamed of doing. Courts did not yet begin on their holidays. Indeed, when they did, there would be endless hearings in chambers and references and the like, which had been, one by one, shoved over into this "period of peaceful rest," so that Mr. Heeren said it was worse crowded than the heaviest weeks of the summer.

But Mr. Tangier attacked all his little jobs cheerfully, and his great jobs too. He took ten times as much interest in one appeal from Scott Meakin about the finishing of the stage-house, as he did in the grandest letter from Wall street about an investment. He answered Mrs. Dunster's playful, chatty letters in their own vein. He soon found that the practical correspondent, who kept him really enlightened as to Tenterdon life, was Miss Remington. He had, in a manner, forced the correspondence on her, by asking her to attend to sundry and various forgotten and yet essential details in the stage-house, which suggested themselves from time to time. At first, she answered in a mere business-like form, but gradually the letters became more general. And when she did let her pen run, Tenterdon took on its old charm again, and he wondered why he ground at the wheel as he did, and counted the days till "Chisholm *vs.* Chantry" could be over and he could take his carpet-bag again.

"Scott Meakin," she wrote, "is aghast at the idea of a fireplace which shall use all the south wall of the reading-room. You will have to write him a much stiffer letter. As to the 'mop-boards,' as he will call them, I had my own way, — I believe because women and mops go together. Andirons, Mrs. Dunster undertakes; thinks she knows where there are some. Yes, I spoke to Mr. Burdett about the parish library, and we are all to hear the Winthrop music on Sunday. How do you think I came home from his house?

"Tom Pingree brought me. I was lying on my back on his hay-cart. The hay-cart was ou its way through the main street, and not one of my fellow-citizens — not Mrs. Floxam, the omniscient, not Jennie Campbell, the all-observant — dreamed that I was there. Tom Pingree only knew, but never a smile nor a sign from him revealed my secret as he drove.

"You may talk as you choose about being tossed alone on a billow and communing with Nature. I tell you that when you lie on your back on the top of a load of hay — if the load be only high enough — you may commune with Nature in solitude just as perfect and in comfort much more sure. The blue sky above; sometimes a flight of birds; once, really, a lonely eagle; just as we came into the barn-yard, a swooping half-dozen of swallows; and nothing else, but you imagined a possible angel between you and the empyrean. Only, when Tom drove from the north meadows into the main street, the elms came between, and once an oriole's nest swept so near to me that I could have stolen it had I been so mean. It is the only way we can fly!"

"Is life worth living?" said Mr. Tangier, as he read this letter to Morton, who lay in the bows of their boat, as she drifted, and his friend lay in the stern. "Is it not worth living, when there are such chances to fly?"

"As that to fly or as this to float," said Morton. "Touch elbows with the rank and file, live much in the open air, and see every day some man who is your superior. If you will hold to these rules, Mr. Mallock will not trouble you much or often; any way, these three will do for a beginning. It is 'with God, for man, in heaven,' as the padre used to say."

"Yes," said the other, "and that is a good gospel, as indeed you taught me that April night when you sent me into exile so unceremoniously. That was very good practice, Morton. Sagen treu, my dear fellow, I feel much more at home at Tenterdou to-day than I do here. I feel as if I were detached on duty here, but I am pulling at my roots, which are there. Yet I had never seen the place, and hardly heard of it, two months ago."

"Precisely," said Morton. "You are beginning to take on that healthy tone of an Englishman who, in the midst of his triumph in Parliament, when he compels the opposition to cheer — as old Hayes used to say — or, in his grand reception at the Duke of Rigmarole's, is still sighing for his salmon river or his stalking-ground. You do not suppose that man cares much for salmon or for deer, do you? What he wants is a touch of Nature, Nature with a large N."

"You knew poor dear Grace better than I did," said Tangier. "Had he this on his mind when he wrote that letter on which I made his will?"

"Certainly; that was what it came to, or, if you please, came from," said the other, stepping forward now and taking up the oars. "Not that you would ever have put him on gentleman farming. He laughed it to scorn. 'Not I,' he would say; 'I built all the "stun-wall" I shall build before I was sixteen.' But he loved home. He loved the old oaken bucket. He liked to have those people at his home. One of the little boys there sent him down, one year, a salt-box full of shagbarks, cracked and picked, for a New Year's present, and Grace never forgot it. Why, he was as careful in his orders for maple sugar and syrup from those Steuben's Ford hills as he was in his correspondence with Hope or Barings. And this was not the mere sentiment of boyish memory. It was the clear, sheer love of the blue above and the green below; of the smell of the earth. Well, he loved to eat his peas one hour from the vine, and his corn one hour from the stalk. Why, the last time I had Grace in this boat — it was last October — I had covered him all up with rugs, where you lie there, and this man of millions was talking to me about some ground-nuts that he and Mrs. Milnes had found as they were driving up there, and how he had dug them out of the sand with a paper-cutter and a pair of scissors, and how they carried them home and roasted them on the hearth. I could almost hear the great, liveried Thomas cursing and swearing, as he sat on the box and held the horses, while the 'old man,' as he would have said, was digging up ground-nuts with a paper-cutter."

" You see the paper-cutter was all his advance upon Massasoit," said Mr. Tangier, laughingly.

" As to that, I think Massasoit could do it much better than Grace. But Grace was on a good road and was coming on well."

Three hours a day did Mr. Tangier spend in the saddle, or on the bay or the river, thus, or in a hammock under the pine-trees. It was not that he was afraid to meet Morton unless he did this. It was that now this had become a second nature to him, as a cigar is to one man, and whiskey to another, and coffee to another, and sleep to everybody. It was a step in advance in his moral, mental, and spiritual make-up. To Miss Remington he wrote, in "typewriter," alas! one evening:—

"I note what you say about the fireplace. I do not want to seem absurd. But really a large fireplace — a very large one indeed — means generous hospitality; as a hole for a stove-funnel, on the other hand, means parsimony and a lonely cabin. Do not block my wheels, therefore. Scott Meakin makes trouble enough about it. But I am trying to send him over to Oliver, to see a magnificent fireplace by Van Brunt or Ware, or both, in their guild-hall there.

I envy you your power of flying on a hay-cart. For me, the best I do is to ride to the beach on Fear Not or float down the tide in the doctor's boat and count the days until the 14th of July. But it is clear enough that Scott Meakin will not be ready for us before the 1st of August."

BOOK II.

CHAPTER I.

IT was nearly two months, as it proved, before Mr.
Tangier saw Tenterdon again. He said himself
that he had to pay for his spring holiday by summer
work. But he had now well learned Mr. Webster's
maxim that a man can do more work in eight months
than he can in twelve. He had three short notes from
Scott Meakin, long, rambling letters from Mrs. Dunster, and notes or dissertations, as the case required,
always amusing and to the point, from May Remington, to whose care he often intrusted some private
commission.

At last, the complicated accounts in "Chisholm *vs.*
Chantry" were referred to a master. This means, that
in a transaction where everybody is so perplexed that
no one can make head or tail of anything, one competent man, who has never heard of the matter before,
is told to take it off by himself, disentangle the knots,
and tell everybody what The Truth is. It takes some
time for him to find out; and so when a thing is referred
to a master, everybody else engaged has a holiday.
Besides this, it happened that the most important judge
who was sitting in Chambers received a telegraphic
message from the Secretary of the Treasury, asking

him to go off on a Government excursion in the "Tala-poosa." He left Chambers, between night and morn-ing, with a message for some chief clerk to everybody that all cases would be resumed in November. Mr. Heeren himself held a less firm hand on the move-ments of his chief, and so it was that, on the evening of the 31st of July, Mr. Tangier alighted from the ex-press train at Wentworth Junction, and wondered to think how different was his feeling, when Wentworth Junction was so new to him only the May before. Nathan was waiting, as he was then. But this time the meeting was of two old friends, and Mr. Tangier received, well pleased, Nathan's information as to how things went on. As they turned towards the sea, though it was five miles away, the refreshment after the dead, hot air of the train brought a new life. Mr. Tangier wondered at himself that he had kept away so long. And he wondered what spell was on the so-called civilization of the century, that the new and abundant life, which came to him in such a tide of delight, should be counted as the exception, and that the deaf and dumb, nerveless and heartless, drudgery of three or four weeks past should be counted as the expected daily course of hundreds of thousands of people, in those cities which this same civilization affects to call its centres.

But Nathan, and the sea breezes, and the golden lilies, and the blazing cardinals, and the tufts of clematis, with now and then a frightened squirrel or rabbit, now and then a sniff of perfume from an azalea, now and then a flight of swallows flying over the ponds they passed, — these and a world of other interruptions broke up much meditation on social science, or the hitches in social economy, to the undoubted satisfaction of this reader and the equal satisfaction of this writer. Nathan was only too glad to show to advantage the speed of the new horse, which Mrs. Fairbanks had been compelled to add to her establishment; and when they arrived in the yard by the old Sea King's house, over which she presided, there was still light enough for a joyous company to welcome Mr. Tangier.

Another company of "boarders," who had arrived since he left, hung back, because they were later comers, as a sort of plebeian and unworthy circle. Mrs. Floxam, who had all day explained that he certainly would not come, and that it was absurd to expect him, hovered, pendulum-like, between the two.

Mr. Tangier's luggage was disposed of; a mysterious parcel, which really contained rockets and Bengal-lights, was put under lock and key in the closet under the stairs, and he himself had finished the tenth course in a very high tea, which Mrs. Fairbanks and Rachel had provided, in utter contempt of Mrs. Floxam's forebodings. He was doubting, himself, whether he would attack, in a friendly way, the group of new-comers, and so pass his initiation and theirs, when a noisy clamor in the hall announced Mrs. Dunster, Mr. Burdett, the doctor, and May Remington. They had come down, they said, for an early conference, there was so much to be done before to-morrow evening.

To-morrow evening was to witness the dedication of the old stage-house to its new purposes.

"Dear Mr. Tangier, all is ready, though no fatlings are killed, because we had none to kill at this season of the year; all the people are asked; every man and woman and man-child and girl-baby within what you call a radius of five miles. And yet the place has no name, more than a poor unbaptized baby of ten minutes old. What is worse, its godfather has forgotten it in 'Chisholm *vs.* Chantry.' I hate them both, and I hope the court will turn them both out-of-doors. And what are we to do when all the people come ? I do not know 'no more nor the dead,' as your friend Sabriny Wotch would say. And so we have come, before you went to bed, to tell you that all will go to shame and ruin unless you come to the rescue. Why, if you put Nathan in charge of the Channel Fleet, he would know more what to do with it than we know what we are to do with our party."

This was Mrs. Dunster's somewhat eager harangue, as she and the rest arranged themselves around Mr. Tangier, who was still playing with a few blackberries which remained of his slow and long-drawn supper.

"To begin at the end," said he, "the Channel Fleet might be in worse hands than Nathan's, if he handles an iron-clad as well as he does a pink-stern schooner. Dear Mrs. Dunster, have you and I lived to mature years, and do we not know that some things go better for not being managed ? "

"Exactly what I tell her," said May Remington.

"You !" said Mrs. Dunster, with scorn. "You! I should think so ! Do I not remember when you and Peg sold theatre tickets to all the children at school, two for a cent, performance to be in your father's! barn, at two in the afternoon ; and when the poor things began to arrive, your poor, dear mother heard of the play for the first time, and found that no preparation whatever was made for it, not a name, not a plot, not an actor, not so much as a curtain! You, indeed!"

"Precisely," said May Remington, unabashed, though all the others were laughing at her. "And did they not all have their money's worth and much more? It was the first time I ever saw your celebrated performance of the 'Pilgrims of the Tioga Canal-boat;' and, dear Aunt Mary, if you will only do that to-morrow night the fame and the success of the Palace of Delight will be secure."

"But is it to be the Palace of Delight, or what is to be, Mr. Tangier?"

"Why do you all ask me?" said he, folding his napkin slowly, and then leading the way to the western stoop, which was recognized as in some sort belonging to him. "I am only an accidental wayfarer, who happens in on the festivities."

"Oh, yes; as Jack the Giant-Killer happened in on the festivities of Blunderbore. But I do not know what would have come to the lads and ladies in the prison, if Jack had not come along."

"Prison! who is in the prison?" said he.

"How dreadfully literal you are, Mr. Tangier! You are as bad as you were in the spring. I hoped your Mr. Heeren, and your judges and juries, would have taught you something. You are here to answer all Scott Meakin's questions, all Mr. Burdett's doubts, to solve all Mr. Drummond's difficulties, to oppose all Mrs. Floxam's contradictions, and first, second, third, and seventeenth, you are here to give a name to the old stage-house. This name,—it shall be emblazoned on red cambric in white letters cut out of Lowell shirting by these hands, if only you will say what it shall be."

"I thought we settled it all that day you sat on the tool-box. What do you vote for, Mrs. Dunster?" said he.

"Oh, I am firm. There is to be a Woman's Guild formed. The place shall be called Guild Hall."

"And you, Mr. Burdett?"

"I cannot answer as boldly as Mrs. Dunster. But I tell her to revive an old name."

"I declare, he is going to call it the Synagogue," said May Remington, affecting to whisper.

"Oh, no, not that! I want to recall an old name, as we restore an old thing. Call it 'The Nooning House.'"

"And you, Miss Remington?"

"I am first, second, and last for 'The Palace of Delight.' I have changed my mind ever since you made me read Mr. Besant's story."

"And you, doctor, you say nothing, but you keep up a deal of a thinking."

"Like an owl, as I am. I am not quite satisfied, but I say, 'The Club House,' or 'The People's Club.'"

"Have all voted?" cried Mr. Tangier. "Have any changed their minds? Are any more remarks to be made on this subject? Going once! Going twice! Going three times! Gone! The name is to be 'The Old Stage-house.' Let the Knights Templars call it a Temple; let the Masons call it a Lodge House or a Chapter House; let the ladies call it Guild Hall; let Mr. Burdett call it a Nooning House. But the people will call it The Old Stage-house, and for *The Old Stage-house* I shall vote every time.

"At all events, that subject is off to-night's programme. Now for the order of ceremonies."

CHAPTER II.

OF all these devisings and conspiracies the result appeared the next day, and May Remington's reckless forecasts were largely justified. "Trust in that Providence," she said, "which takes care of drunkards, idiots, and the United States."

And Mr. Burdett told her, to her great joy, that there were philosophers who thought that the fall of man followed fast on the introduction by Adam and Eve of an analytic philosophy. Before that, they had faith in the right outcome of all that was well meant. May Remington was delighted to find that any philosopher would have one kind word for her. Without philosophy, what had been done was this : Six or eight young men, well known and generally liked, had been selected by Drummond and other Templars, and had been despatched, some days before, on every road. They had gone literally to every house, and they had carried to each house a printed card of invitation, which read thus : —

HOUSE-WARMING.

You are invited, with all the members of your family, and any friends visiting you, to be present at the opening of the OLD STAGE-HOUSE, on the *Knox Road*, on Tuesday next.

Children from two to five. Adults of both sexes from two to nine o'clock.

By invitation of the committee.

"The wording is clumsy," said Dr. Tillinghast. "But it was the young men's own, and I was not going to lose caste with them by fiddling over grammar or rhetoric." And Mr. Tangier heartily approved of his catholicity.

"My only fear," said he, "is for the three hours of the children."

"Ah, me!" said May Remington. "I wish I was as sure of the grown people as I am of the children. Children do not stand on ceremony. Do you wait, Mr. Tangier, till you see six solid old women and two old men glued down upon your settees in the reception-room, and with mere looks of iron, saying silently to all comers, 'Entertain me, entertain me! I am here to be entertained. Why don't you entertain me?'"

"As to that," said he, good-naturedly enough, "they deceive themselves if they think I am going to entertain them. I shall sit in the smoking-room and read the 'Tribune,' if by good luck a paternal post-office brings it to me. I am not going to entertain any one."

"Not me?" said she, and she dropped a mock courtesy. "After I have made my fingers bleed by basting on the sixteen letters, in 'The Old Stage-house,' upon the elegant magenta background, am I not to be entertained?"

"I think you will have to do the entertaining," said he. "I shall ask permission to smoke, and shall hope for the second chance at the 'Tribune.'"

All the chief conspirators appeared at the stage-house early in the day. Drummond and his friends were driving up large wagons and small, now with furniture, now with provisions for the inevitable banquet, now with flowers. Scott Meakin and his most

trusty men were everywhere, closing rivets up, obey-
ing the bidding of the womenkind, now on the tops
of "steps," now deep in the cellar. Few of the leaders
of society, in one or another of its sub-tribes, sub-clans,
or sub-castes, but were on duty, leading as occasion,
required. Mr. Tangier compelled Scott Meakin to
take time to be praised, and John Michael, the painter
and glazier, who preached, and preached very well, to
the Seventh-day people, to receive his share of congratulation also.

"Well," said Scott Meakin, "it was a queer job, any
way. You know, Mr. Tangier, I said to you that
you never knew where you would come out when
you began on an old hulk like this."

"Yes," said Tangier, "and I took courage when
you were willing to go on."

"Well, to tell you the truth, Mr. Tangier, the
frame is better than I told you. I found, when we
uncovered it, it was one of old Gray's frames. They
still told stories of him when I learned my trade.
He drank like a horse, and he died in the poor-house.
But he knew good work from bad. He knew a good
stick of timber. And in those days he had oak for
the cutting. Yes, Mr. Tangier, you had only to strip
the clapboards from this house to see it was built on
honor."

"Do you say that?" said Tangier, well pleased.
"Miss Remington, come here. Hear what Mr. Meakin says. You must give us a motto to hang in the
great room. Mr. Meakin says this house was 'Built
on Honor.'"

"You are not going off, Mr. Tangier?" said young
Drummond to him, as he was leaving for his lunch.

Mr. Tangier said he was, that he should have some lunch at home, and come back again with the Fairbanks party.

"That will not do," said Drummond. "What is the house for but a club-house? Stay with the boys, try our coffee, and learn how we fishermen make a chowder."

And Mr. Tangier stayed, well pleased that "the boys" were not afraid of him.

There was the usual hush and dread for five minutes of terror, lest, after all the preparations, no one should come to the party. "I call it 'silence in heaven,'" said May Remington, who was, however, awed by this terror which always comes over people who have invited others; and she only affected to feel at ease.

Then came the inevitable first drops of shower; the people came, who had least to do with each other, and were utterly unable to talk with each other, — as when Mr. Rostock, the saw-mill man, arrived on foot with his work-house boy, just as Madame Gunnison, from the house on the hill, was being lifted by her footman from her victoria.

But the doubts of such a beginning were forgotten in ten minutes, when the whole tide of people poured in, when the young Templars and every sort of committee of reception were engaged in every sort of way, when all the visitors were rambling over the house to see what were its arrangements, and the prospects of future "good times." The boys soon found the provision of mask and balls and bats, which had been made by Mr. Tangier's prescience, and two impromptu nines were organized on the green behind the house. In the large room, which had already been called the "music-room," because there the piano from the Gingerlys' had been placed, a great multitude of little children were assembled. Rachel Fairbanks was playing marches for them, and Miss Gurtry moving them to and fro, as a little organized army, in pretty movements such as modern schools understand, and now and then was holding them at "parade rest," while she told them a story. The story invariably required from them much clapping of hands in chorus, answering of questions, and singing in refrain.

Miss Gurtry forgot herself entirely, as she magnetized and swayed the children, and in her abandonment was perfectly charming.

It need not be said that the sound of the music and the screams of laughter from the children drew most of the older people to this hall, and they stood round the sides, or sat in the deep window-seats, watching the movements.

"She is absolutely lovely," said May Remington to Mrs. Dunster. "And that is what they try to teach in Normal schools! They might as well try to teach me to sing the songs of seraphs! I lost my heart to her again and again at the sewing circle and at the picnics. And she has not the faintest idea of my passion for her. But here and now I have lost it for good and all. I shall tell her so; I shall go on my knees to her like Charles Grandison. Really, dear Aunt Mary, I do not see why some of these hulking men do not go up to her and say: 'Let me take you in my arms and pet you and take care of you and keep you out of scrapes and out of trouble for all the rest of your life.' That is my notion of proposing to such a girl as that."

As she ran on, Miss May did not observe that Mr. Tangier had joined them, and was but just behind her. She turned in her enthusiasm just in time to catch his amused smile. But she was not confused. "I hope you heard what I said, Mr. Tangier. I can't make you read novels, but I beg you to see that I read them myself to some purpose. Be assured that when there is as charming a person as that in this world, that is the way in which she should be spoken to."

Mrs. Dunster, who had the far-reaching prevision of a chaperon and of an aunt combined, looked rather critically upon Mr. Tangier as he answered.

He was not thrown off his guard. He was quite too much a man of the courts and of the world.

"Dear Miss May," he said, "have not you and I done our very worst or our very best in intermeddling with Miss Gurtry's affairs? Did we not leave her and Mr. Drummond together for two hours that day here? Did I not, under your instructions, send him on an errand to the school-house about mottoes or something?"

She interrupted him. "My instructions! Never! Do not charge your blunders upon me."

"Some one instructed me, and I had never heard of the mottoes before. I am sure that when I saw him on a chair, nailing them up, and Miss Gurtry handing them to him, I discreetly withdrew, and never once in my inmost heart did I say, 'This is my work.' Meekly and honestly I said, 'It is Miss Remington's success.'"

"Very fine," said she, laughing, as, indeed, she was apt to do. "Very fine, indeed. And pray, where is Mr. Drummond now?"

"Do you really expect to see him next to Master Sam Pingree and leading Lucy Campbell? Do you wish to have him clapping his hands in time, or singing treble in the chorus? When I last saw Mr. Drummond, he was peeping through the crack of the orchestra door in the gallery yonder. I think, if you like to speak to him, you will find him there now."

"Really, is it so, Mr. Tangier? You are not making fun?"

The girl seemed more serious than her wont, and much more serious than he saw any occasion for her being. She looked up at the door, which was indeed ajar, and of course gave no token of any espionage on the other side.

"If you are drawing a long bow, Mr. Tangier, you draw it very well," she said, after her survey.

"Why am I accused of drawing a long bow?" said he, with an air of injured innocence. "Was the romance one of my making? Mrs. Dunster, I appeal to you. Was I not on your own piazza charged with dulness, because I did not see the beginnings of it? Have I not been lured, or let me rather say driven, at every point, to assist in an affair which was no business of mine?"

Again Mrs. Dunster looked at him with that doubtful glance of an aunt and a duenna. But May Remington did not notice this, and it may be doubted if he did.

"Let that be as it may," said she, as if tired of the play which she had herself started, "it is, as Mr.

Knightly says in 'Emma,' very unworthy business for a well-educated young woman like me, and I will have none of it, whether I began it or no. Aunt Mary, come with me and let me show you the clever plan which takes off the smell from the range in the kitchen. Really I do not see why we should not have it at home."

She did not ask Mr. Tangier, but, as if of course, he joined them.

And thus, with groups of people who really found each other out in a truly cordial way, the old stage-house dedicated itself in all its various capacities. There were even people who played dominos and chess. There were girls who played with graces, as there were boys who played with bats and balls. When the little children were feasting, there was even dancing in the music-room. For at first some of the girls waltzed together; and then, under a good deal of persuasion, and with a good deal of sheepishness, Eli Whaley was made to dance a regular sailor's hornpipe to Rachel Fairbanks's very spirited music.

At six, supper was served for all the grown people, as some meal unnamed had been served for the children at four. And at eight in the evening, after the rooms had been lighted up, Mr. Burdett and the other ministers and Dr. Tillinghast made each the inevitable " few remarks " of such an occasion. They congratulated the town that it had, almost spontaneously, secured such a place, so long needed for its sociabilities and its hospitalities, and amid great applause old Squire Kenison pronounced the "old stage-house open for every purpose of good-fellowship and a reasonable hospitality."

The different groups of people looked round a little uncertainly, as if doubting what was to come next, when, "S-h-i-r-r," a brilliant rocket blazed up from the farther end of the ball-ground. The sound and the flash summoned all parties to the piazza, and in a minute more another "S-h-i-r-r" delighted them all, and they showed their approval of the unexpected spectacle.

From the open window where she stood, Mr. Drummond withdrew Miss Gurtry, and asked if he might have a word with her.

"Why, of course!" she said, utterly unconscious that he spoke with a high-strained eagerness.

"If you really do not care to see them, though they are so beautiful," he said, apologizing, as he led her away into one of the front reception-rooms, where they were away from all the rest and would be quite alone.

"Oh, no! but was it not a nice thought of his? I suppose it is Mr. Tangier."

"I suppose it is," said Drummond, trying not to be annoyed. But he was in that nervous mood in which he hated to hear the woman he loved even allude to any other man. "He is one of those lucky people who can do all he chooses and have all he wants." Miss Gurtry was amazed at the cynical tone in which he spoke, which was, indeed, wholly unlike his natural manner. It gave her the first hint that she had been called here for anything but some conference about the evening's entertainment. He went on at once. He went on, as if hurried and worried, eager and awkward, but direct enough, to say, "I do not want to talk about him nor anybody — yes, I do — I want to talk about myself and about you. You know, dear Miss Bess,"— he had never called her so aloud before, but he would once if he died,—"you know I must go to New York to-morrow. I cannot be here again till September. I will not go, I dare not go, till I tell you what you know perfectly well, that I love you with all my heart and soul, and I want you to say I may. Do say so, somehow, or try to say so. Oh, if you knew!" And the fine fellow took her hand boldly, as it lay in her lap, as if indeed, as May Remington had suggested, he would gladly have taken her in his arms and carried her to the end of the world.

He looked her full in the face, and, in all his doubt, he fancied that for an instant a flash of exquisite pleasure lighted her eyes. But he was too bold in the fancy, for she withdrew her hand, after an instant, if indeed there were an instant, to say with a tone of utter agony : —

"Oh, George Drummond, what do you say? what have I done?" And the look on her face was of undoubted, unutterable anguish.

Yet to him, aghast as he was in the suddenness and almost bitterness of her answer, there came the strange question, "How did she know my name was George?" For he knew she had never called him so before.

For half a minute neither of them said anything. He looked at her, but she looked at her hands, and dared not lift her eyes to him. He was the first, of course, to speak.

"What do you say? Why, what is it? I knew you would say it. I knew it perfectly well. I said you would say it; and yet, — oh, my dear Miss Gurtry, if you knew what my dreams have been — "

"Oh, do not say that! Because — then — you blame me. I must have been to blame. But if, — oh, my dear Mr. Drummond, I was so lonely. And when you were so kind to me I could not, — indeed, I am so wretched, — I could not tell you not to be."

"Not to be! why should you tell me not to be? Tell me to be kinder to you than ever man was to woman, or woman to man, and see if I do not obey you. Oh, Miss Gurtry, you think I have persecuted you!"

"No, no!" she gasped.

"You think I am pressing you. But you do not know how often I have gone by the school-house for the mere pleasure of seeing where you were. No, nor how often I have been watching you when you did not know I was within ten miles. Tell me, order me to be kind to you. I am so ashamed that I have frightened you. But I was so eager. Let me write to you from New York? But there, I could not write what I can say."

"Oh, Mr. Drummond," the girl almost groaned now, "do not, do not say another word! You torture me. What can I say? I am so sorry; I must have done wrong, or you would not be here. What you ask is impossible. Please let me go, and do not think of this again."

"That is impossible!" said Drummond; but when she looked up he was gone.

And she? Poor girl, all alone now, for she would not call one of her faithful school-boys to help her, she had to hunt up her wraps in the deserted cloak-

room.   It seemed mockery, indeed, that this wretchedness was the end of the dedication of the Palace of
Delight for her.   She could hear the rush of the rockets, and the clapping of hands, while she, poor girl,
was trying to make out whether the sandals she had
in her hands were hers or Miss Remington's.

CHAPTER III.

THE last fire-work had blazed away, the last
cheers had been given, and every one was
thronging to the door of the same cloak-room, but
now so empty. A set of nice boys and girls were
doing their best to pass out sandals and shawls and
cloaks and hats, and the other paraphernalia. Other
boys and men brought up the wagons from the long
sheds, which had survived from the old stage-house
days. Mrs. Fairbanks's two carry-alls were among
the rest, and Mrs. Dunster's one.

"Mr. Drummond, will you find Mr. Tangier? He
is to drive us home. And he has no other carriage.
But we are all ready, and he is lost."

But Mr. Drummond could not find Mr. Tangier.
He had been last seen with the fire-works, and Nathan thought he had gone in to bring more. But now
he was nowhere.

Sabriny Wotch was washing dishes still, and she
sent her band all over the house to find Mr. Tangier.
But Mr. Tangier was nowhere.

"It is very strange," said Mrs. Dunster. "And,
after all the pains he has taken, it seems very stupid
to leave him to walk home. Perhaps he has gone
with some one."

But, as she spoke, she knew that May Remington
was at her side, and she did not believe that there

was any other lady to whom he would have offered his escort.

"May I ask you to drive us home, Mr. Drummond? Tom is not so sure on his fore-feet as I wish he were."

Of course Mr. Drummond would drive. Mrs. Dunster and her niece and Rachel Fairbanks filled up the carriage, and all went homeward, chattering of the success of the inauguration.

"And it all began with the sidewalk," said May Remington. "And it needed Miss Gurtry to show us how to do that. Mr. Drummond, I shall always say that Miss Gurtry is the real founder of the Palace of Delight. You men could talk, but Miss Gurtry did."

Of course she meant to say the thing most agreeable to him; in truth she did drive a dagger into his heart. He did, however, mumble some answer.

"I wanted to bring her home with us," said Mrs. Dunster. "We could have made room for her. But she must have walked. Look, May; perhaps you can see her on her own sidewalk in the moonlight as we pass."

All parties looked out on the left as they crossed the Wentworth road, up which Miss Gurtry's sidewalk ran. All parties saw, not her, but Mr. Tangier, alone on the sidewalk, coming toward them.

Had Mr. Tangier walked home with Miss Gurtry? This was the private question which every one asked. Drummond struck the horses suddenly, and they did not stop to inquire.

CHAPTER IV.

FROM this point, for several chapters, this little story of a little town might be told in four different ways, according as the incidents which concern our readers were told from Mr. Tangier's point of view, from Miss Bessy Gurtry's, from Mr. Drummond's, or from Miss Remington's. Most stories may be told in many ways, as Mr. Browning's poem of "The Ring and the Book" has proved so well. The counsel for the prosecution will see a shield of lead, while the counsel for the defence sees a shield which is of very bright gold.

But the story is of Mr. Tangier's Vacations. The reader has seen with his eyes thus far, and has gone only where he has gone. So it shall be, for one chapter more.

Mr. Tangier walked home that night somewhat thoughtfully, nay, a good deal surprised that Miss Gurtry should have been so anxious to go home, and should seem so nervous and dispirited. He had run into the Stage-house on some errand concerning the fire-works, — had entered it from the front, while all the spectators of the exhibition were on the other side, — and he had met her, alone, as she was descending the steps of the front piazza. She would have been glad to pass him unnoticed. But, even in his haste, he could not but see that something disturbed her, —

she did not even walk steadily, and he offered her his arm. He tried to persuade her to go back to the house, but she said she felt faint and tired, and should be better at home. She would not let him bring one of the carriages for her, but he insisted on going home with her. As he returned, his return had been observed, as the reader knows, but as he did not.

Quite unconscious that he was challenging the attention of his neighbors, he went up to the schoolhouse the next day to ask how she was. It was clear enough that she was not well. Her face was flushed, and she was ill at ease. But she explained that the summer school was now over. It had indeed been kept open much longer than usual, by a special subscription made among some of the parents.

"And it has been quite too long, I am sure," said he, in his good-natured way, "if the result of the extra schooling is that the schoolmistress breaks down. Nervous prostration, my dear Miss Gurtry, which had not been invented ten years ago, is now the order of the day. I do not think it speaks very well for our wit or prudence."

She hardly answered him. She was — or she affected to be — busy with locking her drawers and putting things in order to leave in one or two cupboards. One or two of the big boys were waiting to help her, or to offer some rustic attention to her in parting. It was impossible for Mr. Tangier not to see that his presence was not needed or desired by these boys. Miss Gurtry gave no intimation that she wished it. And so, with some other expression of his wish that she might have a real holiday, he went on with his walk, — went quite around White Pond, stopped to see how the workmen came on with Sabrina Wotch's new house, and so was rather late to dinner.

Little did he suppose that the mild police of the boarding-house had noted his entrance into the school-house. The same mild police had not noted the moment of his departure, and credited him with an interview with the schoolmistress for the two or three hours which followed that entrance. The mildest police will sometimes err.

It was so ordered that, on that evening of all evenings, Mr. Tangier received from Mr. Heeren's substitute, who was left in town to watch the mails, a parcel of papers which needed his personal study before he sent off his return mail of the next day. So it was that he did not take his walk across the way to the piazza of Mrs. Dunster, where he spent certainly three evenings out of seven, as she and her household spent three more on the stoop at Mrs. Fairbanks's. The next morning, with his stiff hand, Mr. Tangier forged out a long despatch to Mr. Heeren's substitute, and then turned his steps to the Old Stage-house, otherwise called the Palace of Delight, to see what might be its attractions on a hot morning in August.

Not very cheerful, not at all delightsome, was the Palace of Delight. Mr. Burdett had been made to select a nice old lady, who in her advanced life preserved a certain dignity and the regard of all her neighbors, though she were very, very poor, and he had placed her as keeper in the Palace, to see that no one actually took the chairs and tables into carts and carried them away.

She occupied herself with her own sewing and knitting. She had a little bedroom behind where the old bar of the stage-house stood, and as she sat in the reading-room, so called, she could say, "How do you do?" and otherwise pass the time of day to each and all comers. But for the rest, there was no one to offer any welcome at the Palace, and the wayfaring man must delight himself when he arrived there. Mr. Tangier could not but notice that some of the newspapers which he had himself ordered and paid for, were not yet taken out of their wrappers. He also observed that no person but himself and Aunty Turner were the occupants of the house at the moment of his visit. But this, indeed, was as it should be. For these were the working hours of the day, and the house was not dedicated to laziness.

Aunty Turner's report of the last evening was not, on the whole, unfavorable. The Templars had been there and had occupied their room for a session, which was of course private. Some of the fishermen had come up, one or two who were not at the "reception" the night before. Mr. Tangier could not find out that any of them had played chess or dominos. They had preferred to sit on the long settees of the piazza, or on its steps, smoking most of the time. Two or three girls had walked in together and had walked out, as if a little frightened that they found no others there. On the whole, the most encouraging report as to the Palace seemed to be that the boys had played baseball all the afternoon before — till it was too dark to see, indeed. Mr. Tangier well knew that they would have played thus in Seth Campbell's pasture, and that nothing had drawn them to the Stage-house but the provision of free bats, masks, and balls. Still, this had drawn them, and here was a good beginning of a habit. They might, when darkness closed in on the green diamond, come in and look at the "Harper's Weekly" or the "Graphic." They had not done so last night, but possibly they would in some halcyon future. For himself, he consecrated the reading-room by opening his "Tribune" and reading it there; he wrote a note to Mr. Stevens, 4 Trafalgar Square, that he might inaugurate the note-paper which he had himself provided with the printed heading, "Old Stage-house, Tenterdon;" he put this in the letter-box, that Aunty Turner might see that the letter-box meant something. "They will begin to come," he said cheerily to her, "when we get the Library running." "I hope so," said the old lady, "for it 's kinder lonely here." A sad verdict this on the Palace of Delight. To say the truth, she missed the visits of the children who generally looked in on her in her own old home, as they passed by, and for whom she had generally a bit of molasses candy, or some other toothsome luxury. With such comfort Mr. Tangier left her, and determined at once to devote himself to his plans for the Library.

He went up to the Dunsters' for such advice and consolation as he might find there, but the Dunsters had all driven over to Knox. The day was hot, and Mr. Tangier doubted. But on the whole he determined to see the doctor. The doctor, as he might have known, was off with the second horse of the day. He was in the North Precinct, making the long circuit of it, and would not be back before four or five o'clock. Mr. Tangier needed advice, and knew he did. These people understood the town much better than he did. Naturally he would have turned

to Mr. Burdett. But his home was a mile away, on
the other side of Mrs. Fairbanks's, and so Mr. Tangier
acted without advice; or rather went to seek it at
the lips of one who was herself concerned, — Miss
Elizabeth Gurtry. She was boarding at the Nathan
Campbell's, which was only the second house beyond
the doctor's. Of this visit of Mr. Tangier's, also,
the mild police of Tenterdon took immediate notice,
as it had done of his visit at the school-house the
day before. The mild police keeps no record of its
observations, but it had casually mentioned before
twelve hours were over, to every person of the large
number who were engaged on its staff, that Mr. Tangier had visited Miss Gurtry three times in as many
days.

The interview was, in fact, one which might have
taken place in the parlor of the Old Stage-house.
To tell the precise truth, Miss Gurtry kept Mr.
Tangier waiting a little while in Mrs. Campbell's sit.
ting-room, and when she did come in showed the
slightest possible sign of annoyance, if that pleasant
face could show such a sign. But her manner was
still cordial, as she excused herself for her delay.

"I was in the midst of packing, Mr. Tangier. And
you do not know — or I hope you do not know —
what it is to pack after you have been at home
for nearly a year, when you may never come back
again."

"You never come back again? What do you mean?"
said he, in a man's blundering way. For, in truth,
he had wholly associated Miss Gurtry with Tenterdon,
and supposed she belonged there as much as the Old
Stage-house. He had yet to learn as matter of fact

and practice, what he knew perfectly well as matter of talk and theory, that in New England hardly any one holds anywhere by a tenure of more than twenty-four hours. The Viking habit of movement is in our blood.

"Oh, I hope I shall come back! Every one would like to come back to a place which has been almost home. But I am a teacher, and a teacher is like a soldier or a sailor, — she goes where she is sent."

"And pray where are you sent now, if I may be bold enough to ask?" said he. "Really, indeed, we shall miss you so here. I had supposed Tenterdon had a lien on you." He wanted to say, "Does Mr. Drummond know of your purpose?" But he was not wholly left by the powers who had him in hand, and he stopped short here.

There was an uncomfortable pause for a moment. He broke it.

"Do you not — is your engagement over? When does the school open again, and who will take care of the children then?"

The girl seemed puzzled. Was she annoyed perhaps that he was breaking up her pressing work with questions which it was really hardly his right to ask? But they were good friends, of course, and she answered at once: —

"Do you understand your own country so little? No teacher in a country school holds place for a mo-ment after the end of the term. Why, here all the district committee are my friends, — Mr. Norton, as you know, my near friend, — but I do not think that one of them would commit himself a week in advance of the committee's meeting in November. Still, I suppose," — said the girl, with a certain archness which seemed a little more like herself, — "I suppose that if I want this school I can have it, or another in this town." She stopped a moment, and then went on with more hesitation: "It is I who am uncertain. I do not know. My father is an old man, and he has no one but his little girl to care for him. Mr. Tangier — no, you cannot know how hard an old man's life may be made. My mother died when I was very young, and — well, Mr. Tangier, his second wife was not good to him, and now she is dead too. And that is the reason why I am going home."

Mr. Tangier of course sympathized with her, could not but sympathize, — who could? But how could he advise? nay, what advice could he have given had he any right to advise? That was a question he could not have answered had he put it in form. Still, he was conscious that all this was wrong, that she was with the best of friends in Tenterdon, and among others he thought of Drummond, who was a man whom he thoroughly respected. He knew that she must really begin a new life with her father. He determined at once to advise, whether he had any right to advise or no. And he said, a little abruptly perhaps, "Could not your father come here? Is there anything to bind him there?"

Strange to say, a flush which seemed to express pleasure passed over her face. But she repressed it, and in a troubled way, again, she answered, "Oh, no! I am so fond of my life here, and of my boys, that I had thought of that, — I thought it all over. But how could it be? He would be quite without friends here. He is not strong. And I — oh, Mr. Tangier,

I have sent him a little money, but you do not know,
a young girl like me can earn so little!"

Is it a wonder that, as the slight creature spoke
with this despair, May Remington's words came back
to him, when she had so eloquently described the way
in which some man ought to take Bessy Gurtry in his
arms and tell her that her struggle was over? He
did not, however, make this proposal himself. He
did, judiciously or not, advance the conversation a
step by saying: —

"I do not see why I should not say what I came
for. Certainly not to interrupt your packing. I had
no idea that you meant to go home so soon; indeed,
that you meant to go at all. I came, because — well,
let me begin at the beginning. I was at our club-
house this morning, the Old Stage-house, and I was
the only visitor. There will be no one to come there,
unless somebody is there to take care, and to make it
inviting. Well, I thought of the Library again. I
knew your school was over, and I thought you might
undertake to be librarian. You see — let me explain
before you answer. For a thousand books, of course,
a librarian would have very little to do. But, my
dear Miss Gurtry, if the right person were there, say
if you were there, and with nothing else to do, while
you would be called librarian you would really be
teacher and helper to half the children and young
people in the town. Don't you see? You would
have your Sunday-school class there, you would have
the King's Daughters there, you would have some of
these boys who worship you," and she smiled gravely
now, "and you would make a Wadsworth club of
them. You would have a microscope, don't you see,

and teach them botany. You would be just as much a teacher as you are at the school-house, and you would justify the pains we have all taken in fixing up the old shell; because, with you to welcome them, they would come to be welcomed. They did not teach you to do this at the Normal School, but I should think it as good a mission as to teach little Nahum Pingree that b-a-t spells cow."

He pretended to laugh, but he knew that he was in earnest. When he began, her face had seemed listless and sad, but her expression had wholly changed when he closed his little appeal. She took him up at the moment when he stopped: "Oh, Mr. Tangier, you read my own thoughts, only your plans go farther than mine. I told my girls, only on Sunday, when I bade them good-by, that they must meet there Saturdays to go over their Sunday lesson together. I told the base-ball boys to be sure to go in whenever it rained, and read aloud. I even gave them a list of books that were not all nonsense, you know. Why, I had a long talk with — a friend," — she would have said George Drummond had she dared, — "and we had planned it all out; there was to be a Shakspeare club and a Chautauqua circle, and some one was to teach us botany, as you say. But really, it seemed like a dream — and seems so now," she said more sadly, as her enthusiasm expended itself a little.

"I do not see why it is a dream," said he. "If it is, it is a dream late in the morning. And morning dreams come true, they say. For it was to propose this to you in definite form that I walked over. I wanted to talk with the doctor first, but that is no matter, as I have missed him." Then he went on to say that though nothing was systematized about the Old Stage-house, he was heartily interested in the plans, even the boldest, which had been made for it. He did not want them to fail. If an experiment was tried, and succeeded, why, any board of management which might be appointed would take it up far more cheerfully and confidently than if it were all on paper. He had thought that perhaps she would stay in the House so as to cheer up Aunty Turner to begin with. Then — well, she saw what could be done every day. "Just for your vacation, you know," he said, almost urging her. And he asked then what was her monthly stipend as schoolmistress. She told him that it was twelve dollars a week. It was not much; but she said it was all she was worth as schoolma'ams were paid now. Mr. Tangier at once proposed to her to take on trial, at that rate of salary, for three months or a year, as she should prefer, the post of librarian at the Stage-house. "Librarian" she was to be called, but her function was to be much wider than the charge of books. It was to be what he had blocked out in his talk — it was to be whatever she should find best to be done in the way of levelling up the lives of the young people whom she could make to consort there. "It will be," said he, "in the end of the afternoons, and in the evenings. It ought to be, and it will be. They will be at work in the morning, and you and Aunty Turner will have the morning to yourselves."

Mr. Tangier was really eloquent, in his quiet way, as he urged this. But Miss Gurtry gave him no encouragement. She had made her path, she said, or

God had made it for her, and she would walk in it.
Her father needed her, and to her father she would
go. And so he bade her good-by, — wondering at her
force, and admiring her for it, — and he returned to
his lodgings, asking himself if it could be that he was
never to see her again.

CHAPTER V.

AND now the reader must follow our story for a little from the schoolmistress's point of view. Miss Bessy Gurtry, as her prime favorites among the girls were permitted to call her, started on her journey for a long August day, and what seemed a much longer night, heart-sick and broken-down. She had borne herself in Mr. Tangier's presence with a pretence of courage which was much more than she really felt, and the reaction when she was alone made her the more cowardly. The parting with these good-natured Campbells, who had been kind to her for the last eight months, did not help to re-inspirit her. She dropped her veil when she found herself with the other passengers in the mail carriage which took them across to Wentworth Junction; for if the tears chose to come, she wanted to let them come with no one the wiser. And they did come; and all the passengers, sympathetic or unsympathetic, knew that the poor girl was crying.

The great express swept along with a rush, but condescended to stop for a moment to take her on board. Then followed thirty hours of smoke and dust and cinders, of boys with figs, boys with cracked walnuts, boys with packages of candy; other boys, or the same boys, came with poor novels in stiff covers, then with poorer novels in paper covers, then with fashion newspapers and other weeklies, and then with daily papers. Each boy, as he passed, scanned her face, till he could judge from it what sort of novel she would like, or what newspaper or magazine, and when he had determined, he left it with her. The thirty hours included one night, as any thirty hours south of the Arctic circle must do. Just as night came on, an army of Canadians, men, women, and little children, invaded the car. They took possession, as so many locusts might have done, seeming to disregard the presence of the people who were there before, as if they had been so many images. The new-comers did not speak to their predecessors, nor heed their inquiries. A young woman with a baby on each arm sat down abruptly by the side of the schoolmistress, waking her suddenly from half-sleep, and crushing the little hand-bag which she had placed there; nor did the Frenchwoman seem disturbed that it was under her. Both babies screamed lustily. Bessy Gurtry took one of them to try her newly-acquired Kindergarten experience. But it was all one who took the child. It screamed as a cricket would have done, and as all the five babies around did. Of a sudden a veteran Frenchwoman appeared on the scene with a bottle of milk. A stout man, who seemed to be a sort of major-general of this organized invasion, poured out a little tumbler full for each screaming baby. Each in turn took what was given, as the six horses of a rapid stage-coach might take their water when it was brought to them at a relay-house, and then each of the six sank to sleep. "The complete satisfaction of any personal appetite is followed by sleep," says Dr. Hammond, and so it proved now. In three minutes all was still.

And with such adventures the night went on, and the day which followed.

But there is an end to every lane, to every night, and to every day ; and so it was that, just as the sun went down on the second day on the station, called a "deepo," at Newfane, she was at last released from her moving prison, and stepped timidly from the car upon the platform. It was an insignificant station, at that lowest of grades in the order of commerce, known as a "flag-station." The "depot-master" evidently expected no one by this train, — generally it passed him without even stopping, leaving its thin and consumptive mail-bag by a mysterious mechanism of intelligent iron rods on hinges. He took the girl's trunk in one hand, and the lean bag in the other, — so small were they both that he needed neither barrow nor assistant. She looked round timidly and rather anxiously, and then asked him with frightened surprise if there were no one there from Tecumseh.

"Tecumseh! No, lady. No! We don't often have folks from thar. Most of their folks goes by the great Northern."

She knew this, she said, but on this occasion she had written to her father that he should drive across country for her and meet her here.

"Ye farther? 'n' wot sort of man may he be ?" asked the good-natured agent, curious, and trying to show sympathy. "Does he wear a straw hat ? "

The girl intimated that she did not know. As it was August, he probably did.

"Don't you think he will come ? But of course you cannot tell," she said, trying not to sob.

"Wall, I donnoh," said the good-natured fellow in

answer. "P'r'aps the mail broke down. They don't have no daily mail, any way, to Tecumseh; on'y every other day, and onsartin at that. Has ye heern from him since ye writ?"

No, she had not heard, but she had given time enough. If her father was well, he would certainly be here himself.

"Wall, ef ye don't mind waitin' alone, ye can sit here, 'n' I'll leave your things jest ware they be. I'll go over to the house 'n' git suthin' to eat; onless mebbe you'll come too. We can leave the things, 'n' nobody'll take um till he comes. Guess you'd like a cup o' tea, mebbe?"

Poor child; she was, indeed, faint and heart-sick, and hungry and thirsty. But she did not know who might appear if she turned her back, and she said so.

"Oh, don't be afeared. We should see um, ye know, ef anybody come along. Et's only a little way. You come with me, and the ole woman will be all ready."

And actually the good fellow, on hospitable thoughts intent, expected her to leave all her worldly wealth on the platform, while she shared his unnamed afternoon meal. But while she dreaded the risk, and on the other hand could not bear to seem disobliging, the welcome sight appeared, half a mile away, of a horse and wagon. It was enough to induce the station-master to wait, and eight or ten minutes more showed that waiting was not in vain. The driver was, as had been hoped, John Gurtry.

Alas! the least inspection of the whole equipage and of the man was enough to tell the whole story.

His face was thin and skinny, as if he had a new attack of malaria or "shakes" every month of his life.

His dress, always neat indeed, but wretchedly worn wherever dress can show wear, brought back in fabric and in cut memories of years gone by. The horse and wagon! One wondered that either had survived the rush of the advancement of the West, and why or where it had been thought that they were worth keeping in existence. He pointed out, as an excuse for his delay, the broken trace, which he had to mend by nailing the bits together on his way from Tecumseh. The good-natured station agent lifted the little trunk into the wagon, pressed them both again to go round and try the tea, as he had pressed her before, and then bade them good-by in a tone, however, which showed how little hope he had that, with that establishment, they would soon arrive anywhere.

"Better hold up in the hollow, and git Hiram to take a stitch in them traces. 'Fi was you I would put in another of them big tacks now. Hold on a bit." And he came out from the office with a brick, a hammer, and two sharp tacks with which he himself improved on the insufficient botchery which he condemned.

But poor Bessy Gurtry was so happy in seeing her father again, in her surety that no accident had happened to him, in her freedom indeed from all the doubts of the last half-hour, that all those new doubts and fears passed her unnoticed. She had travelled nearly a thousand miles to be with her poor worn-out father. She was with him now. And, whatever happened, she asked or needed little more.

"He was as God-forsaken a critter as ye ever did see." This was the comment of the station agent, when at last his wife poured out for him his long-delayed tea. "'N' after all, anybody could see thar was the right stuff in him. Played out, that's all."

Yes, poor John Gurtry was played out. This was the end of his gallantly going into the war rather older than most men. For four years he pulled on as a soldier, coming out as a Captain, Brevet Colonel indeed. All the four years were in sickly regions. All the quinine in the world could not have broken up the deadly poison of those swamps.

Yet no lucky bullet had so much as scratched a little finger. There was no injury "received in actual service" for which a grateful country could make reparation. Nay, John Gurtry was himself too proud to have asked for any, had a grateful country wanted to give it. And by this time the surgeons were dead who would have known how, and who could have told where, were sown the seeds of malaria which had all but unmanned him, and would not cease to germinate until he died.

A grateful country had made him postmaster of Tecumseh for some twenty years. But this was all over now. Politics had changed, and nobody at headquarters now was so very grateful. And somebody else wanted the place, and John Gurtry had no friends at court, nor would have used them, had there been any.

To this man, after a second marriage, which had turned out wretchedly, the only relation left in the world was this slight girl, our Bessy Gurtry, who was made for the moment perfectly happy because she was sitting by his side. The woman who took the place of her mother had fairly driven her from home. Better for her that it should be so. By hook and by crook she had used her time in the Normal School, till at the youngest conceivable age she could try her powers as a schoolmistress; and how well she had succeeded, and to what grade she had risen in her calling, our readers know.

It was more than two years, nearly three, since she and her father had met. For her these were the most eventful years of life. She had been sent from home, not to say driven, under the constant wearing antipathy of her stepmother. At one and another academy and normal school she had fought her way to the position which she was now able to hold, and to hold well, in charge of a school. In the vacations of these training-schools, by hard work, either at some shop counter, or as a book-keeper or cashier, once as a private governess, she had earned the money with which she lived for the rest of the year, and had paid her modest school fees. A year before, "this woman," as the second wife was generally called when people spoke of Mr. Gurtry's family, had died suddenly. All along, Bessy Gurtry's correspondence with her father had been close and dear. For the last year and more she had been able to remit to him something from her earnings, enough to give her the feeling that she lightened a little the pressure of the harrow that was dragged over him. But, till now, they had not met since she was a school-girl with long braided hair hanging down behind, with a school-girl's short skirts and boy's boots. In place of that school-girl John Gurtry now welcomed, and he hardly knew, this mature, graceful, rather elegant young lady.

With quite unnecessary detail he plunged into a long second explanation, to tell why he was late, and why he did not drive a certain span of horses which would have been much quicker than the broken-winded wretch, which was in fact yoked in with their destinies at the moment. But the girl hardly cared what he said. For months she had been longing to hear his voice and to see his face. She had been homesick for the sight and the sound. She could not quite persuade herself that the poor, thin, shaken man looked even as well as he did three years before. But the voice had not changed. Voices do not change. As they rode slowly on, she did not see the face. She heard the familiar tones; there were the old spurts of humor, of exaggeration sometimes, of self-depreciation always. It was wholly her own father. And whether they arrived at Tecumseh at eight in the evening, or at four the next morning, it was all one to her.

This joy was a little dashed, as must be confessed, when, at half past-nine o'clock, they did arrive. Poor John Gurtry had done his best to make his modest apartment fit for a lady's presence. He had a bunch of summer lilies in a wash-pitcher as an ornament. While his daughter opened her trunk, he repaired to the well, and brought up a plate of butter and a dish of berries which he had lowered in a private tin pail to keep them cool. These dainties he had ready on a tin waiter covered with a neat napkin. No sign appeared of any other host than he, and she knew, from what he had told her, that she and he would reign monarchs supreme of this household while she stayed. Perhaps she would like to make breakfast and get tea here. As for dinners, he had arranged with Mrs. Whitcomb, the other side of the way. The girl praised the skill of his masculine housekeeping. She did not need to feign an appetite, and applied herself to the bread and berries while her father took the horse and wagon to the stable.

Everything was of the simplest and cheapest in this modest establishment of her father's, in which now for some weeks she made her home, but it was of the neatest also. At first, the joy of being with him again was enough to leave her indifferent to personal comfort. She brought in one and another trivial improvement in the daily routine, but simply and accidentally, so that he might not think she found fault with his ways. With every morning, the poor fellow addressed himself, with a sharp spur of conscience goading him, to the helpless and futile task of finding something to do. One day he was at court, dressed in his best, in the vague wish that he might be necessary as a talesman, when the jury was called, as by good luck he had been a year before. But it was a Democratic sheriff this time, and he had no eyes for the old Republican postmaster. One morning it was a long tramp over to Sidley's, where their cashier had been drowned in a freshet, and there seemed reason to hope that in the promotions a copying clerk might be needed. Five miles' walk to Sidley's and five back, — that was all John Gurtry made by it. He would not complain to his daughter. He dropped not a word about hard usage, or an ungrateful sneer. But when he did come in, perhaps at four or five o'clock in the afternoon,

after one of these daily tours of useless homage at the .
great altar, after she had given to him the bowl of soup
she had ready to warm up for him, and the eggs she
scrambled on the little kerosene stove, he would bring
out his papers with such solid satisfaction, he would
explain to her the drawings in the "Scientific American" so eagerly, and try to make her understand where
the last inventor had missed the critical point which
Gurtry himself would so willingly and eagerly have
applied, that the girl's heart — half glad, indeed, to
see him happy — was by turns almost broken when
she wished that he were somewhere, in some place
where he might not have to pretend to be the man
of affairs which he was not, and where he might have
the solid joys of the life of the dreamer that he was.

He did not often permit himself, even to her, to open
on the endless vistas of his dreams. But once as she
sat, really on his knee again, in the darkness, after
twilight had almost faded away, she had lured him
into telling her early stories about her mother, and he
gained courage to repeat to her some verses he had
written to her mother on the last Valentine's day before she died. It was, indeed, a long poem, — so pretty,
she thought it, so tender, — and, in the midst of its
dainty, loving flatteries, it was all so true. He had
sent to Bessy herself pretty verses on her birthday
and at other festival times; and more than once he
had written songs or hymns for public celebrations.
But even her love was surprised at the reach and the
depth of this poem which he had sent to her dear
mother, and she assailed him, with glad severity, pretending to blame him that he had never read it to her
before. In the end she made him light the lamp and

bring out the old portfolio and the school copy-books
into which he had copied, while her mother lived, and
since "this woman" died, several poems, more than
pretty, all alive with his love of Nature, with his reverence for duty, and with his intimacy with God, and,
in the midst of joy and reverence, just flavored now and
then with the tonic bitterness of a life which seemed
to have failed entirely, and which wondered what its
seeming failure was. Bessy Gurtry knew all this was
in her father; but till now she had never known that
he had succeeded in expressing it in words.

Alas, and alas! Her own daily life was not very
different from his. What had she come home for?
Because she was not satisfied to send him a check for
twenty dollars every now and then, when she could
earn it, and stay away from him, not knowing when
he was sad, or hungry perhaps, or sick, with nothing
but a guarded, uncomplaining letter once a week, to
tell her of his life. Because she was not satisfied
with this she had crossed the country to resume her
home life. Ah, me! because she was not satisfied to
leave him alone, what had she not surrendered that
night George Drummond spoke to her so eagerly?
And now, what was coming of this sacrifice? The
very first day she was in Tecumseh one and another
gossip told her, half a dozen times, that the place of
assistant preceptor in the Academy had been given to
Mary Brodenheim, and these gossips all knew that
Elizabeth Gurtry had been spoken of among the can-
didates. She had thought it would be so good if she
could take her father to live with her in the Academy
dormitory. Morning after morning, while he was
walking to Sidley's and to other such places, seek-

ing employment such as a broken man might take, poor Bessy was writing to old school friends, or now and then visiting school trustees, to offer her services anywhere where there was a market. And she had no better success than he. The market in Education was in the hands of the "bears," and poor Bessy was not the person to "bull it." She was provoked with herself, but she was ashamed as she made one and another such visit, with the same certain result, — the causes were different, but the sequel was the same. Either she was too young, or they had decided to take a man, or the funds had shrunk and they must economize, or nothing could be changed before the spring. Bessy came to that point, bitterly strained as she was, that, as she rang the bell or knocked on the door, she could construct in advance her sentence of dismissal.

Was it possible that, after all, she must stand behind the counter and sell thread and needles and writing-books and slates and pencils and straw hats and horse-rakes and hoes and pitchers and basins and tumblers and knives and forks and the ten million other necessaries of life which the Meldrums sold at their store? They had had a sign out ever since she came to Tecumseh that they wanted a "sales-lady." Bessy saw it in every walk she took, and at dinner at the boarding-house, every other day, that cross Miss Sylvia Smith asked her why she did not go to Meldrum's and talk to him about it. She was afraid that the public opinion of the village would settle down upon Miss Sylvia Smith's opinion that it was her duty to go there. But Bessy hated shop-keeping. She had been a shop-girl, and was not unsuccessful in that affair; but it tired her, her very bones ached, and her head swam, — it tired her so that she could not even sleep. It confused her. She would sell scissors for the price of forks, she would weigh forks like raisins. She hoped, she even prayed, that she might not have to go to Meldrum's.

She remembered, all along, her promise to Mr. Tangier, and the similar promise she had made to Mrs. Campbell, that when she was settled she would write to them. She was not settled yet, but she must write something; so on a rainy morning she wrote two letters to Tenterdon.

And the mild police of Tenterdon, which kept a very capable force at the post-office, announced at once that Mr. Tangier had had a letter from Elizabeth Gurtry.

CHAPTER VI.

LIFE at Mrs. Fairbanks's house went on with the usual limitations, and the usual joys of summer life among people of whom the one point of agreement was that they had nothing to do, and that they wanted to make the best of a holiday only too short. The few gentlemen went fishing, all day long perhaps, carrying their luncheons with them. The many ladies collected toadstools of different colors, and arranged shields or other trophies with them; one or two of them slopped with water-colors a little; two of the most eager collected ferns and pressed them. Miss Anna and Mrs. Bates were good botanists, and studied grasses successfully and intelligently. Miss Jane Tunstall, who was the least bit strong-minded, or was supposed to be so, was rather the admired centre of the women of the company. This was because she kept a subscription for the summer at Harper's and at the Seaside Library, and so received, almost every day, two new novels. Most of them were wretched, as need hardly be said. For even the brave nineteenth century, with all its corre-lation of forces, has devised no machinery which shall produce more than ten good novels in a year. So that four thousand and nine hundred and ninety of the year's manufacture must be bad, most of them very bad. But for this the "Boarders," as Mrs. Fairbanks called them, cared but little. So that there were two heroes, two heroines, a difficulty in the middle, and two weddings at the end, they were satisfied. As why should they not be? The novels cost Miss Tunstall but fifteen cents each, on the average, and cost the Boarders nothing. For Miss Tunstall left them all, for general use, on the table of the "sitting-room."

"And who did you find at the Stage-house?" said Mrs. Floxam to Jane Fairbanks, in the contemptuous tone with which she spoke of everything excepting General Cervantes and Northern Mexico.

Jane Fairbanks answered cheerfully, but with a sort of mechanical cheerfulness, that she found the girls of her own Bible class, who were all she expected, that they were all there, and that they had a very pleasant hour all together. Jane Fairbanks said this cheerfully, because she knew that Mrs. Floxam would have been pleased had no girl attended, and if she had gone to the appointment for nothing.

"Of course they came. Poor things, I suppose they had to come. I did not mean them. I meant how many were in the reading-room, and how many were playing cards, — I believe you let them play cards, or you will some day, — and how many were in the conversation-room." All this was said with a sublime scorn, because these places were not "patios" or "salas de recreacion."

Jane Fairbanks said that she did not go into either of these rooms, that she had told the girls to meet her in the anteroom of the library, and that she had met them theré. But Mrs. Floxam's bolt had, none the less, struck home. She knew it had, and Jane

Fairbanks knew it had, and an uncertainty in her voice, as she made her reply, showed that it had.

"I knew no one would go to your Palace," said Mrs. Floxam, replying to the quiver of tone rather than to the words. "I told Mr. Tangier so, and I told Mrs. Dunster so. I told Mr. Burdett that when we lived in Mexico, General Cervantes consulted my husband about erecting a shed where the cavalry men might sit in the shade when they played with their jack-stones, and Colonel Floxam told him it would not answer. And it never would have answered. But I suppose Mr. Tangier wanted to throw away his money, and Mrs. Dunster, she always wants something to fool away her time with, so they have got what they want. Where is Mr. Tangier?"

Some one explained that he was out with a party who had started early on quite a long voyage, hoping to find bluefish.

"Bluefish!" said the indomitable Mrs. Floxam. "They will get no bluefish to-day. They will get wet jackets, and they will be lucky to come home with them. If Mr. Tangier was not so heady and obstinate it would be better for him. To go out in the teeth of a gale after bluefish!"

Mr. Stratton, a meek little freshman from Yale College, who had arrived only the day before, and did not yet know Mrs. Floxam, said, because no one else replied, that the weather report was favorable, that it promised light winds from the southwest, and that this was just what the fishermen wanted.

Mrs. Floxam looked with sad pity on this new adventurer into the ocean of conversation, and then expressed her contempt of the Weather Reports. They

were always wrong, she said. When the telegraph
was first established in Mexico, General Cervantes
consulted her husband on the question whether there
should be any arrangement attempted for observations
on the weather. But her husband had wholly discouraged General Cervantes, and from that time to
this there had been no Weather Reports in Mexico.
It would have been better for this country if it had
followed the Mexican example.

Poor little Mr. Stratton said no more. His first experiment was a sad failure, and his voice was not heard
again for twenty-four hours.

Mrs. Floxam, with a certain pride in her victory,
looked up and down the table in search of new adventure. It would not be right to say that she was
trying to think what was the most disagreeable thing
she could say. Jane Fairbanks would have given this
account of the momentary pause, but Jane Fairbanks
was young, and so was not fair. Such people as Mrs.
Floxam say disagreeable things without any effort.
They are so accustomed to look on the worst side, or
the blackest side of everything, that if they speak
what is in their thoughts, they must say something
disagreeable. They would be much surprised if they
were charged with conscious effort in the matter. The
truth probably is that utter selfishness, or the habit of
thinking of one's self only, ends in a habit of thinking
with contempt and dislike of all things else or all
beings. Then, if one speaks at all, one speaks with
this contempt or dislike. Indeed, such a person must
speak so, or be silent, or indeed be untrue.

Now, Mrs. Floxam never chose to be silent. She
liked to talk. And because she liked to talk she said

disagreeable things, — "from native impulse, elemental force."

But she was not on this particular occasion to have her own way absolutely. That is, she was not to have all the talking. Mrs. Hasey appeared on the field a little late. So soon as her plate of soup was brought to her and finished and as, with the refreshment thus afforded, she was able to engage in the more serious work of the day, she took up the wondrous tale of life, which she always approached from a point of view different from Mrs. Floxam's.

"Jane! my dear child, why did you not wait for me? I got talking with the girls, and though you know I never say anything, they lured me on, and I stayed till after one. You should have come and called me."

This little joke, "I never say anything," was one of Mrs. Hasey's stand-bys.

Jane explained that she supposed Mrs. Hasey had come home long before her.

"Well, it is better for you that you did not come in, for you would not have come home before this time. I should have set you to work, as I did them. I always set people at work, Mr. Stringham." This was to Mr. Stratton, who had been presented to Mrs. Hasey the evening before. "I shall set you at work, unless you run away. Yes, I only ran in for a minute to see Aunty, and to ask what she did for chilblains."

"Chilblains!" cried Jane Fairbanks, "surely you have no chilblains now."

"My child, when you are an old woman, you will know enough to prepare for war in time of peace.

I can show it to you in Æsop's Fables. Only my Æsop is locked up and stored with our things in Derne Street. No matter, dear. I went to see Aunty Turner, and dear Mrs. Fairbanks here had given me a couple of pies for her — "

"No matter for them," said poor Mrs. Fairbanks, who did not care to discuss her charities before the Boarders.

"— and while I sat at Aunty Turner's, — that is really a very cosey little room of hers, she says it was once the place where the bar-tender sat, and where his especial favorites came in and played poker with him, and really, Jane, I am not sure but just the charm and attraction of the wickedness hangs round the place, though the wickedness is gone — is not that interesting? Well, Aunty had brought in for herself a cup of tea, and she opened the little cupboard where those old wretches used to have their private tipple of Hollands — I have seen them, my dear, you need not laugh — and she made a very nice cup for me. Really, your Mr. Tungy must have friends in the India trade. He has provided Aunty with the best tea this side Canton. I know tea if anybody does. It is almost a shame to waste it upon Aunty, who does not know, but I do. But, well, none of you know, except dear Mrs. Fairbanks, whose tea is always so good."

This was Mrs. Hasey's second thought. For in truth, if there were a weak spot in Mrs. Fairbanks's armor, it was the tea-hole; and this all the feminine boarders knew perfectly well. Mrs. Hasey, even, tripped an instant on her own white lie, and thus was brought back to the story on which she had begun.

"While I was sitting, talking about winter and chilblains and oiled silk, and I do not know what else, another old woman came in, as old as I am. You need not laugh, Jane, there are old women as old as I am, and I hope you will be some day."

"I hope I shall," said Jane, boldly, "if I am half as nice as you are."

"Well, my dear, you do not know how much nicer I was when I was nineteen. This other old lady, — well, I think perhaps she had come with some little comfort for Aunty. I found she had not seen the house. And after she had taken Aunty Turner out, and they had had their little talk, I undertook to do the honors. That was when I looked in on you and your German class, Jane."

"German! dear Mrs. Hasey, I do not know any German! It was my Bible class. We were reading the book of Proverbs."

"Very good reading, it is, dear Jane, and I hope you will make them commit to memory the thirty-one verses about the good woman, and what comes before them. Much better that is for their albums than this stuff of Swillburne's and Halt Whitman's, Mr. Stringham."

Poor Mr. Stratton blushed to his eyes, afraid that his verses in the last Yalensian were alluded to.

"Well," continued the monologue, "I am never strong about names, and if Aunty Turner knew who this was she did not tell me, in introducing her, but all the same, name or no name, we went all over the house together. And then it was that there came in, while we were sitting in the reading-room, that tired-looking Mrs. What's-her-name, — you know, Mrs.

Sigfried, she gave you the hymn-book last Sunday ; they live in the house with a big chimney, beyond the duck pond. Yes, that is the woman ; she stopped in her wagon, coming home from the Junction, to pick up her girl, Jane, who was in your class. And she knew my friend, or seemed to, and we all three fell talking, and talking, and we talked till now.

"And really I am ashamed to tell you, but I promised the woman that has no name that I would come there to-morrow, with your tapestry book, Mrs. Meldrum, if you will lend it to me, to start for her a mantel fringe. She had tried to do one, and had made a mess of it. And we were looking at that pretty thing which one of the girls made for the reading-room, and I told her that with that for a pattern I knew I could show her how it was done. In fact, I told her that that was what old women are good for."

"My dear Mrs. Hasey, do you know what you have been doing ? " said Jane Fairbanks, with an air of mock surprise and curiosity.

"No harm, child, — I have done no harm. I have promised Mrs. What 's-her-name to teach her some stitches in crochet. But I have not even done that. And I have come home late to dinner. But your mother is so good-natured that my chop is a little warmer for that, so I shall probably sin in that way again."

"Mrs. Hasey ! " cried Jane, in a sepulchral tone, "you have been reconstructing society."

They all laughed, for it was quite clear that Mrs. Hasey had been, without knowing it, inveigled into the drift of the conspirators who had founded the Palace of Delight.

"You may make all the fun you choose," said she. "I shall never reconstruct society. I shall knit baldrequins, or, if Mrs. Meldrum will lend me her book, I shall crochet them. Perhaps I shall do both. And as for the Old Stage-house, if Mr. Tunis was not all the time fishing, I should give him a piece of my mind."

Every one listened, curious to know at what deductions or inductions the old lady had arrived in her morning's observations.

"I shall tell Mr. Tunis that nothing goes unless there is a driver. You girls will all pile into the carry-all this afternoon, but Peg will not start till somebody takes the reins and says, 'Get up, Peg!' And the driver must not go a-fishing every day, or every other day.

"Now old Aunty Turner has never succeeded so well in making her own home comfortable that she will make other people comfortable. She cannot drive this wagon. I do not suppose that Mr. Tunis means to leave all his courts and lawyers, and clerks and people, and come and live in the Stage-house. But somebody must live in the Stage-house that has a head and two eyes and two hands and two feet. Now, what was the little schoolmistress's name? I had a notion that if she were there, she would make things bright and pleasant, and I mean to say so to Mr. Tunis; and I mean to say to him that all that has been done will go for nothing, and will be remembered as the shadow of a dream, as Dr. Watts says, or somebody else, unless there is a captain, and I mean to propose for this captain the little school-mistress, — if she had any name, I have forgotten what it was."

One of those terrible silences fell over the assembly that will come when exactly the wrong thing has been said. However ready all these people were to discuss the relations of Mr. Tangier and the little schoolmistress when they were in separate groups, none of the different groups cared to state their views on the matter in the presence of the whole company. What was known was, that the little schoolmistress had written Mr. Tangier a letter; what the letter was about nobody knew. What was also known was, that Miss Remington had left Tenterdon, and seemed to have lost all interest in the old Stage-house and in the reconstruction of society. What Mrs. Dunster thought nobody knew, though many people guessed. The general impression on the mind of everybody was, that Mr. Tangier had been flirting with May Remington, as he never should have done, and that he had been flirting with the little schoolmistress, as he never should have done. But all that was known was that May Remington had left town, and that the little schoolmistress had sent Mr. Tangier a letter.

Alas! the mild police of a country village is apt to find out a great many things which do no good to anybody; and is equally apt, like other detective bodies, to lose the clews to the things which might help along the world.

CHAPTER VII.

GEORGE DRUMMOND had left Tenterdon sick at heart. Yet it is not enough to say that he wished he were dead; it would be more precise to say that he wished he had never been born. He had been struck very heavily, and he could not guess why. But he made one and another guess which had no reasonable foundation. And George Drummond had sense enough to know that these guesses had no foundation. If he had been a woman, he would have had to stay at home and brood and cry. As he was a man, he had to do his duty in the world, just as if he had not received a terrible disappointment the night before, which would change his whole destiny. He could not believe that the ticket-seller at the station did not know that something had happened to him. He could not understand why the boy who sold newspapers offered him the same paper which he would have offered him a week before. It even seemed strange to him that the sun shone as it shone yesterday. But he had, all the same, to go to New York to renew the contract about fresh fish which he and his friends made with their agents, or refuse to renew it and to make a new contract. Fish would swarm, and nets would be drawn, and ice would keep the fish cool, and the trains would take them to New York, and people would buy them and eat them, whether

George Drummond were happy or were not happy; indeed, they would do so whether he lived or whether he died.

He was tempted to stop over a day, and go to see his mother. No misfortune had ever happened to him in life but he had done so. This was a misfortune, however, which he could not believe that even she would appreciate, and for once he undertook to bear his burden alone, and to do without the support which any man or any woman gains from the sympathy of another; which one begins to gain, indeed, as soon as one states one's trouble in words. No, George Drummond went on to New York, took the room that he was in the habit of taking at the little private hotel on a cross street, and the next morning went down to see his fish people as if nothing had happened.

The contract was not to be renewed exactly in the form in which it had been made the year before. Times change, fish change, and people's tastes change. All this George Drummond knew when he came to New York. He knew, too, that his agents respected him, and in a certain sense he respected them. He found, also, to his surprise, that he could talk about fish as well as he ever could, and that a certain numbness, which he was aware of as he walked up to his hotel and back, disappeared as soon as he was making plans for next year's work and adventure. The young man of whom he saw the most at the office was a person he had always taken to, and who had always taken to him. It was impossible for them to complete their arrangements in one day or in two; and this gentleman asked Drummond one afternoon, a week after his arrival, if he would not go up and spend the evening with him at his little "box," as he called it, on the Hudson.

"You will see my wife and children," he said, "and that will be better for you than trying to laugh at Hart and Harrigan's. It is pretty hard going to the theatre in the middle of August."

Drummond accepted the invitation as cordially as it was given, and thus it was that the two fell into talk more wide than they would have done in the counting-room, where every moment was precious. The visit ended in a proposal which the New Yorker made to Drummond, which really suited his present mood more than he could have supposed would be possible.

"Why should not we recognize what is? Why should we undertake to do business on the old lines, when there are new lines all around us? Here is this Canada row, as the newspapers call it, meaning our row with the provinces of Nova Scotia, New Brunswick, and the rest, which, by the way, are hardly Canadian. We do not know, nobody knows, what our Government will do, or what the Dominion of Canada will do, or what England will do. What we do know is, that people in New York want fish, and people in all parts of America want fish. If Americans cannot fish in such and such waters, Canadians can. What should you say, Drummond, to going to a place, which I will show you on the map, and establishing yourself there? What should you say to owning such part in a dozen vessels, in which we are interested, that they could go and come as yours? What should you say, in a word, to making yourself a Blue Nose, in partnership with us who are here, if I could make such a proposal to you, — well, for a good many years to come, — as would please you as to terms, partnership, and a share in the profits ? "

Drummond listened to him as if he were fascinated. He had time enough, and he had habit of analysis enough, to be amazed and amused. A fortnight ago, had such a proposal been made to him, he would have said it was the most absurd suggestion that ever was made. It was made to him now, and it fell in with all that dismal thought of his on the ride, and every day's walk up and down Broadway, that he wished he were dead, or rather that he wished he had never been born. Here was the other life which he had half asked for in his prayers; here was a life with no Miss Gurtry, with no fishing-gang, with no Tenterdon, with nobody who ever saw him or heard of him. He should begin all over again, as completely as if it pleased God to lift him out of this world and to carry him to the planet Mars.

His New York friend was accordingly a good deal surprised at a certain feverish eagerness with which Drummond replied to him. Drummond pressed questions which were natural enough, but it looked almost as if he had accepted the plan, though he had not. They had the chance of the long ride down the river, and afterwards on the Elevated, to talk over the possible details of such a plan, and it ended, when they parted from each other at the counting-room, by Drummond saying : —

"Well, you see I am interested. Give me a few days to turn it over. Let me correspond with my friends, and I will see if any of the boys would like to go with me." So he went back to the hotel.

His walk up Broadway was different from what it

had been any day since he had been in New York. And when he came to the post-office he crossed the street and took the Elevated to the Park. He knew every corner of the Park as well as he knew the walks in Tenterdon itself. Such is the great hospitality of the great metropolis to thousands upon thousands of people from all parts of the country. He found himself a quiet nook where he could turn the whole matter over; and he did turn it over. He was offered a place where he might forget, if forgetfulness were possible. Of course the poor fellow thought that forgetfulness was not possible; but it would be something to live where he was not reminded of old days in every hour; and it would be something to live without seeing Bessy Gurtry two or three times in every week. In the half-insane chaos of a man's thought in such a crisis, it was not very likely that George Drummond would make a wise decision. But his good angels had not wholly deserted him, and without deciding anything he did something, and this something was, as it proved, the right thing. He took out of his pocket the pocket writing-case which he always carried, and then and there, sitting on that shaded bench in the Park, he wrote to his mother a long letter.

It was a pleasure to the poor fellow to open the whole story of his hopes and his disappointment. It was a pleasure to tell his mother how he first knew Bessy Gurtry; how she had impressed herself upon the whole neighborhood; how he had been surprised to find that he thought of her in every minute of his work and of his life; how he had thought that she had at least a certain esteem for him. All this was a real pleasure to write.

To this had to be added the miserable story of the downfall of his castle. And he begged his mother to understand that the thing was final. He begged her not to think hardly of the girl. He begged her to think that he was a fool himself, and that he never ought to have pressed so far. That episode was over; a curtain had fallen on that play. Now he must take life in its reality. He must go about something like a man who does not expect happiness any longer, but, as he had heard somebody say when he did not believe it, instead of happiness he must seek for blessedness. His mother would be surprised, but he thought he must go into exile; and, just at the moment that he thought so, exile under honorable conditions was offered him. Such was the letter which the sensible, tender, unselfish, far-seeing woman, who lived from day to day in the hope that the night's mail would bring her tidings of one of her sons or one of her daughters, — such was the letter which she was to receive as her mail came in on Thursday evening.

George Drummoud could not have chosen a wiser counsellor. He did not know that he had written for counsel; but as it proved he had. His mother wrote him the tenderest, kindest, and wisest letter in reply. She did not tell him that it would break her heart if he went off among the fogs and the icebergs; but at the bottom of her heart she knew it would. She did not tell him that ten thousand other men, unknown to him, had suffered in just the same way on the very day in which he suffered so. She knew this was true, but she was his mother, and she was too kind to tell him so. She wrote to him as he wrote to her, as if this were such a calamity as had never fallen to man before. She did not say to him that she supposed his little schoolmistress was a wicked, foolish, selfish flirt, though she did think so. Most mothers, receiving such a letter from such a son, would have thought so. On the contrary, she wrote as if Bessy Gurtry were the noblest woman God had ever sent into this world, and as if her son had honored himself by his regard for her.

But she told him that he had perhaps surprised Miss Gurtry; she told him that he had had to do what he had never done before, and that perhaps he had been too quick or too slow; she told him that he must not risk the fortune of his life on an accident. She asked him to remember how often in novels a poor blunder had complicated the whole thing, because nobody of sense advised the principal parties to begin all over again. "Now," said she, "your poor old mother is the good fairy. I tell you, before you decide on any great change, to see Miss Gurtry again, and to ask her to reconsider her determination. At all events, say to her that, if she do not reconsider it, you become an exile from your own country."

These words she wrote with an aching heart, not to say a breaking heart, though with a firm pen, in her own regular handwriting, which was so dear to her boy. And the one hope which this poor woman had that she might not lose her boy, was her hope that a foolish, flirting, selfish girl, as she imagined his peerless queen to be, might be glad to welcome back the lover whom she had played with, and give him a chance for such a broken life as he would spend when married to such a woman.

CHAPTER VIII.

THE business of George Drummond's exile did not proceed as rapidly as if he had been a Nihilist on his way to Siberia. Many things were to be considered on many sides. He had many interviews with different members of the firm, and with other advisers. He wrote many letters, and many answers came from one and another bay between Anticosti and Eastport; and all this time George Drummond himself had the recollection of what his wise and kind mother had said to him.

At last it seemed quite certain that what had been little more than a dream between the two young men, as they talked and walked together, might be wrought out into a plan which should circumvent diplomatists, and overcome international difficulties. The thing came to so nearly a point of action, that George Drummond had the distinct offer made to him as to the terms on which he should enter into this new partnership, if at the same time he gave up his allegiance to the United States, and became as loyal a subject of Queen Victoria as that other loyalty to the Dominion of Canada and the province of New Brunswick might imply. Before he could make his decision, he told his friends in New York that he would see some of his old companions in the fish-gang at Tenterdon, and that he would give them a distinct answer within a fortnight. And so he bade them good-by, and broke up this visit in New York, which had lasted so much longer than he or any of his Tenterdon friends had thought possible.

But, strange to say, instead of taking the express train for Wentworth Junction, which would have been his direct route to Tenterdon, he took a ticket by the New York Central and its more western connections. He rode by night and he rode by day. He had the guidance which the use of the railroad guide offers, and skilfully studied the impossible rival railroads, each of which made its own line perfectly straight, and the line of its competitor as crooked as the letter Z. His objective point was Tecumseh. He took a route a few miles nearer to it than that which Miss Gurtry had taken some weeks before, and he found a conveyance more readily than she did. He made his way to the Prophet House, which was a rather decrepit fourth-rate hotel, pretending to be something that it was not; he registered his name, washed and dressed himself, and then inquired where Mr. Gurtry was to be found. He found John Gurtry was perfectly well known, and had no difficulty in making his way to the room where Bessy Gurtry had found her father on her arrival; but the door was locked, and George Drummond sought in vain for an answer to his knock.

He then by one and another excursion found, in a somewhat distant kitchen, a woman at work with her clothes in her wash-tub, who was to be pardoned for a certain slowness of apprehension, as by misfortune she was nearly deaf, and understood only with the greatest difficulty the questions or suggestions that

were addressed to her. All that could be learned
from her was that Mr. Gurtry gave up the room
which he had hired from her, on the Monday before,
and that he paid his rent up to that date, as he had
always paid it regularly, that then his trunk and
his daughter's were carried to the same tavern, or
"hotel," in which George Drummond had established
himself, and that certain boxes had been sent to the
freight station. Some articles of furniture had been
disposed of in different ways, but this reader need
not be told how, as this is not a strictly realistic
narrative. In short, John Gurtry and Miss Bessy
Gurtry had gone, the washerwoman knew not whither.
She however pronounced an encomium upon them
both, which, in a dim way, gratified the heart of
Miss Gurtry's lover.

He returned to the "attentive clerk" at the hotel,
or to the very stupid and indifferent functionary who
united the duties of the attentive clerk with those of
porter, hall-boy, steward, head and foot waiter, and,
indeed, every other branch of the administration of
the inn. George Drummond found this functionary
in the stable, rubbing down a horse, and with some
difficulty brought his mind back to the fatal Monday
when John Gurtry's trunks and Miss Bessy's were
brought to rest for a short time under his roof.
What became of the trunks then, or what became of
their owners, he neither knew nor cared. He did
not pretend to know, and he did not pretend to care.
So that George Drummond was left to pursue his inquiries in other directions.

He was not a fool; he was not easily discouraged;
and he understood as well as most men do, the

method of operation of the mild police of a small town. But in this case the police was indifferent, and did not give him what the newspapers would call "available clews." That is to say, he went first to the grocer's nearest to their old lodgings. The grocer's boy, profoundly interested in Bessy Gurtry, and very fond of her, pretended to know a great deal about their going, but only knew that they went to the same railroad station which George Drummond had come from that morning. He went to the apothecary's, to receive a great deal of information about John Gurtry's rheumatism and his hay-fever, on the effect which Townsend's Medicines had produced on the hay-fever, and similar related topics, but gained actually not so much information there as he had gained at the grocer's. The apothecary, however, was able to tell who was the clergyman who would be most apt to know what their plans were, but was singularly reticent when he was pressed as to the names of their intimate friends. He gave the names of two or three lawyers, and two or three store-keepers who knew Gurtry; but, on successive visits to each of these men, while one or two of them remembered that Gurtry had come in to bid them good-by, their answers were to the last degree vague as to his plans. They agreed in this,— that he was going away somewhere with his daughter; but where that somewhere was, — whether she were going to work in the mills, as one man thought, or whether she had accepted the position as principal of the female college, as one man thought, it was impossible to say. Indeed, where the mills were, or where the female college was, were points left entirely unknown, after the most careful cross-examination on the part of George Drummond. At the end of an afternoon of vigilant visiting and inquiry, and of the next forenoon spent in the same way, he found that the last clews had run out, nowhere. Indeed, he found that the clergyman in question, on whom he had relied the most, was absent from town, and would be for the next two months, on a vacation which had been given him that he might visit a son who was mining in Montana. George Drummond had made a journey of a thousand miles for the purpose of asking Bessy Gurtry whether he should go into exile, and at the end of the thousand miles he found that Bessy Gurtry had gone into exile herself. The difference was here: that he knew where the place of his exile was to be, and no one seemed to know where the place of her exile was.

He could see the amusing side of the position, but, as always happens with the actor in such adventures, he was not himself amused. Vainly did he say to himself, " How funny this will all seem a year hence, when we are happily settled in life, and can look back upon it ! " That other question would interpose, " Will it seem so funny if I find myself established in Restigouche Bay and am broiling my own salmon ? "

But he was no man to give up on one day's bluff. What was it, after all, he said stoutly, but to telegraph to Montana ? The communication from Tecumseh by telegraph was poor. It meant the confiding a despatch to the " attentive clerk " when he became the driver of the " Prophet Coach " when that coach went, at nine in the evening, to the Great Northern Station. Drummond readily saw that he had better be his own Mercury. He carried on a long negotiation with the same man whose broken harness had worked John Gurtry's delay, and with a somewhat better horse drove himself across a prairie, blazing with autumn asters on the roadsides, to Centreville. Here was a well-arranged office of the Western Union, and from this point he sent this despatch to the Rev. Zenas Kerfoot:—

" Send me the present address of John Gurtry. Answer."

He left word that he would call for the answer in person the next day, and that no effort need be made to send it to him. With that comfortable feeling which a man in health has when something has been done, that it was the right thing to be done, and that nothing else can be done, he drove back through the blazing asters more cheerful than he had been since Bessy Gurtry had last spoken to him. He permitted himself to build up again the card-house which that night tumbled down. She was not far away. Was she, perhaps, on a visit in this very Centreville? It seemed a pretty place. Which of these pretty houses, shaded with maples, was her aunt's? Or was there no aunt? Was she a teacher in that Female Seminary, of which he had passed the ostentatious sign just before? What a queer Evangeline business this was, if he were passing the house she was in, if she were even looking out of the window without knowing that it was he who was passing! Ah me! If she did know, would she care?

The horse was a better horse and the harness a better harness than John Gurtry's means had permitted the day he brought his daughter to Tecumseh.

No accident detained George Drummond. And with the evening he found himself again in the Prophet House. It was clear enough that he had no more business there. And his last night had been so wakeful that he might well hope not to pass another there, even in the " best room " of that establishment. He knew that the postmaster would return to the post-office to distribute the mail when the Great Northern bag came in, and he rendered himself there to receive his own letters from New York, and to give instructions for any which might follow. Half a dozen other men waited in the office with him, most of them bearing that hopeless look of men who are wishing that something may turn up for them. Such men wait for the mail as the daily drawing of a lottery. It may announce that some one has died of whom they have never heard, and that they have all inherited fortunes. True, it did not announce this yesterday. It never has announced this. But no one of them has anything else to do. It may announce this to-night. And so is it that they are all waiting at the Tecumseh post-office.

Drummond waited for the last of them, took his own letters, and left an order for the forwarding to his Tenterdon address of any letters which might come after he had left Tecumseh. He read this order aloud to the somewhat stupid girl who was in attendance, and the words called forward the postmaster himself, John Gurtry's fortunate successor in his office. He had been filling a blank at a desk in the corner.

"Be you the man who asked where John Gurtry had gone ? "

Drummond said he was.

"There was a fellow here this morning said he had gone with his gal to Auburn. Said he had a sister there, or aunt, or something."

Light from the black clouds! Drummond expressed his gratitude. Where was Auburn?

"Auburn — oh! don't you know?" This with a slight expression of Western scorn for the tender-foot who was so ignorant of a central point in geography. As if one should land in Greenwich, and inquire for London, or at Civita Vecchia, and ask where Rome was. Auburn, it seemed, was a well-known city, not eighty miles away, where were three colleges, two female seminaries, an institute or two, and talk of the State University. The postmaster supposed that Miss Gurtry was "to teach" there — he knew she had been seeking a situation.

Drummond thanked him eagerly, — so eagerly that the postmaster supposed him to be some near friend or relative, and, as he turned away, said, "Be you going to see Gurtry?"

Drummond said he was.

"Then you might take his letters. He did n't leave no orders, but if you's going it's a pity to send 'm to Washington."

Drummond assented, hardly knowing what he did. The postmaster gave him two copies of the "Scientific American" and a letter.

It was not till he packed his valise at the hotel that he observed that the letter was not to·John, but to Elizabeth, Gurtry. He also saw, at the instant, that it was in the handwriting of Mr. Tangier, which he knew perfectly well. He had intrusted himself with the business of carrying to his mistress a letter from his rival.

George Drummond slept even worse that night than he had slept the night before.

CHAPTER IX.

MEANWHILE it must be admitted that the Palace of Delight at Tenterdon was not flourishing as its designers had wished or hoped. How should it, indeed, when the designers were not watching its progress ? Four weeks and more had drifted by since that eventful evening of the dedication. Of all the "conspirators," as Miss Remington used to call them, Mr. Tangier only had held the ground with any constancy. Even he had been once and again called back to his office. George Drummond, as the reader knows, had never seen the Palace of Delight since that night of its blazing fire-works, which had aspired so high and had gone out so suddenly. Miss Gurtry, who built the first sidewalk, had left the week after. Miss Remington had abridged her visit in Tenterdon, and was making a series of summer excursions. Mrs. Dunster had gone to the White Mountains.

Mrs. Floxam's sneers seemed to rest upon some foundation. Mr. Tangier was obliged to confess even to himself that he found but few princes of the Blood Royal in the Palace, no matter what the hour at which he visited it. Aunty Turner even had been heard to complain of loneliness, and there were those who hinted that she looked back, with a sort of homesickness, to the little old house, fifteen feet square, where she was often too cold, often too hot, but where, since she was a baby, she was at home.

Was the New Englander unsocial by his hereditary instinct? Mr. Tangier asked himself this question sadly.

The Iroquois, or Six Nations, lived together in immense "phalansteries." But the New England Indian of Canonchet's type, or of Ninigret's, lived in his separate wigwam, with his own household. Mr. Tangier tried to remember if there were any legend of considerable villages of Indians in the peninsula which is called New England, and he could remember none. Is there, he asked himself, sadly, some astral influences by which all those born under these stars prefer separated roof-trees for their long winter evenings or their long summer twilights? Then he encouraged himself as he could by recollecting such crowded bee-hives of industry as Lowell and Lawrence, and Holyoke and Boston. Still, he could not but remember, at the same time, how much of foreign blood went to the make-up of those communities. And then he recalled, to encourage himself as best he might, that the fathers always began the formation of a town by building the "Meeting-house." He whistled "MacGregor's Gathering" as he walked to his supper from the empty Stage-house, and said aloud, "The magic word is 'Together.'"

Mr. Burdett was away on his vacation. The doctor seemed to have given up his habits of visiting, and Mr. Tangier had to find his comfort, as he could, from Mrs. Hasey's optimism, Jane Fairbanks's willingness, and his own determination that the thing should go through. All the same, Mr. Tangier was bored. Perhaps it would be too much to say that he was annoyed, for a lawyer, trained to defeat as he is trained to success, will not own that he is annoyed by failure. But Tenterdon no longer was to him what Tenterdon was at the beginning. In the first place, he was no longer a sick man; there was not the fresh bath for nerves and brain, and indeed for his whole being, that he had found in the beginning. He said to himself that he liked Mrs. Fairbanks's better when he only met with her and her daughter than he did now, when he had to go through with the daily chatter at the table. He grew tired of Mrs. Hasey, and he found it harder and harder to hold himself back from being rude to Mrs. Floxam, in retort which she was constantly inviting by her own steady rudeness. He missed the society which he had had in the first months of his stay, and he seemed to have no gift in finding new society. He said to himself, as a philosopher, that he ought to find Mr. Stratton a pleasant young man, that he ought to like to go after huckleberries with these children; but he was well aware that he did not like the people around him, or the things around him, as he had felt sure that he should do when the summer began. Yes, one may at least say Mr. Tangier was bored, and, whether he would have said that he was annoyed or not, you or I may guess that he was annoyed.

It was at this time that he wrote the following letter to Dr. Morton:—

DEAR MORTON,—I have your note, and sympathize with your hermit life. I have always wondered how a doctor survived the three months of loneliness of his summer practice. I am sorry to see by the papers that you have enough to do;

but unless you poor medical men meet every night to discuss the qualities of paregoric and Hamlin's Mixture, I do not know how you can occupy yourselves in the absence of your wives and daughters, of theatre and opera and club, and everything else that goes to the make-up of every-day life. I wish I dared say that you would find my kingdom of heaven any more heavenly than your own; but, to tell you the truth, I am badly bored here. The people I liked most have gone away, and the new people are not worth the enthusiasm by which I tried to welcome them. I have lived through the charm of the novelty, and am beginning to wonder whether my Grandmother Fletcher was right when she said "Country folks is fools."

Somehow my new plans do not work as well as you and I thought they would work when we were sitting at poor Grace's that day. If you have in your books any tonic or other elixir which will start a broken-down Palace of Delight into life and energy, be good enough to send down the recipe by telegraph, and we will apply it immediately. Or perhaps you could come yourself. I am hand in glove with a country doctor here who would do your heart no end of good. I venture to say that he would teach you a great many things that you never learn in Paris; anyway, he would make you respect your kind more, for I declare to you that I think that this compassing sea and land, as he rides up and down these country roads, merely to carry with him health and life and new spirit, is the finest exhibition of concrete Christianity. Sometimes he lets me go with him, and they are the best days I have; but of late either he is tired of me, or his calls are too far off, or he has some other companion. You will see, therefore, that I am somewhat bored, and a great deal alone.

Observe that the question is, What is to be done in a community of people who like each other well enough, but who will not any of them go quite half-way for the purpose of joining hand and life with each other?

Always yours,   T.

It is no matter of surprise, then, that Mr. Tangier, on the second day after he wrote this letter, having received a cordial invitation from an old college friend to join him in his yacht, on a cruise which might go to Campobello, which might indeed go as far as the Grand Banks, accepted the sudden invitation with a sort of glee which surprised himself, and that he disappeared from Tenterdon in the midst of the speculations of the natives and the foreigners of that community.

The reader will see that Mr. Tangier was in that condition of an inventor, who, having perfected his model, and made it work entirely to his mind, has sent it to the Patent-office, and has been told in a formal letter that the patent will be issued to him on such and such a day. He has no questions to answer, no investigations to make. He has done what he could do, and he is waiting for the world to pass approval. Or you may say Mr. Tangier was in the position of the artist who has finished his picture for the Salon. It has gone to the man who had to frame it, the framer has sent it to the committee, the committee has approved it, and has hung it upon the wall, and now, that the artist waits to see what the public will say about it, he finds it very hard to direct any interest to a new picture. If, at the same time, all the artist's friends go away, for some mysterious reason or another, and he finds himself all alone in his studio, he is in much the same position, socially and personally, in which poor Mr. Tangier found himself after the dedication of the Palace of Delight.

As for Miss Remington, she had rather unexpectedly remembered this series of summer engagements, as she pleased to call them to her aunt, — it is fair to say, rather unexpectedly to herself. She had joined, as the reader may have seen, in the efforts for the Palace of Delight, with a genuine hearty enthusiasm. She had had the same satisfaction which Mr. Tangier had had, — what Lord Houghton calls "the joy of eventful living," — while they were making all the arrangements, and while she was, so to speak, the chief of his staff in the making. The summer days had flown by while they were planning for carpets and lambrequins and book-shelves and writing-tables and stationery, and all the things which were to be so useful and attractive in the people's club house. Miss Remington had certainly not analyzed her feelings while these things were going on. She had simply waked every morning to the consciousness that there was something to do, and enough to do, and she had done it with good heart and with good spirit. She was not in the habit of analyzing her life, or asking questions why it had been a pleasant one. She was a girl of quite too much sense not to take the present as she found it, and to think, as well as she could, for the immediate future.

But, as the reader may have guessed, she also found a certain deadness in her personal experience when the thing was done for which they had all been striving, and, without asking herself what was to come next, she was willing to acknowledge that life in Tenterdon was not what it had been for the six weeks before. She certainly did not acknowledge to herself that one element in her dissatisfaction arose from a certain distrust of the companion with whom she had been most engaged as those six weeks went by. Miss Remington was no such fool as to suppose that Mr. Tangier was particularly attached to her because he had made use of her hand to write for him when his was lame, or because he had addressed to her, from his office in the city, a dozen letters about tassels, and carpets, and curtains, and other furniture. She would have been angry to the last degree if Jane Fairbanks and Mrs. Floxam had ventured to intimate that Mr. Tangier had been flirting with her, or that she had been flirting with him, — if any of them had had the daring to convey to her any such intimation, which they were free enough in suggesting to each other. None the less, however, was Miss Remington annoyed, on the night of the ride home from the Palace, and in the gossip of the next day or two, when the whole village, with one accord, pronounced that Mr. Tangier was making a fool of Bessy Gurtry, and even went so far, in some of its myriad voices, as to announce that Bessy Gurtry was making a fool of him. May Remington was far too just and well-poised a girl to do any injustice to Miss Gurtry. She liked Miss Gurtry, and Miss Gurtry liked her, though they were by no means intimate. There was a certain shyness about Bessy Gurtry which did not permit her to be very intimate with any one. On the other hand, there was a certain frankness, amounting almost to audacity, about Miss Remington, which led her to claim rather more than she ordinarily found in the people who were around her, and in the same proportion restricted, and restricted very severely, the number of persons who would venture to say that they were very intimate with her. So, though she and Miss Gurtry had met each other almost every day in some of the recent arrangements for the Palace of Delight, they had never come even near the point in which they should call each other "May" and "Bessy." It was still "Miss Remington" and "Miss Gurtry," and "Miss Remington" and "Miss Gurtry" it would long be. Yet, though they were by no means intimate, or maintained any of the forms of tenderness with each other, May Remington liked Miss Gurtry with a very solid esteem and respect. She had said to her aunt a dozen times that a girl like that, who was earning her own living, and was able to do something for a father who was far away, was a person of a great deal more account in the world, and deserved a very much higher place in the circles in which Beatrice sits so high, than a girl like herself, who was leading merely an ornamental life, was manufacturing a set of duties for herself, and who, as one of the gentlemen had said, could not earn five dollars a week by any service which she could render to society in any of its demands. Her aunt, who believed in her thoroughly, and was passionately fond of her, would controvert this assertion, and would even scold her for it, as if it were a bit of mock modesty; but Miss Remington was really sorry that circumstances had so placed her in this world that she had not to fight any battle for herself. That means that she was sorry that she had a father who idolized her, a mother and three or four brothers who loved her, as much money as she wanted to spend, — within reasonable limits, — and nothing to do, as she said, but to make a fool of herself, and wish that the hours might go by. She respected Miss Gurtry, and hoped that they should see more and more of each other.

For her to be told by anybody, then, that Mr. Tangier, whom she also respected, whom she respected very thoroughly, and whose purposes she thought she understood, — that he and Miss Gurtry had been carrying on, under the rose, what Jane Fairbanks called a flirtation, this irritated May Remington. Perhaps she did not know how much it irritated her. She did know that on Mrs. Floxam's interrogatories on the subject, addressed to her personally, as they met in walking one day, she fired up with rage, and almost lost herself so far as making a tart reply. She said to her aunt, when she came home, that she almost bit her tongue out in order to keep silence, and this is probably literally true. It was after this that she came down to breakfast, announcing that she was going to make a visit with an old schoolmate, who had asked her to come to Pomfret, and if she could persuade her to join in the party she should go to Mount Mansfield with the Appalachian Club on an excursion which that club had projected for the exploration of that mountain.

It seemed necessary to say this, that the reader might understand the social position of the Tenterdon to which Mr. Drummond was returning, after his fortnight for decision was nearly ended.

CHAPTER X.

MR. DRUMMOND had very foolishly taken it for granted that the unknown counsellor who had told the postmaster that Auburn was the new home of Mr. Gurtry and his daughter, knew what he was talking about.

It sometimes happens that we take a thing for granted when it is told us at second or third hand, which we should not believe for a moment if we heard it from the lips of the person who first made the assertion. In this case, Mr. Drummond had been so much discomfited by the expression of scorn which followed his inquiry where Auburn was, that he had supposed that his informant was as well informed on all other matters relating to this affair as he was on the point of geography. He went back to his disagreeable quarters with the fixed determination that he would go to Auburn as soon as the morning train would carry him there. When he arrived, as has been told, he found that he had to carry with him a letter which he wished might be at the bottom of the sea. But he did not change his plan. He bade the stable-keeper send him over to Centreville the next day, and from Centreville proposed to take his departure to the seat of these various seminaries and colleges.

He was not so certain, however, when morning came, with its colder suggestions, but that he went to the telegraph office to find what was the answer of the travelling clergyman. In this, however, there was nothing encouraging; there was simply an office despatch, which said that no such person could be found as the Rev. Mr. Kerfoot. Drummond was now comparatively indifferent; he had not to wait for Montana to send him upon his way; he had merely to go to Auburn and meet his fate like a man. The never-failing railway guide gave him the information he needed, and between three and four in the afternoon, after many transfers which were not close connections, he found himself in the university town.

Here, as before, obedient to the laws of what we have ventured to call the mild police of such places, he inquired at the post-office if any person of the name of Gurtry had asked for letters. His first disappointment was in finding that the name was wholly unknown. It then occurred to him that if this Mr. John Gurtry were as dreamy and unpractical a person as he had begun to infer, he might have neglected to ask for letters, by the same law by which he had neglected to give directions for their being forwarded. His next step was to inquire at the various inns and hotels of the place, of which there were not many, if any such persons as Mr. John Gurtry and his daughter had arrived there in the week before. To this question his answers were equally unsatisfactory. He did not permit himself to be discouraged, however. In fact, the zest of a search did him good, after the stupidity engendered by the long journey. He ordered a carriage, with a driver, to take him from point to point, and began a series of inquiries at the seminaries and colleges, winding up with the institutes. The seminaries were "female seminaries," and the colleges and institutes were conducted on the principle of co-education. Both of the colleges were quite out of the village; one of the seminaries was two miles away.

Ulysses did not meet more fascinating Circes in ten years, or Calypsos less fascinating, than Mr. Drummond met in the several institutions of learning which he visited. He found each seminary somewhat jealous of each other, and very ignorant as to the other's affairs. But each seminary and each institute was equally certain that no such person as Bessy Gurtry was within its own walls, or ever had been expected within its walls. Indeed, there was generally a certain air of cold reproof observable in the manner in which this news was conveyed to Drummond, as if his mistake on the matter involved a certain moral obliquity, for which any man of character should be ashamed. After each interview he had to shake himself together, to be quite sure that he had, indeed, done nothing so far which was disgraceful. Auburn ended, though it were the loveliest village of the plain, as Tecumseh had ended, — there was, very certainly, no Bessy Gurtry there.

He came to this conviction late in the evening, as the tired horse stumbled back to the Auburn Hotel. He went to bed wondering at his own readiness to be deceived as lately as the morning of that day. With the next morning he repaired again to the post-office, and examined for more geographical light the postmaster's register. It was only to learn that there are forty-four different Auburns in the United States; one in Arkansas, one in Alabama, three in Illinois, and so on. A cyclopædia in the Christian Association reading-room showed that many of these were the seats of academies or high schools. Clearly, even the most intrepid lover must falter before so many. Certainly Mr. Drummond must not attempt them, for he had only nine days left now, for the forty-three of which he knew nothing.

No! For him the thing is to do what he should have done first. He must go back to Tenterdon, to start thence anew. There must be people there who will know !

Day and night, therefore, night and day, he rushed back, or was rushed back, eastward, into the same frenzied haste in which he had come westward. True, it seemed as if the hours would never go by. But they did go by. And at last the express faltered a little — faltered more — " it is surely stopping — yes, it stops," and the conductor calls " Wentworth Junction."

It was two hours after sunset. Drummond felt his steps carefully as he left the rear of his car, almost stumbled upon a man who was descending from the next platform, and started as he saw that it was Mr. Tangier.

The yacht had been becalmed off Corlies Head and Mr. Tangier had been set on shore there.

Both men were surprised. They even laughed and shook hands. A moment after, in the lantern light, another man, who seemed confused, asked them some question, and when Mr. Tangier in answer turned to guide him and to explain, it proved he was in turn wishing to help from the steps of yet another car a young woman who was Bessy Gurtry. This time Mr. Tangier left to George Drummond the duty of caring for her. As he himself led her father to the great heap of trunks, which were already piled upon the platform, the two, in the deceptive lantern light, joined another lady who was holding out her check for inspection. She turned and said:—

"Mr. Tangier?"

"Indeed! is it you, Miss Remington?"

Yes, it was Miss Remington. In the mysteries of palaces, and sleeping-cars, and parlor-cars, and cars not palaces, the five had ridden together for the last hour or more, and had not known how near they were to each other. George Drummond's friends had sent one wagon across for him. Mrs. Dunster had sent over her carriage for her niece. And in these two conveyances the five must make their way to Tenterdon.

CHAPTER XI.

THE situation was complicated and to the last degree delicate. George Drummond, with the accurate knowledge of a native, had telegraphed to one of his friends of the fishing-gang that he was coming, and Nahum had been sent over to the Junction from Tenterdon to take him and his traps home. Here was one carry-all, which, if people were good-natured, would seat three of the travellers. Mrs. Dunster had sent over her carriage, with Rebus, the "hired man," who directed her destinies. Two could sit within, and, if necessary, one could crowd in on the seat with Rebus, with the baggage. Six seats for five travellers. But how were these travellers to be arranged? Mr. Tangier had left the becalmed yacht unexpectedly, at a little cove, which gave him as few opportunities of telegraphing as Leif had, the first time when he sailed up the waters of the Back Bay.

It was a delicate question, and was the more difficult because there was no one of the five travellers who wanted to take the responsibility of decision. Mr. Tangier did not want to invite himself to ride home with May Remington in Mrs. Dunster's carriage. He felt, rather than knew, that, in Mrs. Dunster's bearing toward him in the two or three weeks since the party had broken up, there had been a certain coldness. He had set down that coldness, as men will, to that general account of "Profit and Loss" which they head "Women's Ways," an account which, on the whole, stands them well in stead, so that they do not grumble so much because it is wholly inexplicable to them, and because they sometimes have to charge to it great misery and misfortune. Mr. Tangier would not offer, himself, to ride home with Rebus, nor would he suggest that Miss Gurtry should ride with May Remington. Indeed, he pretended to be occupied with the station-master, and to be making some inquiries about freight expected for the Old Stage-house. As for John Gurtry, he had never in his life proposed any course of conduct in a difficult exigency. That was, indeed, exactly what John Gurtry could not do. And here in a foreign land, stranded like Robinson Crusoe on the beach of an unknown station, with the hiss and steam of the receding tide announcing to him that his fate was irrevocable, John Gurtry was the last person in the world to solve any problem.

As for George Drummond, as the reader knows, he would have been glad to take Bessy Gurtry in his arms, and say to her: "Dear child, let me carry you wherever you like to go. We will leave all these people and places, and I will carry you to a home of my own. There I will watch over you and defend you from all evil. You shall eat of the best, you shall look out upon the grandest prospect, you shall read from the most charming books, you shall paint the most beautiful pictures, and all you shall have to do shall be to love me truly." This is what George Drummond would have said in a genuine romance. And it is because the George Drummonds of another day said such things, and, what is more, because they could and did take their Miss Gurtrys in their arms and walk off with them into the forest, — because of this is it that the romances of Amadis and Huon and Esplandian are as good reading as they are. In a parenthesis it may be added that because the heroes of to-day do not do such things, nor say them very much, is it that such stories as this in the reader's hands, and other stories, not unlike, are not always finished by that reader.

The dictates of modern life, and other circumstances, prevented George Drummond from addressing Bessy Gurtry in this way, as he was suddenly aware that he had not spoken to her, since with tears she had passionately begged him to leave her, and had told him that this life he proposed could never be.

George Drummond therefore, while he assiduously helped Mr. Gurtry with his trunks, offered no suggestion as to the way in which the trunks should go to Tenterdon, nor intimated, indeed, that Mr. Gurtry and his daughter were not to spend their lives at Wentworth Junction.

As to poor Bessy Gurtry, her courage failed her. It was dark. It was late. It was raining. She was tired out. She had telegraphed to her friends that she and her father were coming. But the Western Union Telegraph, true to that great policy of discouraging the small customers and working for the large ones, whose payments are worth working for, had not hurried with the message, which, in fact, appeared the next morning. And so poor Miss Gurty all but broke down. She did not cry. She would have cried, had not George Drummond been on the platform. She did pretend to ask the station-master whether he could send her over, knowing perfectly well that he could not if he would, and would not if he could.

May Remington was mistress of the position. She would naturally have asked Miss Gurtry to go with her, and would have asked Rebus to let Mr. Gurtry sit on the seat with him. But two instincts dissuaded her, rising from two utterly different hypotheses, and yet reinforcing each other, as diverse instincts will. If, as she had sometimes thought, as she had certainly thought the night when Mr. Tangier was seen returning from Miss Gurtry's home, the night when George Drummond cut the old horse so savagely with his whip, — if George Drummond hated Mr. Tangier, he might kill him in riding home in the carriage with him. On the other hand, suppose she should ask Mr. Drummond to take home Miss Gurtry and her father? Would not that be a palpable bit of match-making, too gross to be pardoned, observable even by the station-master? The thing to do would be to put Mr. Gurtry into that carriage with his daughter, and ask Mr. Drummond to sit outside with the boy who drove. But for that she had no courage. So May Remington gave no advice, and I do not know but Miss Gurtry and her father might have sat in the ladies' room all that night, as they had sat in the ladies' room at Abydos half the night before, but that Rebus came to the rescue of all parties. Rebus was used to directing the destinies of women, and therefore always moulded, to a large extent, the destinies of men, who are principally dependent upon women.

"Nahum," he said to the boy from the fishing-gang, who had come for Mr. Drummond, "back up here. Take this bag on the seat with you. You get in here, Miss." This to Miss Gurtry, who obeyed as meekly as if a giant in one of those old romances had given to her his orders. "Miss May, I shall leave your large trunk for the stage; you will not need it to-night. Please get in; they are waiting." And he handed the passive May Remington to her seat. "Now, sir, get up with him;" this to Mr. Gurtry, who obeyed as meekly as the others. "Mr. Drummond, Mr. Drummond, they are all waiting. Mr. Tangier, I take you, if you will get in," and he thrust Mr. Tangier in to join May Remington. He bade Nahum keep behind him in the darkness. He took his own reins and drove off, and left George Drummond to enter the other carry-all with Miss Gurtry, to be shut in by darkness, and to follow in the darkness.

Do such people as Rebus solve the great questions of life intentionally? Or does some demiurge, working behind them and by them, compel them to these movements of sudden determination, in which they become, for the exigency, the directors of the world ?

CHAPTER XII.

MR. TANGIER entered the dark carriage, amused and not disconcerted. He had not chosen his companion, but he had the very companion whom he preferred, without having to show that he had made the choice. As for Miss Remington, she hardly knew whether she were annoyed or not. She was too conscious that she and Mrs. Dunster and all that family always obeyed the directions of Rebus, to struggle much against his authority. There flitted across her mind a sense of how funny this would be if she saw it upon the stage, and she could not but think that, a moment before, she would have bitten her tongue out, before she would have invited Mr. Tangier to ride with her. But as she had not invited him, and as he knew she had not invited him, — indeed, as he knew perfectly well how great the powers of Rebus were, and how desperate was any attempt to oppose him, — she acceded to the inevitable, as, in such cases, she had often done before.

As to Mr. Tangier, he was in the happy condition of a man who had done nobody any harm. He suspected, indeed, that everybody in Tenterdon thought that he had done everybody harm. As has been said, he was quite conscious of a certain coldness in Mrs. Dunster's bearing towards him, and he was quite conscious that the people at the boarding-house discussed his affairs, not in the absolutely friendly tone with which he was regarded at the beginning of the summer. But he had done nothing wrong to anybody; and he knew he had done nothing wrong. He was straightforward in his life, and without crime, as Horace says, and although he did not ever quote Latin to himself, he entered the carriage with the readiness of a man who has obtained exactly what he wants, without having put out his hand or wagged his tongue for it.

"I am so glad to see you," he said to May Remington. "It seemed as if I were never to see you again. And, as I could not tell in this darkness whether you were Miss Remington, or whether you were Lucretia Borgia, I am very well aware that I use a figure of speech in saying that I see you at all." May Remington, a little grimly perhaps, expressed the hope that he was not crowded by her parasol, her little carpet-bag, the roll of prints she was carrying home, or the basket of pears which had been sent as a present to Mrs. Dunster.

Mr. Tangier saw that she was disposed to be either on the defensive or on the aggressive, he was not quite sure which. But he was still light-hearted at the good chances of the interview, and determined that he would find out, before the ride was over, what the matter was with Miss Remington and Mrs. Dunster. For three weeks he had been aware that something was the matter, and now was the time to find it out, if any time there were.

"You have been quite a traveller since I saw you," he said. "We have had rumors of you at the Mount Adams House; I met Ferguson, who saw you at Berlin Falls, and some one said that you had made

the ascent to the topmost peak, if peak there were, of
Mount Washington."

May Remington had meant to be cross, was cross.
But, all the same, Mr. Tangier was a gentleman, and
he spoke with the light-heartedness of a gentleman
who was innocent of crime.   She had been at all the
places indicated; she had forgotten herself, and enjoyed every moment while she was there; and, with
the true passion for Nature that characterized her in
all that she said or did, she forgot, for the instant,
that she had meant to be cross with him, and launched
out in that enthusiasm with which a person who is
fond of Nature must speak of the mountains at any
time.   In Miss Remington's case, the enthusiasm was
the more pronounced, because, as it happened, this
was her first visit to our little Switzerland.   Before
she knew it, she was running on in an eager account
of the glories of the mountains, as if Mr. Tangier had
been the best friend she had in the world.

Mr. Tangier was himself an old mountaineer.
There were few of the passes in the White Mountains
which he had not himself explored.   He had gone
through the well-known notches with gay parties, on
horseback, on foot, or on the top of a stage-coach,
when everybody was in high spirits.   He had gone
through the woods alone, by a spotted trail, with no
guide but the brook which he traced, or his compass,
or his good sense.   He had made his own fire when
night came, and slept happily by it till sunrise.   May
Remington's animation waked the memory of these
old experiences, and he eagerly compared notes with
her about Pulpit Rock, and the Carter Notch, and
whether she went up this valley or down that, about

that wonderful garden of orchises which is high above the Tamworth valley as you cross to Sawyer's river, and so on and so on. Both of them for the moment, in the eager memory of what they had so much enjoyed, forgot that there had seemed to be a cloud on their cordial friendship. And matters were thus well prepared for a return to the experiences, more mundane, but not more commonplace, of Tenterdon, and the reorganization of society. Rebus had to stop to leave word with Jonas Wesley about some post-holes which were to be dug the next day; and, from a sunrise view on the top of Mount Washington, Mr. Tangier and his companion had to descend instantly to the present condition. They were not looking at the sunrise. They were sitting in a close carriage, with a pile of hand-baggage on their feet and knees, while Rebus was pounding at the door of the Wesleys. The Wesleys had gone to bed.

Mr. Tangier accepted the interruption. He meant to be at the bottom of their misunderstanding, if misunderstanding there were. If there were not, he meant to know that there was none.

"I am afraid that you do not hear very favorable reports of the Palace of Delight," he said. "Either we planned wrong, or our plans have not been carried out wisely."

"You know I have been away," she said, recollecting, a little indignantly, that she had meant to be cold and reserved, and had not been cold and reserved at all.

"Perhaps that is what is the matter," said he, good-naturedly, but not with the air of compliment. "I have been away more or less. But that ought not to have made a difference. If the plot were a good plot, it should have worked well, even in the absence of the chief conspirators."

"And why do you think it does not work well?" said she. "We must not expect too much, as my aunt is always saying."

"No, I hope I do not expect too much. But I had hoped that, if there were a reading-room, somebody would read; if there were a conversation-room, somebody would converse; if there were a music-room, that somebody would play on the piano. Now, as far as I can find out, Aunty Turner is the only person who frequents the house, and every time I go there I am afraid she will have left it in despair, and that I shall find the key hanging behind the door. I did find it so once, when she had gone for an outing."

"Can it be," said Miss Remington, "that people have grown unsocial, and that they are so shy or so proud that they do not want to see each other? Certainly, that night every one was cordial enough," and then, by a sharp surprise, there came back to her the memory of George Drummond's blow on the horse when she and he together saw Mr. Tangier returning from Miss Gurtry's house at the end of the evening.

"I wish," said he, "that I could unravel the mysteries of that evening. I left all of a sudden. In the midst of the fire-works I found your poor Miss Gurtry, faint and all knocked up. She would not ride, but she would go home. I did not dare leave her alone, and walked home with her. But it was later than I thought, and I met all of you as I went back again." He spoke with perfect simplicity and evident frankness. Fortunately, indeed, he was wholly ignorant that this walk, to which he had ascribed no importance in the social problems of Tenterdon, had, in fact, been the subject of endless gossip and speculation.

May Remington was indignant beyond measure with herself, that she had ever permitted herself to think a second time of a matter of which he spoke with such frankness and indifference.

Fortunately, it was so dark that he did not see her face. She had nothing to say, and she said it. He broke the moment's silence himself, and went on in the same unengaged and frank way.

"It is all over now, but I may as well tell you another plan I had, though nothing came of it.

"I saw the tide ran against us at the Palace. I saw that Aunty Turner was homesick, and that nothing worked well. And I had a notion, I rather think you or your aunt started it, that Miss Gurtry would be a good element there. I knew about her classes at church, and it was plain enough that her boys worshipped her. So I went round to see her, and I asked her why she could not go to the Palace of Delight, and live with Aunty Turner, instead of living with the Campbells. Oh, I blocked out quite a scheme, — that she was to be called ' librarian,' but really she was to be Director of the Hospitalities. After all, there is no hospitality unless there is some one to be hospitable. And I thought then, and to tell you the truth I think now, that a bright, engaging person like her, young herself, and who gets on well with young people, would find endless ways and plans which would make quite another place of our poor gloomy old Palace. But I don't know, I have no art of persuasion. I should have done better with a jury in a mill-dam case. She would not hear to me at all, and went back to her father."

So, simply and openly again, did he unfold and discuss that interview which had set all Tenterdon on the *qui-vive* of inquiry. Again May Remington bit her lips in indignation, that she had ever, for a second time remembered that Mrs. Floxam, in her hateful way, had told her of this visit.

Again she said nothing. But Mr. Tangier, honest soul, did not remark on her silence, perhaps did not observe it.   After an instant's pause, he went on :

" Seeing her here makes me almost feel as if I would open on the matter again. She wrote to me from Tecumseh, where her father lived, a letter which she had promised to write, because she had some feeling that I might be able to advance his fortunes. I know some of their political leaders out there, and I might perhaps serve him. I got her letter promptly, and I answered it promptly, but I have never heard from her again."

Once more he spoke without the least hesitation on a matter which all Tenterdon discussed in whispers, and of which even Mrs. Dunster had spoken in writing to her niece.

And once more May Remington felt the blush which she was glad no one could see, which would have shown her mortification that the mild police of the town had made so much fuss about a matter of no importance.

"Now that she is here again," said Mr. Tangier, as innocently as before, "I shall turn you ladies upon her. I wanted Mrs. Dunster to see her, but she was away somewhere, and Miss Gurtry left so suddenly that I could not negotiate. I did not understand that she was to come back; indeed, the exact thing which I did understand was that she was not to come back. And now she has brought her father with her. I wonder whether he is to stay."

May Remington roused herself to a consciousness that she had said nothing, and that she must say something. She succeeded in remembering that Miss Gurtry was very much attached to her father, and had once told her that she was anxious about his health. She thought Miss Gurtry had said that he and she were all, that there was no mother, nor any brothers and sisters.

"He seems delicate," said Mr. Tangier. "But when we were together a moment, there was something very attractive about his face. Clearly a gentleman — you might have guessed that, for she is clearly a lady. How would this do, Miss May, — ask your aunt how this would do. Might not he and Miss Gurtry both live with Aunty Turner in the Stage-house? Would not that cheer her up — I mean your dear old Mrs. Turner — so that she shall not die of loneliness? Might not Miss Gurtry maintain the elegant hospitality, be the 'Hospitaller,' as Ivanhoe would call her, and then this quiet, poetical father see to the books, the checkers and chessmen, talk Shakspeare in the Shakspeare club, Mozart in the music club, and science in the Stevenson club? Really, I begin to take heart again."

May Remington was self-rebuked again. If Mr. Tangier had been flirting with Miss Gurtry, he certainly had the most open-handed and public way of announcing the several steps of his flirtations.

CHAPTER XIII.

IN the other carriage, very different conversations were going forward.

On the front seat, Mr. Gurtry made one or two inefficient efforts to engage Nahum, who was, however, now taking the direction of affairs largely into his own hands. He was indifferent to Mr. Gurtry's approaches, until he felt that he had completely established his own superiority. He then took the lead in the conversation himself, thinking he had sufficiently subdued the Western man. In a long monologue, he eventually told Mr. Gurtry the ups and downs of the enterprise of the saw-mill man, how far it had been conducted as Nahum thought judicious, and in what points it had wholly failed. In this monologue, Mr. Gurtry was compelled to pretend to listen, but was hardly able to say a word.

The other two, George Drummond and the woman he adored, were seated so close to each other that it would really have been more convenient, had propriety permitted him to fold her in his arms, as the books say. Propriety did not permit, and he did no such thing. And here they had a ride before them of half an hour or more, with only the faintest opportunity for him to say what he wanted to say, and with all the thought, quickened to agony at times, of the days of his pursuit. He had not now so arranged thought or purpose that he knew how to address her, when he must speak what Nahum and Mr. Gurtry might hear as well as she.

The whist-players have a maxim, "When you are in doubt, take the trick."

A similar maxim in life would be, "When you do not know what to say, tell the truth."

George Drummond did not care if all men knew what all good angels knew, and so he said bravely, "I am so glad you are here. You do not know it, but I have been to Tecumseh to see you."

Was she, for a moment, exquisitely happy? Or was there a sense of exquisite misery? In a book, she would have started; but in fact she did not start. If he had hoped she would start, he was disappointed.

"To Tecumseh — really to Tecumseh?" she said. "Why, when were you there? We have only just come away."

Then he explained in some little detail that he knew on what day she left Tecumseh, and he certainly surprised her by his accurate knowledge of her movements while she lived there. He told her of his false clews afterwards, and of what he had done, — not in undue detail, but carefully enough to make her understand how thoroughly he was interested in his search, and that she, and only she, was his object. The story was long enough to give her some little chance at self-command.

Then there was a pause, which seemed to them interminable, but they could hear Nahum lecturing in a monotone on the price and quality of oats. Drummond would not break the silence, perhaps could not. As has been said, he had been preparing for fifteen hundred miles what he would say. But he had been preparing for a private interview, and not for the chances of being overheard if the prices of oats should adjust themselves. Miss Gurtry on her part said nothing, because she was very much frightened. She hardly knew why, but none the less was she frightened. At last, however, when it seemed as if the top of the carriage would fall upon them and crush them both if neither spoke, she screwed up all her courage, and said : —

"Have you friends in Tecumseh ? " She was sorry, of course, the moment she had said it, for George Drummond answered in a flash : —

"I thought I had one friend there, for I thought to find you."

Then she said again that they left on such and such a day; for it is one of the oddest things about an embarrassed conversation, that people continue to repeat the same statement of facts, either in new words or in the words which have been used before. It is somewhat as in a weak or embarrassed newspaper, when you have read one paragraph, you find the same paragraph put in a second time, under it.

"Yes," said George Drummond, more bravely this time, "I went to Tecumseh only to see you." George Drummond was willing that Mr. Gurtry should hear this acknowledgment, and Nahum, and the horses, and all good angels. In fact, also, Nahum was by this time lecturing on the saw-mill, and Mr. Gurtry's thoughts were far afield in the intricacies of a decision in the Patent-office.

"I wanted to consult you," said George Drummond, boldly, "about an important proposal which has been made to me, which will require me to go to Newfoundland or to Cape Breton."

Miss Gurtry of course should have said, in a tone of rebuke, and with her head thrown up as if she were a schoolmistress trying to confuse a pupil: "Pray why should you consult me?" But being rather a human person, and being taken rather by surprise, she did say, "You leave Tenterdon, — and for how long, pray?"

Once more George Drummond defied Nahum and Mr. Gurtry. "As long as I live, unless you say no."

But Mr. George Drummond, being, indeed, as ignorant of women and their nature as he was of the more recondite problems of quaternions, had gone too fast and too far.

Miss Gurtry was well-nigh alone. She was in low spirits. She did not know what the next day would bring her. She was without a home and was looking for one. But for all this she was not to be crowded, and so Drummond found.

"I do not think so ill of you as to believe you," she said. "You ought to know yourself better than I do. But I know I will not let anybody else make up my mind for me, and I do not think you will let anybody else make up your mind for you."

These words might have been said priggishly or harshly, but they were said gently and pleasantly. For Bessy Gurtry was not a prig, and she was George Drummond's true friend. He saw, in a moment, that he had gone too fast and too far, and that he must begin again.

"Let me tell you," he said, somewhat apologetically this time, as if he would withdraw the hasty remark she had censured. "Let me tell you. Do you know, have you read in the newspapers, or has your father told you of this trouble there is about fish? Part of it is about treaties, part of it is the jealousy between men of one nation and another. Practically, as Mr. Burdett would say, the bottom question, the real question, the question for the angels, is, How can the codfish and the mackerel, which are now crowding each other in the waters for a thousand miles, more or less, to the northeast of us yonder,"—and he pointed to the light-house which they could see in the offing, — "how shall these fish, amiable, innocent, and indeed not unwilling, be brought most easily to the plates, not to say the mouths, of hungry people? That is the bottom question. Now, as you know, I am a fisherman by profession. I went to New York, after I saw you last, about our little business here, and there I saw some men who want to establish a Yankee colony down on the coast yonder. And they have proposed to me that I shall be the Captain John Smith of the new Jamestown, or, if you please, the John Winthrop of this new Boston. Of course it is all in good faith. But we know how to fish, or we think we do, quite as well as they do. Why, it is in my blood," he said proudly. "The first Drummond dried codfish on the Isles of Shoals before Mary Chilton put her foot on Plymouth, — before Mary Chilton was born."

Then he laughed at his own eagerness, which had indeed implied that Mary Chilton was to blame for coming into the world no earlier. But the sudden outbreak of his enthusiasm in this matter was fortunate for him.

It pleased Bessy Gurtry, even in the reserve which she had assumed. She had always liked this pride of Drummond in his occupation. More than once, she had heard him boast that the fishing-gang was employed in direct answer to men's daily prayer for daily bread; and more than once she had heard him run back on little odd bits of the history or romance of fishing, like this allusion to Mary Chilton and to the Isles of Shoals. But the girl said nothing, and so forced him to go on. After a moment's pause, he said: —

"And I really wanted counsel. I withdraw all I said before, but I did want the best advice from my friends, and I think you are a true friend."

This time she could not help saying, " You are quite right there," and she said it so gently and sweetly that the poor fellow took it for more than it was perhaps worth, poor little crumb of comfort that it was! Unfortunately, at the same moment Nahum had come to a pause in the saw-mill lecture, and gave to his audience what the old Lyceum used to call "an intermission of five minutes."

Once more the dead and dread silence brooded over the four, broken only by the pattering of the rain on the top of the carriage, and the plash of the horse's feet as he stepped into the frequent puddles. Once more it seemed to Miss Gurtry that she should die if nobody said anything, but this time she doubted if she could try the experiment; for she could think of nothing to say which she dared say, and she had no such convenient resource as asking Mr. Drummond if he had read the last Howells's, or how he liked the opera.

George Drummond had many things which he

he wanted to say; but he confessed to himself that
did not care to have Miss Gurtry's answer to them
repeated in the stable the next morning by Nahum.
He had taken the measure of Mr. Gurtry well enough,
already, to know that he was dreaming of some far-off
matter, and would hardly know whether his daughter
spoke or what she said.

"I think we all hate to change our allegiance," he
said at last. "I think that is in the blood. We all
talk about our respect for the gracious lady who has
reigned for fifty years, and I suppose I have as much
of it as any man has who is not her subject. But the
idea of becoming anybody's subject is in itself dis-
tasteful;" and then he paused again, to see if he could
draw her answer. But he did not succeed. "On the
other hand," he said, in a tentative way, "I think it
is in the blood of all Americans to wish to establish
colonies, or to wish to go somewhere where they were
not born. You know the Garfields, for seven generations, died in houses they were not born in, and in
most of those generations the houses were built on the
land which had been given them for military service.
The Drummonds have never been soldiers; they have
not always been fishermen; but they have always
been emigrants. I was born in New England, and
perhaps that is the reason why I should die in
Anticosti." Here was another pause.

Again Miss Gurtry said nothing. It was not that
she had nothing to say; but she was a little afraid
of herself. She was not quite sure whether she had
passed her own line in the last words that she said,
and she remembered that—

"The dumb man's borders still increase."

"Then again," said George Drummond, almost as if it were the "thirdly" of a sermon, "there is a certain satisfaction in having a thing done well which is now done ill. I cannot read the newspaper quarrels about this matter with the least satisfaction. In fact, I do not read them. If it would do to say so, I do not think that either government understands at all what it is talking about. I believe that a commission of fishermen, such as I could make among the gang yonder, and my principals at New York, and two or three gentlemen I should like to name in Newfoundland and Nova Scotia and New Brunswick, would settle this matter better than all the cabinets in the world. If we know how to do it, why should not we do it? That question comes up to me sometimes."

He paused again. This time Bessy Gurtry thought she was safe in saying: "I see there are more difficulties than I supposed at first. Indeed, there is more involved than I supposed at first, when I thought you were speaking of absence for the season, perhaps. But, Mr. Drummond, do you know the old story about the law student?"

Drummond said he did not know.

"It is a story my father used to tell when he talked more. It was told to the disadvantage of a young lawyer who lived in our Tecumseh. He was at the law school, and the professor asked him what he should do in a certain crisis. And the poor boy answered, after haggling a little, that he should consult a good lawyer. Women are so fortunate that nobody asks them to emigrate. If anybody asked me, I should consult — well, I should consult Mr. Burdett, or perhaps I should consult Mr. Tangier."

She spoke without a thought of the inference which he would draw from her words, but she plunged a dagger into his heart. Mr. Tangier, as it happened, was the only lawyer she had ever spoken to in her life, excepting as a little girl, when she chanced to see one or another of her father's political companions. But, to Mr. Drummond's ear, the selection of Mr. Tangier as a particular confidant was specially annoying.

Rather grimly and gruffly he replied: "A lawyer would tell me just what I asked him to tell me. He would find out what I wanted to do, and then he would find me a great many good reasons for doing it."

She did not see his annoyance, and she said: "And why do you not find out what you want to do, and do that? That is what Mr. Burdett says. He says we must take the duty next our hands, but between two duties next our hands we must select the one for which we have the most taste and more inclination, and therefore the more ability. I suppose you know whether you had rather stay with the fishing-gang in Tenterdon, or had rather go out on the deep sea yonder."

Ah, me! if George Drummond could have said, "I will stay at Tenterdon, and will stay there forever, if you will stay there; or I will go out on the deep sea yonder, if you will go there," he would have said just what he wanted to. But this he did not dare say in the hearing of Nahum and Mr. Gurtry. If he had told the truth also, under that admirable rule which has been given already, he would have said, "Can you not understand that if you are still cruel and hard to me, I do not care whether I live in Newfoundland, or in Boothia Felix, or in Madagascar; if you are sorry for what you said to me before, one place or another is as indifferent to me." But he could not say this, and another of these terrible pauses ensued. It was broken this time by Nahum turning around to ask Miss Gurtry where she and her father would be left. Would they go to the Campbells', which he took it for granted was Miss Gurtry's home, or where would they go?

George Drummond was only eager to say that if they would come to his aunt's house they should have the spare chamber, and the chamber in the L, and the best room downstairs, and everything else that the house had to give. In a blundering way he started on some such proposal, but Miss Gurtry did not let him go on, — interrupting him, indeed, to cross-question Nahum a little about the condition of things with Mrs. Campbell. She knew that Mrs. Campbell had expected company. She had supposed Mrs. Campbell would have had her telegram. It was clear enough Mrs. Campbell had not received her telegram. Did Nahum know whether Mrs. Campbell had company?

Nahum was by this time wet and very cross. He was dissatisfied with Mr. Gurtry's indifference to his discourse about the saw-mill, and as a consequence he chose to know nothing about Mrs. Campbell and her company and the probabilities there. Then it was that George Drummond again made this suggestion of his about his aunt's, and the chamber in the L, and the rest; but this Bessy would not hear at all, and at this moment, as it happened, Nahum himself decided the question by drawing up at the Old Stage-house to leave a parcel of newspapers which he had brought over from the Junction. It had been so dark that no one, excepting himself, knew exactly where they all were. Aunty Turner appeared at once at the door, delighted to have some company at this Palace of Delight on a wet, lonely evening, in which nobody had chosen to be delighted. A happy thought struck Bessy Gurtry. She appealed rather eagerly to Aunty Turner, to know if they might not have the use of the "guest-room," which had been arranged, in the plan of the Palace, for some visitor caught by accident, just as they were. Aunty Turner was only delighted to see a face or to hear a voice, indeed, and she at once assented. Bessy Gurtry left the carriage instantly, not waiting for George Drummond to give her his hand. Almost with an air of command she compelled her father to leave it also, and did not even take pains to explain to the dazed Aunty Turner how she proposed to dispose of herself in the arrangements for the night. The poor girl was only too glad to cut short the conversation which was so embarrassing; and though it was but for twenty-four hours, she was glad she had found something which she could call a home.

And so poor George Drummond was carried to his aunt's house to look in upon the loneliness of the L chamber, and the best room, and the rest, with the consciousness that Bessy Gurtry had preferred to stay in Mr. Tangier's Palace of Delight, and had declined to accept his invitation.

CHAPTER XIV.

MR. TANGIER came down to breakfast the next morning well pleased with himself and the world. He went through the morning encounter which every one had to have with Mrs. Floxam, in unusual good-nature; and he fell into the optimistic view of Mrs. Hasey quite as if all the world believed, and must believe, that everything would turn out well.

"Why! Are you here?" said Mrs. Floxam, in her usual tone of displeasure, as he entered the breakfast-room.

"Yes," he said, even putting out his hand in his good-nature, "the bad shilling comes back very soon."

"You said you should not be back for a week," said she, with that eager instinct which such people have to prove that every one else tells lies, and loves to.

Dear old Mrs. Hasey interposed:—

"Well, Mr. Tangier, you are welcome indeed; we have missed you badly. I said to Jane that if you did not come back in a day or two, we should have to send for the Ravels to come and amuse us."

"Thank you, dear Mrs. Hasey. Would you like to have me throw a summersault now? If Mrs. Fairbanks will risk the coffee-cups, I will try."

Mrs. Floxam said she wished people would not do such things at table as he proposed. When she lived in Coahuila a conjurer came in to the breakfast-table one morning, and put two eggs under a bowl, and General Cervantes sent him to prison.

Then there was a pause. But Mrs. Hasey could not be extinguished, and she began again.

"The doctor came here the second day after you left, and I did my best to make him talk about the Old Stage-house, and Aunty Turner, — you know Aunty Turner has been sick ? "

No, Mr. Tangier had not known it. And, if she were sick, he believed she would be better very soon. He was too well pleased, — released as he was from the yacht cabin, — to believe that any misfortunes impended.

"That is just what I say," said Mrs. Hasey, "only you are so quick. You go before my story. The doctor said she was not well. He was afraid she was homesick."

"And then," interrupted Jane Fairbanks, "our dear Mrs. Hasey knew that what Aunty Turner wanted was to be petted and fussed over a little ; so she did not say a word to anybody, but drove over to the Palace of Delight and stayed with her till yesterday. And now Aunty Turner is as bright as a new dollar ; and the Palace of Delight was the place of the wildest dissipation while dear Mrs. Hasey was there."

"My dear child," said that nice old lady, "you must not run on so. You are wholly ahead of the story. You have none of the artistic method. I meant to lead Mr. Tangier on day by day."

Mrs. Floxam got a chance to say that it was a

wonder that Aunty Turner had not died. She would use Sanford's Elixir for her cough, while there was certainly mandragora in that elixir, and General Cervantes had known, etc.

But no one would listen to her, and Jane Fairbanks, in her best style, gave accounts, more or less exaggerated, of the varied entertainments at the Palace while Mrs. Hasey had been at the fore.

Mr. Tangier listened with thorough interest now. Had he, perhaps, watched the hatching of the eggs too closely while he was at Tenterdon? Was there, perhaps, a certain awe or suspicion attendant on his presence every day at the Old Stage-house, and was it even possible that Aunty Turner was not at her best in presence of this lawyer, fresh from juries and witnesses? Such questions, while they did not distinctly take form, were suggested for future inquiry. But his mood now was rather that of triumph than of analysis. If the Palace of Delight had delighted anybody, he had not been quite a fool himself. And he was so far disciplined by his experience that he could permit the idea to cross his mind that it was quite possible that Jane Fairbanks and Mrs. Hasey might understand the people in the midst of whom they were born, quite as well as a stranger like himself, to whom their life was in a fashion new.

What there was, in this jovial and social week at the Palace, which showed a difference between its decorous emptiness of a fortnight before, and a certain exuberant and natural hospitality, of which Jane Fairbanks gave a very bright and attractive idea, it would be hard to tell. Simply speaking, and in the words of an ancient Aryan parable, the ox had begun to drink the water, the water had begun to quench the fire, the fire had begun to burn the stick, the stick had begun to beat the kid, and the kid had begun to go. Mr. Tangier declared that he would have one of the artist guilds design a frieze to represent this triumph, and that the frieze should be the ornament of the reading-room.

"And I will pose for the old woman in it," said good-natured Mrs. Hasey.

Jane Fairbanks had met her class of girls there one afternoon, and the same afternoon some of the boys were practising before a match which was to be played at Wentworth. "And, by the way, we beat them eleven to two." And Mrs. Hasey saw the boys, as they washed themselves after the game, and it was just as the girls were going away. And she asked them why they did not all stay and have tea together. And the boys made a fire in Aunty Turner's stove, before she knew it, and had the kettle boiling, and the girls had a table spread before the boys knew it. And they had stopped the baker's cart, as it was going across the lower meadow, and Jem Crothers and Jo Bayley had come up with their arms piled with pies and loaves and buns, and Madam Cradock had sent across a lump of butter, and John had milked his own cow in the pasture half an hour before she expected it, and, in general, there had been such a frolic in the reading-room as had never been heard of since the last picnic in the Ark, before the people left it. And then the girls had stayed, and the boys had stayed, and Mrs. Hasey had stayed, and different people had stayed, who had driven over to bring the girls home, so that so many carriages were in the old sheds that Elkanah Phisbot thought there was a funeral.

Of which staying the secret was that Jane Fairbanks was at the piano in the reception-room, and they had opened the folding-doors, and there was an impromptu dance, girls in their boots, and boys in their tennis-shoes, and they had all had such fun. This impromptu festival, which nobody had prepared for, seemed to have broken the ice. And from that day on there had not been an afternoon in which the Old Stage-house had not some new story of a successful hospitality.

All of which was told to Mr. Tangier with such detail as pleased him well. As the detail went on, he began and he finished a breakfast long drawn out, and the party at last adjourned to the west piazza.

"And who do you think spent the night with Aunty Turner last night?". he said in a mysterious way, when he had heard the whole story of the charade party, which had left the Old Stage-house only an hour before he had stopped there the night before.

"Oh, last night she was alone; but she said she should not be frightened. And Laura and Mrs. Hasey and I are going to spend the afternoon with her."

"But Miss Remington and I have done better than that," he said, with the same smile of mystery. "We did not leave her one night."

"Is Miss Remington here?"

He would not be startled from his artistic way of telling his own story.

"We have left Miss Gurtry and her father at the Old Stage-house. You ladies will know how Aunty Turner packed them away. All I know is, that Rebus and I carried in a big trunk, and left it in the front passage, as you turn in to the bar-room, — I beg your pardon, into the 'conversation-room.'"

"Bessy Gurtry here?" cried Mrs. Floxam in a tone of absolute indignation which would not be suppressed, while the others were too much amazed at Mr. Tangier's effrontery to find words.

"Bessy Gurtry, as you call her, has come back, — I was going to say, has come home," said this audacious man. "But I do not know where her home is now. I only know that her father has come with her. He seems to be a very pleasant gentleman, though not very handy in moving trunks." This was the oracular reply which Mr. Tangier made to all questions. And all questioners felt that if he were carrying on a private correspondence with Miss Gurtry he had a very public manner of announcing it.

Jane Fairbanks was the first person to break the silence of surprise. She had never taken much part with the gossips who had attended most largely to Mr. Tangier's affairs, May Remington's, and Bessy Gurtry's. She was an honest, straightforward girl, who was a little reticent about her own affairs, and did not permit much interference with them. This healthy habit had led to the other healthy habit that she did not interfere much with other people's. On this occasion, her real interest in the Palace of Delight led her a little beyond her accustomed line.

"Mr. Tangier," she cried, "listen to me. I have for once thought a great thought. Why does not Bessy Gurtry fill all the conditions? Let her live at the Palace of Delight, and everything will be Delightful."

Everybody else, even Mrs. Hasey, stared with amaze-

ment at her audacity. Only Mr. Tangier did not see
any audacity. "That is just what I proposed to her
before she went away," he said, "and she said it was
wholly out of the question; and she went off to her
Hoosier or Buckeye Tecumseh after saying so. But
now she is back, — actually in the Palace of Delight, —
I do wish you and Mrs. Hasey would patch her up
some sort of throne there. Have you not got some old
lounges and patchwork that will make a good republican throne ? For it would be an excellent thing if she
should reign there."

"Impudent creature!" muttered Mrs. Floxam, as the
ladies retired. But probably every one else felt that
she had, perhaps, in the talk of the last week, been
a little too busy in the affairs of Miss Gurtry and
Mr. Tangier.

CHAPTER XV.

AT the Palace of Delight itself, no one complained, on this particular morning, that there was a lack either of princes of the blood, of princesses, of courtiers, or of other visitors.

Aunty Turner had been surprised, indeed, at the sudden arrival of visitors. She had been more surprised at the intimation given by both Nahum and Rebus that the two persons whose trunks were landed on the piazza of the Stage-house were to spend the night under its roof. When, however, she saw that one of the two was her dear Bessy Gurtry, whom she loved as if she were her own daughter, her cordiality bubbled over. And the arrangements which she suddenly made for a nice little supper, and for their sleeping comfort, showed that no real mistake had been made when she had been intrusted with the duties of High Chamberlain of the Palace of Delight.

The next morning — the same morning when Mr. Tangier had to undergo the cross-examination of the Boarders, as has been described — Mr. Gurtry, Miss Gurtry, and Aunty Turner met each other at sunrise in a futile effort each to anticipate the other in making the fire in the kitchen stove. Aunty Turner had great advantage in knowing where the matches were kept, and the kindling. Bessy Gurtry had the advantage of youth, and John Gurtry such advantage as is derived from the central truth, around which the civilization of America may be said to turn, — that, in the most perfect social order, it is a man's business, and not a woman's, to attend to this affair. So far has modern civilization advanced upon that of the Aryans in this matter of fit homage paid to Hestia, Vesta, or whoever presides over the family hearth. With three such conspirators blowing the coals together, the fire soon burned, and coffee, omelets, hot biscuit, toast, and other minor comforts and preparations for the day followed in order.

But before the early breakfast, thus initiated, was half finished, a wagon clattered up at the door, and George Drummond boldly entered.

He had a large basket, covered with a white napkin. He said that the moment he saw his aunt the night before, she had scolded him for not bringing the Gurtrys direct to her house. He said that she had been up early, and broiled a chicken, because she thought Mrs. Turner might not expect company. And when the basket came to be opened, it proved that this broiled chicken was a brief expression for a very thorough breakfast. Aunty Turner was by no means slow in placing upon the table these additions to the bill of fare, and she insisted that Mr. Drummond should join in the repast. He did not pretend that he had breakfasted, and it was accordingly a party of four who had, in a very few minutes more, to welcome Mrs. Campbell.

Mrs. Campbell was the good, motherly soul at whose house Bessy Gurtry had always lived. The mild police of Tenterdon had already informed her that the Gurtrys were at the Old Stage-house. She had, come over to remonstrate. She was, however, obliged to confess, in answer to a skilful cross-examination from George Drummond, that her husband's grandmother and two nieces had arrived from New York the week before, that her own cousins had come down from Lawrence, and that she did not know how long they would stay, and that Bessy Gurtry's own room was at this moment occupied by Miss Flanders, who had been ill, and had been advised to try sea air. But Mrs. Campbell made very light of these additions to the usual home circle, and insisted that Mr. Gurtry and his daughter should come up with her to breakfast. When they explained that they had already eaten two breakfasts, or had done their best to do so, she only changed her attack to proposing that they should come a little latter in the morning.

She was the beginning of the series of welcomes which made the Palace of Delight, for that day at least, the central point of the hospitality of the town. News of some kinds circulates fast in a place like Tenterdon; as, by a very curious law, other things will not circulate at all. The moment the boys who had been at Bessy Gurtry's school were apprised, by the mild police, that Miss Gurtry had returned, they and theirs found excuses for going down to tell her how much they had missed her, and how glad they were that she had come. Many were the bids which were offered, with various forms of temptation, that she should make her home, at least for the time, in one or other of the houses represented by these visitors. There were three or four boys and girls talking merrily with her when the contingent from Mrs. Fairbanks's arrived, Mr. Tangier himself driving the horse, and Jane Fairbanks, Mrs. Hasey and Laura Crawford, making the party. Jane Fairbanks offered the hospitality of her mother's home, thus bringing herself into accord with the rest of the world. And Bessy Gurtry was fairly roused from that sort of shyness which generally marked her manner in the presence of a crowd of people by the ludicrous side which presented itself in the multitude of invitations. It was clear enough that she could make no immediate answer, and the various calls on her resolved themselves into a sort of morning levee, such as not the boldest had proposed for the Palace of Delight, even in the most sanguine imaginings. And there was a general burst of laughter when Mrs. Dunster and May Remington appeared, and brought their invitation in their turn.

May Remington was perfectly determined that she would do the upright and generous thing, by way of punishing herself for an unconscious folly. She had told her aunt that she must come with her, to give the invitation full force, and to explain to Bessy Gurtry that there was no place so central and so comfortable for her to stay in, as long as she liked to stay, as was her house. Mrs. Dunster perhaps had a little of May's feeling in the matter that she had been unjust to the little schoolmistress. At all events, she entered very cordially into these plans. It needed only the presence of Mr. Burdett and the doctor to bring all the original conspirators, as they used to call themselves, into the Palace of Delight on this eventful morning; and they began to remember that it was the first time for such a meeting since the evening of the fire-works and the inauguration. Somebody started Aunty Turner on the account of the dissipation of the last week, — of the spontaneous tea-party, and of the various frolics, grave and gay, which had followed. When Aunty Turner was well talking, without much thought of her audience, but with a proper enthusiasm for her story, she was one of the most entertaining people in the world. And while one or another of the party dropped off into one or other of the various open rooms, a large circle cheered her on to her talking, and stimulated her to new enthusiasm as she told the tale.

She was so full of a certain unconscious fun, and talked with such animation, that most of the circle did not observe that the three gentlemen, Mr. Tangier, Mr. Drummond, and Mr. Gurtry, had for the moment withdrawn. But May Remington, who was sitting by Miss Gurtry's side, did notice it when John Gurtry came softly in at the open door, touched his daughter's shoulder, and beckoned her away.

Bessy Gurtry supposed, and naturally enough, that she was called in to the business conference which the three men were holding.

But, to her surprise, her father disappeared the moment they crossed the passage, and she found herself alone with George Drummond.

"It was I who sent your father to call you," he said. "Really I have to make the decision which affects all my life; and I speak perfectly seriously when I say that I cannot make that decision without asking you to go back to what happened in this room when you were in it last. I hurried you then. I was too masterful, I suppose. They say that is my way. But I will not be masterful now. I will be very humble and gentle, and I will wait as long as you say, if I must wait. I will gladly wait, if you will only bid me do só."

The girl looked at him silently, but with an eager expression which he thought was her command to him to be still.

"No, I must speak; and I must speak to-day," he said, more hastily than before. He had finished the speech he had been preparing, and now spoke with more of the pent-up passion of these weeks of loneliness. "I must speak. I cannot live as I have been living. I can bear anything but that. No. You do not know, you cannot know, what it is to go and come always with the thought of another person — always! Why, Miss Gurtry, it was not only in this journey back and forth to Tecumseh and here, it was every step I took in Broadway, which you took with me; you did not so much as know it," he added after a pause, almost in a bitter way. "I would start, when this man asked me about his colony, as if I had never heard him speak before, and it was only from wondering what you would say."

Perhaps it was the surprise of finding him, when she thought she was to meet all the others. Perhaps it was the excitement of the jolly party she had left. But surely she had not that wretched, dejected air which she had when she last sat in that chair. Then she was so wholly broken down. Now she was serious indeed, but she did not look as if she felt all alone in the world.

"I am so sorry to have been such a — such a burden to you, Mr. Drummond. Really, what I said here was true.   Really, I will count you always as one of my best friends."

Ah, me, how many girls have said this to how many boys, and how very unsatisfactory is the promise !

"I know you said it," said he, not wholly discouraged, "and it has done me more good than you thought or than you meant indeed, perhaps."

"Not than I meant, Mr. Drummond; you are not quite fair."

"What did you mean, — what do you mean ? Do you mean that anything parts us that I can remove ? Or do you mean that you distrust me, that any one says anything ill of me, that — that — "

"George Drummond, I trust you as I trust myself. I thank you with all my heart. I am more sorry than I can say — that — "

His face flushed with his delight. "Then the trouble is not with me; it is with you. I have no right to ask, and I will not ask. But now I will wait till you can see — "

"Take care, Mr. Drummond." It was her turn to interrupt him now. "Take care — " But he would not wait.

"No, I must speak now. I am going to say that I am sure of the sympathy, the confidence, of the noblest girl in the world, and the dearest; and she even says that I have her esteem. Sure of that, I shall go to Labrador, if need be, and I shall be happy. For I shall come back twelve months hence, and I shall be in this room with her, and then I shall be so sure, and she will be a little doubtful, and then I shall know that I have won her by my confidence and my obedience."

His face was fairly eloquent, as he spoke with a passion which affected to be satisfied.

"No, Mr. Drummond. I may not be here then. Who knows?"

"Why do I not know?" he replied, as if surprised; and perhaps he was. "Why does not your best friend know? Why not tell the man you honor, in whom you have confidence, whose integrity you are sure of, and whose judgment you respect?"

"Because he wants me to tell him something more," she said sadly; and all the animation, which had been an accident indeed, left her. "I can tell you this, — you saw it last night. I do not know if I ought to say it; but you are good, you are kind. My father — do you not see? He is, — oh, I wish I could make you see! — he is a wonderful man in the real things. But — well — in the world's ways he is a child, and less than a child. He cared for me, Mr. Drummond, when I needed him. I care for him, now he needs me. No one shall come between us, — no, not even you."

"Even I!" he cried in triumph. "You would sooner trust me than any other man! Darling mine, that is all I ask, it is all that I have pretended to ask for." And his face flushed with a joy which the girl never saw on it before. The suddenness of his outcry, and the eagerness of his whole manner, broke her guard; she smiled with a smile which he will never forget, and lost her secret.

She knew she had lost it. "How could I say that? But I have said it, and it is true. Now do you understand, do you see, that I could not, nay, I cannot, talk of myself, talk of you, talk of leading a life for you and with you, when I have him to care for who has already cared for me?"

And by this time George Drummond's arms were around the girl, and he was kissing her, and she did not draw away from his caresses.

Meanwhile, Mr. Tangier was carrying on an interview with Mr. Gurtry.

"What I meant, Mr. Gurtry, was this: If Miss Gurtry lives in this house, — and that was the plan I proposed to her before she went away, — there should be some man here to see to both these ladies, and in general, well, not exactly as protector, but as man of the house, you know, to keep the machine properly running. Why are not you that man? We cannot pay you what would be called a salary; but we can manage that there shall be something to eat and drink here, and fire and beds for all. You have your own business to attend to, your patents, your articles for the reviews, and you can see to them as well as if you were in Tecumseh. There would be no difficulty, if you should want to run on to Washington. Some of the young men would man the house, — Drummond here, or the doctor, or I would."

Run on to Washington, indeed! As if poor Mr. Gurtry could run here and there as he chose! But there was something fascinating merely in the suggestion.

"It must be as Bessy says," he replied. "She is very prudent, and very wise." This indeed was the sum of several little speeches by which he replied to Mr. Tangier's business-like statements and suggestions. Mr. Tangier saw that that was true which he had suspected, — that whatever power of command Captain

Gurtry might have had when he served under the orders of some spirited colonel, such power had left him now. All the same did he press the project, which he had determined on the night before, — that John Gurtry should be established at Tenterdon, and the Old Stage-house should be his home.

"I should like to talk with my daughter about it. She will know what is best. Where did she go? I called her in, and I thought she would like to hear what you and the other gentleman were saying."

Jeffrey Tangier was not without suspicions as to what the other gentleman was saying. And he was so loyal to his friend Drummond that if he had prolonged the discussion till sunset, or till midnight, he would have held Mr. Gurtry rather than have him go in search of his daughter. But it was not needed that he should do so. Just as Mr. Gurtry said, for the sixth time, perhaps, "I must go and find Bessy," the door opened, and Bessy came in, followed by George Drummond. As Mr. Tangier looked at him he saw that all was well. Drummond was himself again. He came directly to Mr. Gurtry, and said: "You must not think I have kept your daughter too long, Mr. Gurtry. I shall want to keep her a great deal longer. I have asked her to be my wife, and she has not said no. She has said that she must not leave her father. There is no reason why she should, unless her father wants to leave her." And he just nodded to Mr. Tangier, with a proud smile, as much as to say, "You understand what a victory. I have won."

While poor Mr. Gurtry was vainly trying to shake himself together, Tangier was eagerly congratulating George Drummond, leaving the girl to her father. yes.

to cry a little, to whisper a little, and for her to make him see that every care she had ever had was lifted from her, and that she was the happiest girl that ever lived — that she did not know why she was so happy.

"I do not see," said Tangier to Drummond, "why this does not make our plan here even more simple. Let us establish him here. You shall establish her where you will and when you will. Clearly, he is a person who will help us on all sides here. And, who knows, he may be the very missing link, which, with Aunty Turner, shall complete our chain. We will leave them for a minute, you shall have time enough with her by-and-by. Come back to the others, and let us hear the rest of their stories."

And so it was announced to assembled Tenterdon in the spontaneous congress which had welcomed Bessy Gurtry and her father, that, at least for the present, they would stay at the Old Stage-house. The caucus even went so far as to indicate the rooms which they two should occupy, and to make some suggestions as to the furniture. New England does not like to be told that any plan has been specifically settled in all its details. New England greatly prefers to have the details arrange themselves, from step to step. So the conclave, caucus, or congress, was well-pleased with this announcement. As for Aunty Turner, she was in the seventh heaven. That she and her dear child, as she loved to call Bessy Gurtry should live under the same roof, — this she had never hoped for. Even Aunty Turner was still blind to the secret, which had been so close under her eyes, that George Drummond had determined long ago that Bessy Gurtry should live under no roof but his.

CHAPTER LAST.

Jeffrey Tangier to Mrs. Dunster.

SHALL I come up to tea to-night? I have some papers about the Palace which I want to show you. May I bring the doctor?   J. T.

On the back this note bears Mrs. Dunster's answer, written in pencil:—

"Certainly. Shall I send for Mr. Burdett?"

And to Rebus, who brought down the folded answer, Mr. Tangier had said, "Yes." So Rebus had gone on to Mr. Burdett's with a note with which he had been provided. Rebus had himself approved of this arrangement, or he would, before this, have interposed with his veto. And so was it that the central conspirators met at high tea.

Into the detail of the conversation, which was almost wholly about the Old Stage-house and its future, and Bessy Gurtry and hers, this record shall not now go farther. But when the last macaroon had been eaten, and the last jelly refused, when all parties went out on the west piazza, and sat in the glory of the sunset, Mr. Tangier produced from his pocket an envelope, and said:—

"I want to show you this. I am satisfied that we have not made fools of ourselves, and that what we have done is, on the whole, a good beginning. I have therefore concluded a bargain for the Stage-house to-day, and it will be mine to-morrow. Sugden, at Wentworth, has been looking up the title to-day, and probably the deed is already drawn and signed. Now, I may die at any moment, and we want no mistakes."

May Remington started, but not observably, when he said he might die. She was not used to a thought which comes of course into a mind well-trained in life, nor to the habit by which such a man as Jeffrey Tangier always leaves a day so finished that any stranger may take up his work on the next day, and know how to carry it on. He was not even looking at her, and he went on without a pause: "I have, therefore, drawn up this deed of trust, which, if you all approve, I will execute before I go to bed." And he read this instrument, which was short and clear. May Remington was surprised, after all she had heard about legal obscurities, that it stated so simply what was needed. She said aloud: "Is that a deed of trust? I could have drawn it myself." Perhaps she could.

It gave the Old Stage-house, with the four acres of land appertaining to it, to six trustees, — George Drummond, Mrs. Dunster, May Remington, Mr. Burdett, the doctor, and Mr. Tangier himself. On the death or resignation of any one of them, the others were to appoint a successor. If they thought at any time that an act of incorporation was necessary, they were to secure one. This was the first article. The second article placed in their hands fifteen bonds of one thousand dollars each of the Chicago, Kansas, & Western Railway, of which the interest was to be paid semi-annually to John Gurtry as long as he lived in the Old Stage-house, and afterward for any such purposes as the majority of the trustees might approve. This was all.

"You are very generous," said Mrs. Dunster, eagerly.

"Hardly so, for I please myself most of all," said he, rising and making a motion that they might return to the lighted room. Why was he in such haste? Had he any premonition of evil? This was the thought which crossed Miss Remington as his manner compelled them all to rise.

In a moment more he was seated by the lamp, which he had himself removed from the centre-table to Mrs. Dunster's davenport. He asked Mrs. Dunster to call two of the children, who were in the other room, to witness the signature by which he completed his share of the transaction. He returned it to the envelope from which he had taken it, and sealed it. He directed it to George Drummond, and asked Mrs. Dunster to hand it to him in the morning. Miss Remington looked on all the time, almost frightened, she hardly knew why. But she hardly knew this resolution and promptness in the man, though there had been signs of the same thing once and again when they had been working on the details of the Palace.

The moment the envelope was sealed, his whole manner changed. "Now," said he gayly, "we can go to bed with a good conscience. Going, doctor, so soon? Can we not keep you, unless we have a headache, or a deed of trust to sign? Come with him, Miss May, to the foot of the avenue; I want to show you the reflection of the moon in the sea."

She ran for a hat and shawl, and joined him. They

walked down the avenue with the doctor and bade him good-by. Then Mr. Tangier led her to a stile on which she had often sat before.

"There is the moon," said he, "and there is the sea. So I have shown them to you. But I did not come here for that, Miss Remington. I came here for the same reason that I left the yacht. You have been displeased with me. I do not know why. If any other woman were displeased with me, I should not care why, unless I were displeased with myself at the same time. But every day I was away from Tenterdon I found myself wondering more and more why you were displeased with me, and eager to put myself in the right. In truth, I only came here yesterday to ask your aunt where you were. I counted it a good omen that I found you at Wentworth. Let me ask you now what is the matter."

"Nothing is the matter," said May Remington, at first a little hardly. Then she was conscious that this was unfair. She had been in the wrong, and she would own it, though she would never own how far she had been in the wrong. She went on more cordially: "I will tell the truth. I did misunderstand you. I was a fool, and a perfect fool. If I were cold in my manner, why, I am sorry, and I wish you would never speak of it again."

"Thank you a thousand times," said he. "Thank you, indeed, a thousand times. You give me more pleasure than you know. But really you have only answered one question. I want to ask another. As soon as you left Tenterdon, I found I did not care about staying. I found, dear Miss May, that it was not Tenterdon I liked, but you. I went away, because

I wanted to try myself. I have come back because I could not stay away. But unless you tell me that hereafter I may come and find you here, I will leave Tenterdon to-morrow, and never set my foot in it again."

She looked at him, and he could see in the moonlight that she tried to smile. But she could not smile. She tried to speak — she could not speak. She stepped from the stile, and walked toward the house; but he was of course at her side.

"What is it," he said; "why do you say nothing?"

"Because — because — I hope you will stay here all summer."

University Press: John Wilson & Son. Cambridge.

www.ingramcontent.com/pod-product-compliance
Lightning Source LLC
Chambersburg PA
CBHW020943120726
47905CB00008B/2658

9 783337 025922